C009228191

Edel Coffey is an Irish journalist and broadcaster. She began work as an arts journalist and editor with the *Sunday Tribune* and has since worked as a presenter and reporter with RTÉ Radio, and as editor of the *Irish Independent Weekend Magazine*, and Books Editor of the *Irish Independent*. She is a regular contributor to *The Irish Times*, a weekly columnist with the *Irish Examiner*, and Books Editor of *The Gloss* magazine. She lives in Galway with her husband and children.

In Her Place is her second novel.

Also by Edel Coffey

Breaking Point

EDEL COFFEY

IN HER PLACE

SPHERE

SPHERE

First published in Great Britain in 2024 by Sphere

1 3 5 7 9 10 8 6 4 2

A CIP catalogue record for this book
is available from the British Library.

Hardback ISBN 978-0-7515-8241-3
Trade Paperback ISBN 978-0-7515-8242-0

Typeset in Sabon by M Rules
Printed and bound in Great Britain by
Clays Ltd, Elcograf S.p.A.

Papers used by Sphere are from well-managed forests
and other responsible sources.

Sphere
An imprint of
Little, Brown Book Group
Carmelite House
50 Victoria Embankment
London EC4Y 0DZ

An Hachette UK Company
www.hachette.co.uk

www.littlebrown.co.uk

For David

Deborah was always supposed to die. But not in that way.

Ann hadn't planned to go north that week. She never went north. She was a Brooklynite. She didn't even like to leave the borough. She preferred to stay in her comfort zone, where people and ways felt familiar. But they say everything happens for a reason.

Prologue

Ann

Ann woke to the sharp attack of her phone's alarm. It sounded like an anvil. She must have fallen back to sleep after all but now she wished she hadn't. She felt as if she had been run over by a bus. The last thing she remembered was scanning the darkness, certain that someone was in the room with her. She had cowered in bed until the reassuring fingers of dawn had crept into the room and calmed the adrenalin pumping around her system.

What had she been so afraid of? It all seemed so innocent in the morning light. She looked to her left – the bed was empty, still perfectly made up on Justin's side, unruffled by her sleepless night. She always slept like this, never encroaching onto his side, even though he wasn't there. He had trained her well, kept her in her place.

A bang came from somewhere in the apartment. Ann jumped up and mentally tracked the noise to the bathroom before she relaxed again. It was just the air vent that regularly came undone. It must have loosened in the storm last night. She adored this apartment but that air vent was testing her love. She swung her legs out of the bed. Her head swam a little as she planted her feet onto the sumptuous dove-grey carpet. As her mind and body realigned, she stomped across to the bathroom, re-clipped the vent, then moved on through to the kitchen.

Once there, she hit the remote to raise the electric blinds and watched as the Manhattan skyline revealed itself inch by inch. It never failed to take her breath away. This was her New York and she loved it. Even when growing up in social housing in Brooklyn's Greenpoint, she still got to enjoy a better view every single day than the billionaires living across the East River in Manhattan. This was the place she came from. Ann never failed to be grateful for the fact that, somehow, she had found her way back here. It hadn't been easy. But this was her home now, and nobody could take that away from her. Not Justin, not Deborah, no one.

She flicked on the coffee machine. She had exactly three minutes' grace before she had to fire up the morning routine – shower, baby bag, Agnes's toy, blanky, pacifier, the dash to the crèche. Agnes was still only six months old but she was such a good baby. Ann had gotten lucky. Very lucky. She didn't like to think about Agnes's eventful entrance into this world and how she might not even be here today. She shook her head as if she could clear her thoughts as easily as that, took a sip of coffee. Her thoughts were as tangled as the bedsheets she had just left. She felt her stomach cramp. Her period was coming. Ann felt on edge, anxious. She knew that this was just a response to the dream, that she would spend the day exorcising the bad memories that had been stirred up, dragging her back to the edge of the dark crater of the past year, a place she didn't like to go. A place that had nearly killed her.

At 8.15 she and Agnes took the elevator down to the lobby. Ann stepped out into the cool morning air and made her way towards the crèche. She waved to her neighbours' children who were waiting for the school bus, their parents sending them off into another day of the unknown. In God we trust. A few steps further on, Ann bumped into Judy, as she often did now on their morning routines.

'Well, good morning ladies,' Judy said, tickling Agnes under the chin as she bounced on the balls of her feet, stopping but not wanting to drop any steps on her smart watch counter. She was kitted out head to toe in the latest Lululemon yoga gear and had tiny weights strapped around her slim wrists and ankles. Judy was lean and thin, compared to Ann's more muscular, compact frame. 'How are we today,' Judy asked in her relentlessly upbeat tone. Agnes cooed in response.

Judy slowed her bounce and said to Ann, 'You look tired. Are you OK?'

Ann swept her blonde ponytail out from where it was trapped under the collar of her coat. 'I didn't get much sleep,' she conceded.

'That spring storm kept me awake too,' Judy said. 'Around for a coffee later?'

'Coffee would be great, but after lunch, I'm tied up this morning.' She leaned on the stroller and Judy took the hint.

'Sure thing.' She intensified her bouncing before starting to move on. 'Have fun at crèche sweetheart,' she called to Agnes, 'and I'll see you later, Ann.'

Ann watched her bounce away into the morning crowds.

Ann had a rare day off from the office where she worked as a features writer for *The Edge* magazine, so she headed straight back to her apartment after dropping Agnes at crèche. The kitchen looked like it had been ransacked by burglars when really all that had happened was breakfast. She sighed, and walked towards the polished stone island, like a glittering cruise liner, so different from the kitchen she had grown up in with her mother and sisters. She kicked off her Birkenstocks and walked back into the master bedroom, which was still rumpled by her sleepless night. Despite the bright April sunlight streaming in through the triple-glazed windows, she felt cold. She couldn't shake the feeling that someone had been here. Just ghosts, she told herself as she stood in the stream of sunlight and waited for it to warm her body.

On the street below, life went on as usual. Busy, shouting, rushing working people crossed over with the bohos who languidly sipped coffees and checked themselves out in their phone cameras. Their lithe young bodies were clothed in the lightest of silks despite the spring chill. They looked like nymphs and it always felt to Ann like they were dressed up like that so that someone might notice them, pick them up and carry them away from these grimy, earthly concerns of mundane tasks and part-time jobs as insouciant baristas, so that their real luxe lives could begin in earnest, the ones they were meant to be living.

Ann walked into the living room and slumped onto the cream bouclé couch that snaked around the perimeter of the room. It was a compact apartment but spacious enough for them. She had redecorated impeccably before moving in; she wanted to put her own mark on things to emphasise the fact that this was her home, no one else's. Ann didn't know how or why her brain always wove its way back down this dark path to the bad memories of six months ago. She had taken pains to move on in her life, to put her mom's death behind her, to put her time in Hudson city behind her, and to look towards the future and her new life here in Brooklyn, the life she had always wanted. And yet there were still nights when Ann blinked into the darkness at 3 a.m. and called out, 'Who's there?'

She scooped up her phone from the couch, and absent-mindedly checked her bank balance. She did this automatically every day; it was a calming device, to remind herself that the money was really there.

$117,500.09 was the checking balance. The monthly lodgement of $10,000 had gone in yesterday, as it did every month now. This was just one of the secrets that Ann kept. She had more secrets now than ever before, but it was a small price to pay to be independent. She would never again be dependent on someone. She would never again forage the bitter fields of other people's cast-off lives in search of one for herself. It was hard to believe that little over a year ago, she had been penniless, childless and technically homeless.

PART I

Getting to know Justin

Chapter One

Ann

Eighteen Months Earlier

The day before Ann first met Justin was a record low. It was two months since Ann's mother had died and she still hadn't gotten a foothold on returning to work. Her writing had dwindled to nothing during the years her mother was ill, as she slowly surrendered even the smallest journalistic assignments, her mother's illness consuming everything. Ann spent her days reaching out to old editors whose emails bounced back, or who had since moved on or up or out of journalism altogether. She started from scratch with new editors, most of them younger than her thirty-eight years, trying to establish a connection, a relationship and ideally a paying job.

She took on every assignment in the hope that she would become known as the girl who never said no, a reliable go-to woman. She desperately needed to build some security. She was terrified most days of the daunting reality that her mother was dead and she was now alone. She had no safety net, nobody to rely on, nothing to fall back on. Previously she and her mother had lived frugally on her mother's disability insurance, but that payment had stopped the day her mother died and now Ann was struggling.

If she didn't have an assignment to follow up, which was not uncommon, Ann walked the streets around Williamsburg, in an attempt to escape the confines of the apartment. When she stayed in, she felt herself losing her grip on reality, as if her life was no longer real and nothing really mattered. On days like these, she felt like a flimsy figment of someone's imagination. On days like these it was easy to believe that it made no difference if she lived or died, and she wondered if she found her way off the edge of her apartment building, would she just float up and away like a paper figure or plummet to the street below? She knew this was a dangerous mindset. All she could do in those moments was get out of the apartment until the feelings subsided.

She walked past shops filled with things that nobody needed, labelled with prices that seemed incomprehensibly prohibitive, and yet these were everyday items – a teapot, a swimsuit, a writing set. Could ordinary people actually afford these things? She felt utterly alienated and excluded from this world. She lived outside of it, viewing it as if from behind a pane of glass.

She stopped outside a shop that sold delicate jewellery, and beautiful things that she wanted to touch and smell – candles, tarot cards, paperweights. Items for young, unjaded girls with silky hair. Girls who were doing post-grads at NYU. Girls who wore rings on their knuckles and thumbs. Girls whose willowy limbs were oiled and beautiful, and smelled like jasmine but only if they allowed you to get close enough. None of it was for Ann. She felt the drabness of her life humming like a magnetic field. No matter how much effort she made with her long blonde hair or a perfectly executed eyeliner flick, she still felt her inner sadness radiating through her veneer like a lie she couldn't hide.

She simply could not go on like this. Not in the way that people said they could not go on, but in the most literal interpretation of the concept. She could not go on. She would not go on. She stared at her fragmented reflection in the shop window, a mosaic of sadness.

If I do not get a sign today, she thought, are you listening universe? Today! – that things will get better after all this shit, I will give up.

Ann had never seriously contemplated suicide but lately when she thought about it she identified a feeling of relief, that she would no longer have to think about things, that she would be spared the worry of how to pay next month's rent, and forget the gaping hole that was the absence of her mother and the guilt that seemed to fill it.

Her phone vibrated. She looked down and saw a request from an old editor, asking whether she was able to drive to Hudson city tonight to preview a play that was causing a local stir and was coming to the Brooklyn arts festival in the summer. 800 words. $400. She had been hoping for a more exciting sign from the universe, like winning the lottery, but she had asked for a sign and the universe had delivered, so she would have to keep her side of the bargain now.

Maybe it would do her good to get out of town for a night. A change of scene. Her writing felt wooden and she was certain it was because her life had become dull and repetitive. She had little to say and even less to write about. The sound of the heating creeping through the vents in her mother's apartment. The endless streams of cyclists ferrying food to and from people like her, hiding from life behind apartment doors.

She typed out a brief reply on her phone; yes she would go to Hudson city tonight, see this play that had a small town up in arms, interview the writer-director, before turning around and driving back to the safety of Brooklyn.

She had to start moving on, rebuilding her life, and her finances. She had to start saying yes to work, to life. She couldn't live in her mom's place for ever. Her sisters were already dropping hints about selling it. She could give in or she could try. Just put one foot in front of the other, she told herself. Just get through today.

As she sent the message back to the editor, she automatically flipped from her email to social media, scrolling quickly through the posts of former friends. She had watched her peers move smoothly through the gears of their lives, finding the turbo-boost just as Ann's mother became unwell. She had watched them advance precipitously towards successful adulthood as she dropped out of her own life to care for her mother. Some of her friends had bolstered their earning power with marriage to power players, lawyers, plastic surgeons, tech bros, people who could support their hobby careers as writers. Some even had children, which they quickly handed over to nannies so they could refocus on solidifying their earning power and success. Ann tried not to think about lost opportunities, about how that might have been her now, had she somehow had the insight to know that coupling up, allying early on, was like adding a booster pack to your life. But Ann had known nothing back then, when Richard had proposed and she had thought that part of her life could wait. Now she was a nobody who had to street-fight her way back into her career against interns and youngsters who were arriving thick and fast like CGI mercenaries to be dispensed with.

Ann had little direction now, without her mom's

twenty-four-hour care schedule to keep her busy. The hours stretched endlessly, and, with little or no money, there was nothing to do. She couldn't go to the cinema or ask a friend for lunch or dinner, or even buy a new outfit to cheer herself up. It felt important to plot her own life on the graph of everyone else's. She looked up all of the people she could remember from high school, college, early jobs, every single peer she could find as a comparative. In high school she had been voted most likely to be prom queen, most likely to marry, and most likely to be rich. She knew these were ridiculous metrics to base her hopes and dreams on but she had believed it too. Now, she was one of the few people from her graduating year who was single, and the only woman. The other two were men, one a foreign correspondent (everyone knew not to marry them) and a journalist who had sold his news app for forty million dollars straight out of college. Most of her former classmates also appeared to have kids in their profile pictures. Some of them had teenagers! Were they really old enough to have teenage children? It seemed like an impossibility to her. She supposed it *was* an impossibility for her now. At the age of 38, single, broke, she would likely never have a child, a husband, or a home of the kind that her friends all seemed to have – large enough to accommodate not only several children, but the dream of family life – sports equipment, musical instruments, favourite toys and teddy bears, pink duvets and lighting for girls' bedrooms, a sailing theme for the boys, Christmas decorations and camping equipment stored in the basement, double-door refrigerators stuffed with food for regular family dinners. That had been her dream. More than that, it had been her assumption.

She clicked on image after image, searched profiles of husbands, partners, husbands' families, friends, co-workers and found these people were surrounded by concentric circles of money. Rings of wealth reinforced by rings of wealth. This was the worst thing for Ann to be doing at a time when she was grieving and directionless. Compare and contrast was not a good game for right now. These social media images were not real, she told herself. Just the best parts of other people's lives. But still, the best parts of her life had never looked this good.

She shut her phone off and shoved it into her pocket. Hunching her shoulders, she pushed her hands deeper into the pockets of her coat, a cheap knock-off from TK Maxx. She looked up the street, which was covered with yellow and orange leaves, nature's confetti to match the Halloween decorations that hung from every doorway, the pumpkins and gourds that sat on windowsills and benches outside coffee shops. The weather had been unseasonably mild but this week it had turned and now people huddled into their sleeping-bag coats and looked down at the pavement instead of into each other's faces.

She stepped inside the boutique for something to do, instinctively picking up a decorative glass plate, hand-painted with a watercolour of a flower, and with no apparent function. Ann was fondling the trinket appraisingly when she heard a voice say, 'Ann? Is that you, Ann?'

She looked up to find a luminous woman looking back at her.

'Ann, it's Judy. Judy Kepler.'

She dropped the hand holding the plate down by her side. 'Judy!? Oh my god, Judy you look amazing!' Judy looked the kind of amazing that people looked only after a committed investment. This was not the impact of a week-long juice cleanse. This was a lifestyle.

Judy seemed lit from within. Ann's hand went to her hair, which was swept up in a messy bun. She had poked a mascara wand at her eyes and swept a lipstick across her mouth but apart from that she hadn't put make-up on. She was wearing a pair of jeans, some Birkenstocks with socks, and an old cashmere jumper with a fraying cuff. Before she had bumped into Judy, she had hoped to look just the right side of cool, blending in with the young crowd, but faced with Judy's glowing presence and crisp white outfit, Ann knew that she just looked like what she was – beaten down, impoverished and unloved.

Judy hugged her and Ann inhaled her rich, clean scent – something Japanese, she wondered? It was so delicate and yet so … expensive. Ann tried to imagine what Judy might be smelling – top notes of unwashed hair, bed linen that hadn't been changed in too long, base notes of failure and career slump. Judy's skin looked like oil had been freshly rubbed into it at a beauty salon. Her cheeks were splendidly rosy.

'Judy, I had no idea you lived around here?'

'Well, I don't; I'm a bit off my beaten path. We just bought a place in Dumbo but I wanted to come up because I love the jewellery in this store … do you live nearby?'

Ann allowed the Dumbo statement to sink in, keeping her expression neutral. She and Judy both knew what buying a place in Dumbo meant. That little patch of streets between the Brooklyn Bridge overpass and the Manhattan Bridge was the exclusive reserve of the super-rich. Even back when Ann was in university a one-bed could set you back as much as a million dollars. And that was *before* the place was gentrified and smothered by an algal bloom of wealthy Manhattanites.

'I'm still at my mom's old place, just up off McCarren Park, remember?'

'Oh yes, of course I remember! How is your mom?'

Ann paused. This was always hard. Harder on the people she had to tell, she thought. 'She … died.' She rushed to stop Judy apologising, and they both grabbed at each other's hands, wanting to erase the other person's awkwardness.

'Listen,' Judy said, cutting through it, 'do you have time for a coffee? There's a gorgeous little diner a few blocks away . . .'

Ann had nothing but time, and as she took in the quality of Judy's outfit, her glowing complexion and tasteful highlights, she knew that she wouldn't have to worry about paying. 'Do you know, I'd really love that,' she said. 'It's been so long.'

'Great, let me just grab these and we'll be all set.' Judy handed a candle, some tiny dropper bottles of mysterious liquids and a couple of gossamer-thin gold rings to the assistant, who rang it up.

'That's five forty,' she sang. 'Cash or card?'

Judy paid without blinking.

In the diner, Judy shrugged off her jacket to reveal a tanned body that looked sculpted by reformer Pilates and ketosis.

'You look amazing,' Ann said. 'I can't believe we're the same age.'

Judy laughed and batted the compliment away. Ann made a mental note to start exercising again but her inner voice noted that Judy's appearance had as much to do with money as exercise.

'So, how are you doing, Ann? The last few years must have been very tough on you. I'm so sorry about your mom. She was always so nice to us girls when we came over after classes.'

Ann smiled. 'Thank you.' She had learned the easiest way to reverse out of this conversation. Say thank you, acknowledge it was hard, but express stoicism and gratitude that you were one of the lucky ones who had your parents in adulthood. Most people moved the conversation on after that.

'What are you doing these days? Do you keep up with any of the old crowd from Columbia?'

Ann shook her head. 'I kind of lost touch with most people when my mom got sick. There just wasn't time.'

'I see Adriana in the *New Yorker* all the time now,' Judy said. 'And what about Leena's website?! She was always clever though. That journalism MA had a lot of talent on it, including you. Ever since you won that writing prize in final year, I've been expecting a collection of essays, a novel perhaps . . . '

Ann grimaced. She knew she had failed to meet her potential but it was easier to believe that she didn't have that much potential to begin with. Judy had always been kind to her. They became friends when they realised they were on the same train in and out of Brooklyn. They bonded over their fandom of Joan Didion, which was what had brought Judy to the journalism MA, but Judy soon realised while she loved Joan's writing, she was more in love with Joan than with becoming a writer herself. After graduation they had lost touch.

'Still no book,' Ann replied. 'I'm just dipping my toe

back into work after ... What about you, Judy, are you working?'

Ann wanted to put off the moment where she would have to reveal the full extent of her own failure.

Judy actually blushed. 'Oh god no, I haven't worked in a long time. I gave up when Chris and I got married. I was working at *New York* magazine for a few years but it took me so long to research and write the articles that I figured out I was earning less than the minimum wage. It just became kind of embarrassing to be working eighty-hour weeks and constantly broke. Chris and I both agreed that if we were going to have a family, one of us should be at home with the kids, so I quit writing to stay at home. We've got three kids now, hence the move to Dumbo.' She rolled her eyes and bared her teeth beneath her iridescent, plump lips. She said it as if it was all a step down – the rich husband, the kids, Dumbo. Ann wondered where Judy had lived before.

Ann realised it was her turn to speak. She had been mesmerised by the sheen of Judy's line-free face.

'Wow,' she blurted, 'congratulations. Three kids. How old are they?'

'One, two and three – I know! – but we both wanted a few kids, and we wanted them to be close, so I sacrificed my body.'

'Wow,' Ann repeated dumbly, 'that does not look like the body of woman who bore three children.' She thought Judy's body did not look like it had been a part of any sacrifice, except maybe a sugar one.

Judy laughed. 'Thank you.'

'So, where are they now, your kids?' Ann asked.

'Oh,' Judy said, and her eyebrows would have jumped if they were capable of moving, 'they're with the childminder. She's fantastic, like a member of the family. I love being a mom but it's really important to be the best mother I can be, and that involves a little bit of self-care time.'

She punctuated the well-practised statement with a beaming smile.

'Tell me about your husband. Who is this Chris? And what happened to Jeff, the finance major?'

Judy's face darkened. 'Don't even mention that name. It's actually thanks to Jeff that I met Chris. I had just turned thirty and I thought Jeff was going to propose. He was a hedge fund trader by that stage – already super wealthy – and I had invested a lot of my time in him, under the understanding that we'd get married. I thought he was going to propose at my thirtieth birthday party, but instead I caught him in a bathroom cubicle with a twenty-year-old waitress from the club. I dumped him there and then. If he wasn't even going to set me up and marry me, how was I going to put up with him cheating?'

Ann's mind boggled as she replayed that line over and over in her head a few times. Was Judy saying she didn't mind him cheating but did mind him not paying her?

'. . . Anyway, he made a huge scene as he was leaving – on my birthday, can you believe it? – and I was just in tears and this beautiful, kind guy who was having some quiet drinks with his friends at the bar bought six bottles of champagne to cheer me and my friends up. We've been together ever since.'

'Wow,' Ann said for the third time. 'What does Chris do?'

'Oh, he's an investor, like his dad was before him. He invested big in Apple in the eighties and so Chris just picks and chooses his projects. He loves working as an angel investor, helping social justice innovation.'

Ann stopped herself from saying 'wow' again and instead said, 'That's amazing. Obviously you're kept busy with the kids but do you get to do anything for yourself?'

'I don't really have time for anything, to be honest, Ann.' Judy looked at her watch – Cartier. 'I've got a Pilates class in about thirty minutes, and then a treatment with my aesthetician, but I need to get to the bookstore before that. Do you want to walk with?'

'Sure,' Ann said, grabbing her purse, but Judy put her hand on Ann's, telling her, 'I'm getting these!' Ann smiled and thanked her.

They walked the few blocks to McNally Jackson where Judy rapidly went through a selection of fiction, non-fiction and literary journals, until she had a stack. She returned to find Ann reading the back of Elizabeth Hardwick's *Sleepless Nights*. 'Oh, do you want that one? Pop it on my stack.'

'Oh no,' Ann said, 'I'm just browsing.' Judy gave Ann a no-nonsense mom face and said, 'Hand it over.' Ann didn't dare disobey and waited as Judy went to the desk and paid $200 for the pile of books. At this rate Judy would have clocked up a cool thousand on knick-knacks by lunchtime, Ann thought.

Outside, she pressed the book into Ann's hand. 'It was so amazing to catch up. We'll do it again. Come to Dumbo next time. Follow me on Instagram and we'll keep in touch, OK? My surname is Kraus now. I'm the one with the blue tick.' She kissed Ann on both cheeks and Ann watched her little coiled sinews bounce down the street to her Pilates class.

What the fuck just happened? Judy was not a supermodel, even though she looked like one now. She was an ordinary girl, but through what Ann imagined was procedures and hours a day dedicated to her personal wellbeing she had become a human macaron – glossy, attractive, perfect and sweet to taste. Ann looked down at the book in her hand. Judy had bought it as if it was nothing. After Ann paid the mortgage and utilities on her mom's apartment, she was usually left with just a few hundred dollars to live on for the rest of the month, which had to go on carefully allocated travel and food.

She imagined what it might be like to walk into a shop and buy a handful of trinkets on a whim for $500 or a stack of books that you planned on reading at some point because you didn't have to work or clean or do anything else. How much more disposable income might Ann have if her bills were shared with a partner, or paid for by a partner like Judy's were? A lot, was the answer. She could buy some good moisturiser, maybe get a facial or manicure from time to time, invest in a capsule wardrobe. Judy had set herself up nicely, Ann thought. Ann used to tell herself she was the clever one, avoiding marriage and children, but actually, when she looked at Judy, and her sisters and their friends, she knew it wasn't true. The combined forces meant they were living in beautiful homes, having two holidays a year, and driving EVs. How had Ann's life run aground at this point? Was it fair that Judy looked like the glossy singleton while Ann looked like the haggard mother of three kids?

Chapter Two

After Ann drove the three hours to Hudson, she caught the early-evening showing of *Theatre of the Flesh*. She could see why locals were up in arms about it. Not because it was offensive but because it was offensively bad. She tried to keep a straight face as the director talked through his vision of 'theatre made flesh' and how each actor became a 'limb of the body of the play'.

She had planned on driving straight back to Brooklyn but found that she needed a drink after that experience. She went to a bar next door to the theatre. She wanted to avoid the miserable damp of late October, the kind of cold that seeped right into the marrow of your bones. The heating system in the theatre just seemed to make the air smell different rather than make any impact on the temperature. She wanted warmth and the illusion of company.

Ann liked her own company. She felt at ease in a restaurant, cinema or bar by herself, even though for her sisters it was a form of social suicide, something that signified you were one of life's losers. They didn't know the sheer joy of being alone in a room full of people, the bliss of just being in a communal experience but insulated from it all, not having to make exhausting small talk with anyone. She could never tell her sisters that she actually chose to do these things alone, that she never even tried to invite a friend.

She sat at the bar and ordered a glass of wine. She looked down the bar at a man, a bit older than her, who was reading a book and sipping a glass of wine. She tilted her head to see the title. Oh. She was a deep believer in judging a person by the books they read and he was engrossed in a collection of essays by an older New York writer with a distinctly feminist bent. When he glanced up and caught her eye, he gave her a friendly smile but returned to his book without saying anything. Friendly, relaxed, but not in any way trying to capitalise on an opening.

Ann found her gaze returning to him as she sipped her wine. She was trying not to draw attention to herself as she took in his profile from the corner of her eye. She chastised herself, took a notebook and pen out, tried to jot down some thoughts from the interview but the 'theatre of flesh' description kept getting in the way.

Ann surprised herself by speaking first.

'Good choice,' she said, nodding towards the book.

He looked up and smiled again. 'Thanks,' he said then continued reading.

Let the man read, Ann thought.

'I had an early review copy,' she said, not able to stop herself. 'I'm a writer.'

What the fuck are you saying? she thought. You're a *hack*. Someone who used to believe she would be a writer and is now lying to a complete stranger.

But so what? She would never see this man again.

This time he closed the book and turned on his stool to face her. 'Oh really? Would I know your work?'

She took in the full breadth of him. He was built. His chest was hard and wide under his soft blue shirt and she noticed how his thighs and arms stretched the material of his jeans and jacket. As an unconscious response she pulled her shoulders back and squeezed her stomach tight. She crossed her legs and thanked herself for wearing her chic black heels that she liked to think made her look French.

'What do you write?' he asked next.

She realised she hadn't answered his first question. Shit. Her bullshit had been called so quickly. She couldn't tell him that she mostly rewrote press releases for local newspapers. What would Judy say if she was here with Ann?

'Essays mostly. I'm working on a collection right now for Knopf – well, my agent says they want to pre-empt since I won a writing prize for an essay a few years back.'

A few years back? Are you kidding? She shushed her inner voice and was encouraged to go on by his widening eyes and his body language.

He stood up. So tall. Ann swallowed. 'May I join you?' he asked.

She smiled. 'I'd love that.'

He carried his book and his glass towards her, and Ann swore the chemistry in the room changed completely when he sat within her space. She knew right there and then that they were going to sleep together. She just knew. She always knew. It was her gift. So, she accepted this fact and decided to just enjoy the lead-up. She inhaled his scent: strong but no-nonsense, nothing too complex, just clean and very male.

She snapped her attention back and held eye contact. Could he feel it too? Did he know what was happening here? Yes, she thought, as he looked back at her. Ann was good-looking, petite in stature with an athletic figure and long blonde hair, she knew she looked good when she made an effort, which she had done today, but he was out of her league, model-handsome. Sometimes it just happened like that. Some nights the chemistry was just right. She hadn't slept with anyone in two years. Caring for her mother seemed to have shut down that part of her. She hadn't even registered desire on her spectrum of emotions in that time. Until now. Strangely, though, she didn't feel at all nervous.

'So,' he asked again, 'would I know anything you've written?'

She smiled. 'I don't know, what have you read?'

He laughed and said, 'OK, I'll start. I'm Justin, Justin Forster, it's nice to meet you . . . ?'

'Ann,' she said. 'Do you ever think someone is named the wrong name?'

'What, like instead of Diana they've been named Ann?'

She laughed. 'Touché. I just mean, when I was watching you from across the bar I thought you would be called John or Tad or something like that. I didn't expect Justin. But it's nice, I am intrigued, Justin . . . '

'Can I buy you a drink, Ann?' he asked, pointing at her nearly empty glass.

'That would be lovely, thank you,' she said and he made an imperceptible gesture to the barman, who replenished their drinks.

'So, what's your favourite essay in this book,' she asked, giving the volume on the bar a nudge.

He smiled and made a little groaning noise and she thought she could feel a dynamo ignite and charge around her body. 'I'm, ah, a little embarrassed to say.'

Ann wondered if she had hallucinated him as a way of bringing some joy to her bleak little world. He was perfect, impeccable, casual but crisp, sexy but non-threatening, the kind of effect that usually only Italian men can muster with any success.

She remembered the essay about the discovery of female pleasure, the author's sexual awakening and insatiable desire for a particular man, her weakness for him, her uncharacteristic abandon around him.

'My favourite was "The Sea Shell",' she said. She remembered reading it and crying in her childhood bed, longing for anything that might make her feel something as her mother lay dying in the living room next door.

Theatre of the flesh, she thought, and was about to laugh when Justin leaned in. Before she knew what was happening, he had kissed her gently and briefly. He pulled his face away just an inch or two, so that their eyelashes were almost touching as she blinked in surprise. A question was asked and answered without any words. Justin paid the bill and took Ann's hand in his as they left the bar.

Ann had read about moments like this, moments where people felt they were no longer in control, like something important was happening and they were simply there to comply. He led her to his car and said, 'Can I interest you in a nightcap?'

She smiled and leaned into him. 'I'd love that,' she said and the rest was swallowed. She couldn't deny it was her who had made the first move. He had politely batted away two or three efforts at conversation before he had finally relented. Ann had forced it. She had approached him. And maybe looking back that was what he had intended all along. Play hard to get, leave the door to the trap wide open so nobody can tell it's a trap.

Chapter Three

The anticipation on the drive back to Justin's house was exquisite. He reached his hand over and let it rest high up on Ann's thigh, his fingers silently telling her he was looking forward to it too. She arched her back slightly. When he parked the car in the thick darkness of his driveway, he looked down at his lap for a moment, then lifted his gaze to hers as he leaned in slowly to kiss her. She unbuckled her belt and was kneeling on the seat by the time their lips met, hungrily kissing him, high on the moment.

'Wait,' he said laughing. 'Oh my god, I want you so much but let's go inside, otherwise it will be too late.'

She loved how mature he was, how confident. There was no embarrassment. This was grown-up. Ann adjusted her clothes and smoothed her hair and opened the car door. She stood up and looked at the house that seemed to disappear into shadows. Off to the right there seemed to be several smaller buildings as well as the original house, which looked like a massive gothic mansion, but she couldn't be sure where it began or ended in the dark. One thing she could tell: Justin was rich. Not just normal rich. *Rich* rich.

He took her hand and guided her around the back of the house, past the set of sweeping granite steps that rose to the front of the house. He stumbled a little himself. He was so big, Ann thought, and she really loved that about him. She hadn't experienced that feeling of being small, enveloped by someone, since she was a child.

'Watch your step here, these steps are old and uneven ... my w ... ah ... I keep meaning to get them fixed.'

He brought her around the side of the house to a kitchen entrance and then up a narrow staircase, which opened up into a hall of such grandiosity Ann actually gasped. On the drive up they had passed white concrete modernist homes, 10- and 20,000 square feet blocks of minimalist style. Hard edges and glass as thick as walls. Justin's house was different: old-fashioned but still grandiose. The interior was beautiful. Completely decadent, the soft heart underneath a foreboding exterior. Like Justin himself, she wondered. And maybe that's what the house's exterior was for. To keep everyone out, except for the people you wanted inside. In the light of the chandelier, a momentary chill crept into her veins.

Nobody knew where she was. *She* didn't even know where she was. She was in the middle of nowhere with a stranger. Somewhere north of Hudson? West? Her phone would tell her but she herself had long ago lost the ability to locate herself in space. She didn't even know his surname. Could she trust this guy she had just met?

What had felt sexy a minute ago suddenly felt foolish. She could be murdered and never found. Justin seemed to notice. 'You OK?'

She tried to shake it off. 'Sure . . . ' He smiled and she felt herself relax again. His smile was like a tranquiliser.

'Hey, we don't have to do anything. Let me just go pay the sitter . . . '

She was about to say, 'What?' when she heard a female voice.

'I thought I heard somebody.' A woman who looked to be in her mid-fifties appeared from behind a doorway, looking sheepishly at Ann. 'Sophie was in bed at nine and asleep by nine thirty. All quiet since then.'

'Thank you so much,' Justin said, handing her a wad of cash. 'There's some extra there. I really didn't expect to be so late. This is my friend . . . ' he turned to me and smiled.

'Ann,' she provided. Had he really forgotten her name?

It was the kind of introduction you could only make OK if it was before midnight and came with a full backstory. The sitter tried to be polite but Ann could see the seediness of the whole situation and embarrassment set in. This had been a bad idea.

There was an awkward moment as the babysitter got her coat and bag and left.

Ann didn't really know where to start. 'You have a child?' she asked.

He hadn't mentioned a child, and if he was a father, was there a mother? Ann's devil-may-care, let-your-hair-down attitude was neutralised. She felt sober and not in any way turned on.

'How could you invite me back to your place without mentioning you had a child that needed a babysitter,' she asked.

Justin looked genuinely shocked. He shushed her and dragged her closer with a smile. 'I didn't realise it would be a big deal – does it make a difference if I have a kid?' he asked. 'I mean, you're married too, right?' He pointed at Ann's mother's wedding ring and engagement ring, which she had worn on her ring finger since her mother had died.

Ann was flustered. 'Oh these, no, no, no, of course not, these belong to my late mother. I'm not married. And of course it doesn't matter that you have a child; it's just strange that you didn't mention . . . ' He pulled her closer to him, and began kissing her.

Ann kept her hands on his chest, trying to push him back. 'I didn't tell you because I didn't want it to be an issue. I haven't connected with someone in a very long time, Ann. You're so smart. And beautiful. Truthfully, I didn't think you'd come home with me if I told you.' He pulled her gently towards the double staircase. God, he smelled fantastic.

Ann was torn. Why did everything have to be complicated? Why did she have to overthink everything? Couldn't she just have some straightforward no-strings fun? This is what one-night stands were for, right? She heard her sisters' voices in her head – why do you always have to be so picky, Ann?

She pushed all of the questions and red flags to the corner of her mind and submitted, got lost in Justin's smell and his kisses until she heard a small voice from the top of the stairs.

'Daddy?' Justin leapt away from Ann as if she had burned him.

'Sophie! Darling, Daddy's here.' He turned to Ann. 'I'll be one minute. Please wait. Let me explain.' He bounded up the stairs and picked up the most beautiful little girl. She was around six years old, Ann guessed, and looked tiny in Justin's arms as he carried her back to bed.

Ann looked at the photographs in the hall. A little girl playing in the sand, standing on a podium, riding a pony, first place. Another picture a few feet along the hallway of Justin in a morning suit and a beautiful woman in white, unmistakably a bride. So, there was a wife.

She heard Justin come back down the stairs and turned to face him.

'Sorry about that,' he said. The moment had officially fizzled.

'Is she OK?' Ann asked.

'Oh, she's fine, she often gets up looking for water or the bathroom. She won't even remember tomorrow.'

'Phew,' Ann said.

Justin laughed and broke the tension. 'Why don't we have a drink?' he said, running his hand through his hair. 'At least let me explain. It's not what you think . . . '

She laughed. 'It never is.'

That was probably the point at which she should have gotten her coat, but for the second time that night, she felt that she had no control over the situation, that she lacked the power to say no to this man. What's more, she didn't want to. She wanted to be near him. She hadn't felt this alive in years. And so she followed him back downstairs to a basement-level study, a gloriously masculine joke of a room kitted out in leather furniture and plaid carpet. It was warm and cosy. Justin opened the vent on a stove in which some embers were glowing and took two logs from a basket full of chopped wood by the grate. He threw them inside, and sparks flew up before he slammed the stove shut quickly. They watched the logs combust instantly, staring in silence for a few moments.

'Please, sit.'

Ann took a tall leather armchair, at one side of the fireplace, and Justin poured two generous measures of whiskey, sipping from his as he passed one to her and took the chair on the other side of the fire.

'To answer your question, yes, I am, technically, married. But my wife and I . . . we aren't together,' he said.

'Well, these things happen,' Ann said. 'No big deal. You didn't have to keep it a secret that you're separated. I've had relationships in the past too you know. I should probably tell you now, I'm not a virgin.'

He laughed. 'No, it's not as simple as that; it's not what you think.'

'That's the second time you've said that,' she said. 'Maybe you should just tell me?'

'We're not separated or broken up or divorced. She's . . . dying.'

'Oh.' Ann was genuinely shocked.

'She has a rare illness that has slowly stolen her from us over the last couple of years. Sophie was just four when Deborah – that's my wife – went into hospital. She's been there ever since. They've tried everything, but the problem is they don't really know what caused her illness. It could be genetic, it could be environmental, whatever it is, it's incredibly rare and unpredictable. They still don't entirely understand it. They've tried every drug, they've had her on all sorts of experimental clinical trials, but nothing has worked. She's slowly degenerated, to the point that her doctors expect her to die within the next few months.'

Everything Ann had felt in the bar had disappeared. This was not what Ann had expected. She felt flustered. She couldn't even do a straightforward one-night stand. She realised Justin was waiting for a response but she didn't know what to say.

'My mom died,' she blurted out, 'recently. And I never even knew my dad. Or, well, I don't remember him. He died when I was even younger than your daughter.'

He looked slightly confused by Ann's non sequitur. 'I'm so sorry,' he said, leaning forward. 'He must have been young.'

'I'm sorry, I don't know why I told you that. It doesn't have anything to do with . . . I know it's not the same as your wife, it's just . . . I was my mom's carer for three years before she died so maybe I can understand a small bit of what you're going through . . . And there's really nothing the doctors can do for her?'

He shook his head gently. 'So, you see, I'm married but . . . not?'

The full impact of what he was saying hit Ann. Could she really blame him for not telling her this upfront? She was flooded with empathy. She hadn't told him everything either, hadn't told him that she had blitzed her career while looking after her mother, or about her anger at her sisters for abandoning her, or about how she was struggling to find the motivation to keep going, while all of her friends effortlessly ticked off the boxes on the checklist for a successful life.

These thoughts played through her mind as she stood up to cross the few feet between her chair and Justin's. She thought she understood something of what he might be feeling, the sense of duty to someone you once adored but who now resembled nothing of that former person, the lack of any meaningful relationship.

'That is so awful,' she said, taking his glass and putting it down before climbing on top of him and kissing him gently. 'I'm so sorry.' She punctuated each word with a kiss and was pleased that he responded. It was much better than the forced passion of the staircase. It felt deep and dizzying and everything she had ever wanted all at once.

Something was opening up in her as he undressed her and lay her down on the floor by the fire. Her thoughts were flickering. She wanted to look after him, but more than anything she wanted to be looked after, protected.

One thing she knew for sure: she didn't want to be alone any more.

Chapter Four

Ann woke up with the dawn, the fire collapsed in on itself, the embers still gently glowing. She had slept more deeply than she had since her mom had died. She stood and looked out of the window to see the light creeping up from the water, mist curling up from the edges. She hadn't noticed the setting in the dark last night but now she could see the house was perched at the edge of the river with spectacular views.

'I'm so sorry but you're going to have to leave,' she heard his panicked voice say from behind her. She spun around. 'I can't let Sophie see you. It might upset her.'

Ann was horrified. 'Of course!' she said quickly. 'I'm so sorry. I didn't mean to fall asleep. I'll order an Uber now.' She tapped at her phone – 'wait, you don't have Uber here?'

'I'll call you a taxi,' he said, laughing as she scrabbled together her belongings.

'It was lovely meeting you,' she said. 'I had a good night. I didn't expect to, you know, what with the secret wife and child and all that!'

He laughed too as she pulled on her clothes. He spoke authoritatively into his phone. 'It'll take about ten minutes to get here.' She shrugged her coat on and said, 'Well, I can wait outside. I hope you . . . '

What *did* she hope?

'I hope you'll be OK,' she said.

'Wait,' he said, smiling, 'can I at least get your number?'

Ann was wrong-footed. She had thought that this was just a one-night stand. He was too handsome for starters. And Ann, while pretty, wasn't the kind of woman that millionaires dated. So, what was in it for him? She felt a strong desire to see him again but her suspicion held her back. Did he think she would be a convenient hook-up? She felt she was standing on a precipice and once she stepped off there would be no going back. She stalled for time.

'Well, do you think that's a good idea? I mean, you've got a lot going on and I live, like, two hundred and fifty miles away . . . '

'I know, but I had fun too. Couldn't we just . . . have fun again? You've got a car, I've got a car . . . ' He smiled and, god, his smile felt like healing.

A world went through Ann's mind in those two seconds of hesitation. What would her life look like if she responded, 'Thanks, but I think it's best we just leave it. Too complicated. Let's just remember it as a nice night'. Safe, uncomplicated, unchanged.

But as his smile beamed down on her, she found herself doing something she never did. Instead of being level-headed and reasonable, always doing what was right for everyone else, she decided to do something for her, regardless of the consequences. Doing the right thing had gotten her nothing except a boring life of grinding boredom and near-poverty. She was so sick of being the responsible one, the one who always said no to pleasure, rash decisions, bad ideas.

She thought of her sisters again, and how they always said she was holding out for the perfect man who didn't exist. She was pretty sure they wouldn't approve of her hooking up with a married man, or hooking up at all. They disapproved of what they called 'putting out' on first dates or one-night stands.

Easy to disapprove from the comfort of their marriages, Ann thought.

She thought of her cold life making ends meet, the last few years spent caring for her mother, the deep crevasse of pain that had divided her body from her mind when she'd died. What harm would another hook-up do? Couldn't it just be a case of two people helping each other through a tough time, some affection, some fun, no strings, no commitment, no expectations? Justin had said himself it was fun. He clearly had no expectations of her, and she was not in any position to commit to anyone. Besides, she could do with a little bit of no-strings fun in her life. It might not fill the vastness of her grief but it might go some way to bridging it or at least distracting her from it.

She looked at him and smiled and in that moment her whole life changed, though she didn't know it yet.

'Sure,' she said. 'Why not? What's the worst that could happen?'

The following weekend, Justin came to Brooklyn. He booked a hotel close to her place. When she said on the phone, 'you could have stayed at my place,' he said, 'I didn't want to make any assumptions.' She liked that about him.

She booked a local restaurant with a traditional Italian menu. It was cosy and intimate, lit by candles, the kind of place that doubled up as a bar and let you keep your table for as long as you wanted if the night was going well. She arrived ten minutes early. It was particularly freeing deciding to see someone like this, someone she knew was not a boyfriend option. She didn't have to worry about looking too keen or cool enough or strategising about turning up ten minutes late so she wasn't the first one there. None of this stuff mattered any more. They had both tacitly accepted the terms and conditions and agreed that in each other they would find some distraction, some comfort from the demons they were both on the run from. That's all they asked from each other.

Ann was surprised to find Justin was already there, a drink in his hand on the mahogany bistro table. When she saw him she felt a jolt run through her system. She thought somebody should have shouted, 'CLEAR!' like they do on medical TV shows so nobody got hurt. She was glad though, that he was as handsome as she remembered, that she didn't feel any aversion, that she just felt excited about the evening ahead and what was to come.

He stood, leaned over the table and kissed her on the cheek. The heat of his face, the memory of his scent, the touch of his clothes all made Ann bubble inside.

'Hey.' She smiled, sat down and he ordered her a drink. She loved his ease in the world, how he knew what to do, how he knew what she wanted. It felt like being looked after.

They relaxed quickly into easy conversation. Ann noticed how the waitress watched Justin, flirted with him, checked on them regularly. She tried to push her own questions about what a man like this was doing with a woman like her to the edges of her mind. Just take things at face value, she told herself. It's not serious, so you don't have to worry about his motivations. Just have some fun for once in your life.

They talked about their lives, what took Justin, who had studied in New York, all the way upstate to

Albany first and then to Hudson. He loved New York but his family's real estate business had been in Albany, he told her, and its surrounding towns and cities for generations. 'I can come to New York any time I like. But Albany and Hudson made me, Hudson is home. They talked about Ann's ingrained aversion to leaving the five boroughs.

'It's hardly Timbuktu,' he said. 'Hudson is actually a city, you know. In fact, Hudsonites will tell you it is the very first city that officially existed in the United States.'

Ann knew this, of course. 'No, no, don't get me wrong,' She said, laughing, just as the waitress brought their starters, 'I like it; it's just a different way of life to what I'm used to.'

'I get that,' he said. 'I never thought I'd end up there either . . . but the more I was away the more I realised it is part of who I am, it's where I'm from.'

She wanted to lift the tone back up to light. 'I spent a summer in Hudson once, when I was in college.'

'What? Why?'

'It was my first year and a group of us decided to head north to resort towns to get work. We had an idea in our heads that we would earn a fortune in tips waiting in the seafood restaurants. We didn't do too badly. A thousand dollars in tips every week was a small fortune back then. I think my mother had an idea that I would meet a nice boy and start dating someone who was marriage material.'

He looked intrigued. 'And did you?'

'There was a local guy, who I met in Hudson that summer. We actually dated for a few years. He even asked me to marry him, but after finishing his law degree in NYU, he wanted to move back to work in his family's firm. But I couldn't do it; Brooklyn owned a bigger piece of my heart than he did, it turned out. I still had big dreams and I didn't think I'd make them happen in Hudson. I needed to be at the centre of things. It was genuinely a source of distress for my mother.' Ann laughed. 'She was old-fashioned that way and he was from a very good family. I don't think she ever got over it actually. Now I think she might have had a point,' Ann said, with a roll of her eyes.

'What do you mean by that?' Justin asked.

'Oh, just that my two sisters married in their twenties and followed the nice straight path of career, marriage, children, and they've both done well, they're well set up now. I was going to be a writer. The rest would come later, or so I assumed. But it never did come.'

'There's still time, surely,' he said carefully.

'Well, I'm thirty-eight, so realistically I don't think there is time, but I do sometimes think life might be nicer shared with someone ... Everything I do, I do for myself, and I do alone. I'm not complaining, but sometimes it feels like I'm being punished for being independent or being single. Everything costs twice as much and people assume there's something wrong with me because I'm not married and they feel sorry for me because I don't have a kid. I kind of have to fight against that feeling in myself sometimes, like, tell myself that I'm OK, there's nothing wrong.'

'Well, I think you're fascinating, Ann – successful, creative, independent . . . beautiful.'

She laughed to cover her embarrassment and he reached over and took her hand. She felt the jolt again.

'It's true, you know,' he said, and squeezed her fingers.

She didn't think anyone had ever been this kind to her. She felt close to tears. She had been so focused on looking after her mother for the last three years, unsupported, that she had completely abandoned herself.

She felt emotional all of a sudden. It was still only a little over two months since she had lost her mother. She probably shouldn't be out in the world so soon. She felt like a gaping emotional wound, walking the streets, seeking anything that might staunch the bleeding, anything that might make her feel better. Which is perhaps why she found herself here with Justin. He was just the kind of person she needed in her life right now: no demands, no responsibilities, just fun, affection and some human kindness. She hadn't realised how starved she had been of all these things over the last few years. She was wrung out but she was also desperately trying to connect with every bit of stardust that was whizzing through the universe, anything that might give her life some meaning right now.

They lingered long after dinner, sipping cocktails and getting to know each other better. Laughing and sharing their histories, the things they hadn't spoken about at the bar the previous week. She told him about her mother, her sisters, and how she was just getting her career back up and running, and he told her about Deborah, Sophie and their lives in Hudson.

By the time they were asked to leave the restaurant because it was closing, she felt that they knew everything there was to know about each other. So, when Justin asked her to come back to his hotel room with her, she realised she had already decided that she would.

She would follow him anywhere.

Chapter Five

Later that night, as they lay in each other's arms, the white cotton hotel sheets tangled around them, Justin asked about her mother. 'How did you end up looking after her by yourself?'

Ann's face darkened a little. 'I'm still not really sure why, apart from the fact that if I didn't do it, nobody else was going to.'

'But what about your sisters, did they not help out?'

Ann gave a laugh that came out more bitter than she had expected. 'They would say they did ... but they barely spoke to or visited my mom while she was well and only really called her when they needed something from her, usually to take the kids while they went away for a weekend. Mom was always happy to do it, she loved her grandkids, but it really annoyed me how much they took her for granted. They never saw her as more than their mom, the woman they could use and abuse. They never grew up and out of that dynamic. Mom and I had a different relationship; we were friends, probably because I never really needed anything from her once I started working and supporting myself. Anyway, when she started getting sick, Emily and Juliet got together and decided that I should move in with Mom and be her full-time carer . . .'

'What?' Justin said, gently outraged on my behalf. 'But that's crazy, how could they do that?'

Ann could tell him how. 'Because they had kids and I didn't. And they had husbands and I didn't. And they had careers while I had what they saw as a hobby. Writing. It's not a real job like theirs, lawyers and doctors, actually doing things, making real money, helping people in need.'

'Some people would dispute that's what lawyers do,' he said.

Ann smiled and nuzzled her head deeper into his chest. She loved the feeling of his heavy arm around her. She remembered her sisters' arguments so well. When Ann had suggested that their mom should move in to one of their large comfortable homes, they had rebuked her. A noisy, busy house full of young children won't be good for her, Juliet had said. She needs to be in her own home with peace and quiet. Doesn't she deserve that? Emily had added the coup de grace by saying, 'And you'd save so much money in rent, Ann. You know it makes sense.'

'The long and the short of it was they had the perfect defence ... This was the punishment for selfish child-free me, my comeuppance for having white floorboards and sharp-edged, low-placed breakables and candles carelessly placed within reach of small people. I couldn't flaunt all that freedom and expect to get away with it, could I?' She laughed hollowly. 'The fact is, I was the only one who was sacrificable, I was the one who had the least to lose by giving up my life, so I moved in with her and spent the last three years nursing her.'

'They didn't help at all?' Justin asked.

'They would come visit five or six times a year, bearing useless huge bouquets of flowers, books on how to beat ALS with your diet or with God or with crystals, again totally useless. After twenty minutes they would leave again, having done their obligation for the next six to eight weeks.'

'Wow,' he said, kissing her hair gently. 'That's really tough.'

'They paid for everything my mom needed and I think that's how they squared their consciences. Now, though, they want to sell Mom's apartment, which is where I'm living at the moment, but she left it to all three of us. Emily and Juliet think it's better to sell now.'

'But surely they don't need the money,' Justin asked.

'No, they don't but they want it. And I guess that's

their right,' she said. 'I am not looking forward to finding a new place in this market though. I feel like I've been through so much in the last year ... it's just one thing after another. But, look at me, telling you all of my woes. You have enough worries of your own.'

'I don't mind,' he said, squeezing her a little tighter.

How cool this man was, Ann thought, able to offer emotional support without feeling the need to put up walls or push her away. She appreciated it. She smiled and closed her eyes, peaceful against the rise and fall of his chest.

'You know, for the three years after her diagnosis, until she died, I used to dream about finding a miracle cure, a silver bullet that would just repair her, return her neurons, mend her DNA, rebuild her body like a 3D printer, return her to me, my mother as I had known her, the woman I needed more than anyone in my life.'

He took a deep breath. 'I can identify with that. I think I've been the same with Deborah. We've tried every trial out there and I think there is always a part of me that hopes – even though I know it's not rational and all of the professionals tell me it's impossible – I still have this hope that she will get better.'

Ann nodded. 'I think that's natural when you love someone ... I definitely lived in two worlds with my mom. The real world, where I had to stop her aspirating her food, and a fantasy world, where she was my mom again. I used to think about the things we would do together, the places we would go, the holidays, the dinners, the shopping trips, the advice I needed that she would freely give. I think in a way it helped me survive the awfulness of her illness. I held out hope until the very end, right up to the last minute when she told me that it was finally time.'

She felt Justin's body stiffen beneath her. 'What do you mean?' he asked, struggling to prop himself up on his elbows.

She sat up too and looked at him. She trusted this man. She didn't know why, but she did. He had so much empathy. She felt safe. 'She killed herself. She didn't want to suffocate, which was what was going to happen to her. She wanted to control how she died.'

He seemed to understand. 'Did you ever talk to anyone about this?'

Ann shook her head. 'It wasn't possible to tell anyone, even my sisters . . . I see a community therapist from the local clinic once every couple of months. Post-Covid it's nearly impossible to find a therapist and I'm just suffering ordinary grief. There are people out there with much more urgent issues.'

'You poor thing,' he said, drawing her back to him and lying back down again. 'What a time you've had.'

Ann tried not to think of what was lost. It was always hard to acknowledge that she would never see her mother again, that she was exposed to the vastness of life on earth without her mother but, as she fell asleep in Justin's arms, she felt something akin to the protection her mother had offered her. Security, safety, comfort.

And she liked it.

Chapter Six

Walking back home from the hotel the next morning, Ann felt like she was floating on air. She had barely slept and had drunk a lot of champagne, but somehow she felt neither hungover nor tired. She was . . . happy, a bubble of excitement in her stomach. She might cry out good morning to passers-by, or laugh at any moment. There was none of the normal post-date anxiety, excused as she was from those patterns of hoping someone might call and then being disappointed when they didn't, of investing dates with hopes for a relationship that didn't pan out. In this instance, a relationship was not possible, and he lived in another city; it was just what she needed right now. She decided to call in to Juliet's house on the way home. As the less judgemental of her two sisters, she thought it might be a good place to start.

'Ann, what are you doing here? I was just going to take the dog for a run . . . '

'Oh, I was passing and just thought I'd say hi. It's OK if you're busy.'

'No, no, of course not, come in, have a coffee. I can walk the dog later.'

Juliet was wearing sweats, a ribbed golf jacket and a baseball cap. She looked like one of those momfluencers, Ann thought. Fit and pretty and effective in her day. Juliet definitely had a to-do list and Ann was aware that she was putting a kink in it by calling in unexpectedly. But she wanted to talk to somebody about Justin. She wanted every conversation to lead back to him because she couldn't stop thinking about him.

'So, what has you in my neighbourhood?' Juliet said as she ground coffee and shrugged off her jacket. The dog whined and she said to him, as if she believed he could understand her, 'We'll go later, I promise,' so that she almost missed Ann's answer.

'Well, I was on a date last night . . . in the area . . . and I slept over so here I am, still in the neighbourhood.' She smiled.

'Oh my god! Oh my god, Ann! I don't believe it! We have to call Emily!' She had Emily on speaker phone before Ann could object.

'Emily, you'll never guess . . . Ann has MET SOMEBODY!'

Ann waved her hands and rolled her eyes and

shouted, 'MIGHT! I MIGHT have met somebody! It's not cause for celebration.' Emily's voice came down the phone. 'Finally! It's the answer to our prayers.' There was a lot of distorted screaming before Emily said, 'Don't you dare start without me. I mean it. Don't say anything without me, Ann. I'll know if you do. I want to hear everything! I'm leaving now. I'll be there in five minutes.'

It was incredible how they could change Ann's status so easily from being outside of their little group to being in their inner circle. Ann's child-free, husband-free lifestyle had been problematic for both her sisters since the moment they had coupled up. A woman's life cycle was a bell curve. She climbed up one side in her twenties, acceptably single, living out her best hot-girl years. As she curved along the peak in her thirties she had better couple up and procreate before she began the rapid descent into her forties and fifties, if she didn't want to become a statistical anomaly. At this point, friends and sisters ran into marriage and motherhood like they were playing a game of musical chairs and the music had just stopped. Within a year of meeting their partners, they were all engaged, married or pregnant. As Ann had resisted and carried on solo down the bell curve, telling herself she didn't have to conform, she'd realised her social life was suffering. Her free time on weekends was being eaten into by friends who now had kids, desperate for help or a break or some quiet time for themselves. Instead of drinking Prosecco over three-hour brunches followed by a spot of shopping, she was standing in damp cold playgrounds sipping a cappuccino behind sunglasses as her friends complained about how tired they were, how badly work was going and how they never had sex any more. Instead of going for dinner followed by a nightclub, she had dinner off her knees on friends' couches because they were too tired to leave the house.

Despite what her sisters thought, Ann had in fact considered having children many times. To have a family of her own was actually her greatest wish, but it wasn't just a matter of clicking her fingers and everything magically falling into place. Ann had also been taught to be independent, to develop a career, so that her private dream of having a home, a husband and a child seemed embarrassingly gauche, twee, so much so that she had buried it until she could no longer even hear the echo of that desire. It was easier to do when she hadn't met anybody she had liked enough to have a child with. And so it had gotten to the point where a large part of her actually believed that she was fine with not having children, fine with not having a partner, fine with not having a home. But she wasn't.

Her job was the definition of insecure. It was interesting but low-paid, and because she only had herself to worry about, she hadn't really thought about things like long-term earning power, pensions or real estate until her mother had died and she realised she was in a precarious situation.

Her sisters constantly campaigned for her to give motherhood a go, as if all she had to do was fill out a form. What was she dragging her feet for? Ann remembered Kieran's baby-naming ceremony six months previously. Emily had organised a family dinner for them and Juliet, still full of hormones and talking nonsense, had said, 'Oh, Ann, you must make sure you don't miss out on this. It is just amazing.' Ann had thought Juliet looked like foie gras, bloated and stuffed and being nibbled on by her baby. She hadn't quite been repulsed, but she hadn't bought the blissful trip Juliet was selling either. 'Tell her,' Juliet had said to Emily, sensing Ann's scepticism.

'It really is just the big picture, the WHOLE picture. Life in technicolour . . . ' Emily had said, still looking at her phone. Ann hadn't been sold.

She still wasn't sold, but sitting at Juliet's kitchen table now, six months later, and wanting to tell her sister everything about the man she had known for just one week, felt terrifyingly like the beginning of an easy sell.

True to her word, Emily burst through the door a few minutes later and checked the sisters' faces for any signs of betrayal, any sign that Ann had leaked the story to Juliet first. The mode of her arrival made baby

Kieran burst into tears of fright and Juliet had to settle him before Ann could talk. She waited for Emily to fill a coffee cup from the jug before she began.

'OK,' Emily said, 'spill it.'

Chapter Seven

By the time Ann had told Juliet and Emily everything about Justin, apart from the most important detail of course, they were swooning as if she had just read them a Jane Austen novel.

'I just can't believe it,' Juliet squealed, 'It's so perfect. And how lovely to meet him so soon after Mom. Do you think she sent him to you? The fact that you met him in Hudson? It feels meant to be!'

Emily and Ann exchanged a look. Juliet had an ability to get carried away. 'It's early days and we're just having fun right now.'

'Well, that sounds very wise,' Emily said. 'I have some good news this morning too. It looks like we might have a buyer for Mom's apartment.'

'What?! Oh, that's wonderful news,' Juliet said. 'We'll be able to renovate the pool room finally!'

'What do you think, Ann?'

Ann was stiff with fear. 'Where will I live? I'm just getting back on my feet financially. Can't we put the sale off for a year, just until I have built up some regular work and income?'

Emily said, 'The market is so hot right now, Ann. We could be losing out if we wait. And the sale should give you enough cash for a down payment on an apartment.'

She would be downgrading from a three-bed apartment to a studio or one-bed if she was lucky. It was a huge step down. 'Have you seen the prices of three-beds in Brooklyn? And I don't have a stable income. I doubt the banks will give me a mortgage. I'd have to use my portion to pay rent.'

Emily said, 'But you wouldn't need a three-bed Ann, it's just you, surely a studio or one-bed would be plenty?' She quickly changed the subject. 'Tell us more about Justin, he sounds amazing. Really, he sounds like the perfect man for you. He sounds like the perfect man full stop . . .'

Ann smiled. 'He does, but I don't want to get tangled up in anything too complicated . . .'

She cut herself off but Emily had noticed. Nothing ever escaped Emily. It was why she was a brilliant lawyer. Her mind seized on any irregularity, like a hawk seeing a mouse moving in the undergrowth 200 metres below. And with equal elegance and precision, she swooped. The problem with people was they wanted the fairy tale, and any variations or diversions from this would be taken ominously. Juliet looked perturbed. Here it comes, Ann thought.

'Why is it complicated?'

Ann realised her mistake immediately.

'Is there a catch?' Emily asked. 'He does sound too good to be true ... '

'Does there have to be a catch?' Ann asked, mock-offended. 'Maybe he was just waiting for the right one to come along, just like me.'

'Have you googled him yet?' Emily asked, not to be deterred.

'Of course I haven't googled him,' Ann said. 'We're not even dating. We've just hooked up. Neither of us is in a position to be dating. We're keeping it super-casual. I'm not getting into googling him and obsessing over what he has or hasn't told me. I respect people's privacy. Anything he needs to tell me he will in his own good time, I'm sure. Or never. I may never even see him again. We've made no plans.'

Emily made a pitying face as she picked up her phone and started typing. 'What's his surname ... '

But she didn't need it. She had already found him simply by typing his first name, job and 'Hudson', and had his results up before Ann could even refuse to give her his surname. She was a master of search optimisation.

Emily's face fell and she slapped the table, hard. 'Ann ... he's married.'

Juliet screamed, 'No!' and burst into tears, predictably. 'Asshole! I knew it! The ones that are too good to be true are always too good to be true.' She reached across the table and grabbed Ann's hands, squeezing them tight. 'I'm so sorry, Ann, but it's better to find out sooner rather than later!'

'Guys, look, it's not a big deal. He told me he had a wife. I know, OK? I know about her. He told me. I just didn't tell you because I knew you'd react, well, like this.'

'Wait, you knew? You know he has a wife? How can you do that to his wife, Ann? What if she was one of us?'

Ann rolled her eyes. 'This is what I meant by it's complicated . . . It's not what you think. He's married, but he's not really married.'

Emily again. 'It's kind of binary, Ann. He either is married or he is not. There's no "kind of" married.'

Ann inhaled deeply. This was going to be a lot for them but here goes nothing, she thought.

'His wife is dying. What she has, they cannot cure; they've tried everything. Now they just have to wait, which is excruciating, obviously. And I feel for him so much, what he's been through, what he's going through and I'm not going to stop seeing him for silly technical reasons. Don't you think he deserves a little bit of happiness or even friendship and support? Even if it is just escapism. And come to think of it, don't you think I deserve a little bit of fun after nursing our dying mother for three years? I'm not looking for anything from him; it doesn't matter to me that he's married because I am not looking to get married.' But even as she said it she felt the dissonance of the words. She didn't believe them. She already knew that she wanted to marry Justin.

'Well, I would say there is a difference between friendship,' Emily said smartly, 'and sleeping with someone. That's kind of next-level support.'

Juliet was pacing around the kitchen now. 'This is too much. Even for you, Ann, this is TOO MUCH. How can you get involved in this, this … SHIT-FEST?!' Juliet never swore. 'Are you crazy?'

Now it was Ann's turn to feel outraged. 'Ever since you and Emily have been married and had kids you've done nothing but tell me how much I'm missing out on by not dating, by not having a family, by being too picky.' Ann was shouting now. 'Despite the fact that there was no way I could even entertain that because I was too busy looking after *our* mother, a job which you foisted upon me and never bothered helping out with, bar the odd flying visit to assuage your guilt. So, please, it's a bit late to be sanctimonious now.'

'But Ann,' Juliet pleaded, 'are you that desperate for a man?'

Now Ann really was offended. 'No, I am not so desperate for a man that I married the first rich asshole who came along and wanted to marry me – not that desperate,' she spat. It was a low blow. They all knew that Juliet was unhappy with her husband.

'OK, OK, this is getting unnecessarily personal,' Emily said coolly. 'Juliet, apologise to Ann, and Ann, apologise to Juliet.' They muttered childish apologies because it was something their mother had always made them do. Family was family. They were never allowed to fall out, ever.

Juliet was uncharacteristically silent, probably because she couldn't think of anything positive to say. After a few moments, she asked, 'Have you spoken to your therapist about it? What does she say?'

'I literally met him a week ago. I'm not due to see Sarah for another month.'

'Well, why not see what she says, get her take. She's objective, not like us' Juliet smiled weakly, and things thawed.

'Juliet has a point, Ann. It might help you to look at how things will play out, what happens when his wife does die; will he still want you around then? We're only saying this because we care about you; we don't want to see you hurt.'

'I know,' Ann said, 'but I know what I'm doing, OK? We're both on the same page. Neither one of us is looking for a relationship. We're just looking for some company and a little bit of fun. I'm following my heart for once.'

'All we're saying is protect yourself,' Juliet said, conciliatory now. 'Take it slow. There's no need to jump right in with both feet straight away.'

Chapter Eight

But she did jump in with both feet, despite everyone's advice to the contrary. And despite what she and Justin told each other about just having fun, things snowballed. They spoke on the phone every night. They texted twenty times a day. They spent every weekend together either in Brooklyn or in Hudson, and within a matter of weeks they were deeply, inextricably involved. The kind of involved where nobody gets out alive. Hadn't somebody mentioned something about keeping things non-committal, no-strings?

They had spoken about it, tentatively at first but then more freely, as they realised they were both falling for each other. Justin wanted her. In fact, he needed her, and regularly told her so. She was an undemanding presence in his life, someone who listened to him, cared for him, turned up for him and asked nothing of him in return. He had never met anyone like her.

Ann had never met anyone like Justin either. He didn't play games. He said exactly what he felt. Maybe because he was older everything seemed straightforward, smooth, despite the complications that surrounded them. Maybe because of the complications. There were no rows, because there were no expectations. Ann enjoyed spending weekends in Hudson because it took her away from the constant hustle of trying to re-establish her career in New York during the week, and the sad memories of her mother, not to mention the pressing situation of where she was going to live once her sisters closed the sale of her mother's apartment. For now, she pushed it all out of her head. With Justin, she found she could temporarily forget all of her problems.

After they had been seeing each other for two months, Justin invited her to meet Sophie. On the weekends that Ann came to Hudson, Sophie usually slept over with a schoolfriend, but now Justin wanted Ann to meet his daughter. Ann was nervous. She knew on some level it was important for her to like Sophie and for Sophie to like her. She asked Juliet how she should approach it. 'Bring something cuddly, a cute teddy, and a book, and some sweets.' Emily chimed in, 'Just bring cold, hard cash Ann. Kids love currency.'

On the day in question, Justin opened the door wide and stepped back to reveal the most adorable little girl. Long hair, a velvet Alice band, a perfect little dress.

'Sophie, this is Daddy's friend Ann . . .'

'Hi Sophie,' Ann said. She had some sweets, a book and a doll in a bag and offered them to Sophie. 'These are for you,' she said.

Sophie immediately changed her energy, grabbed the toys and hugged Ann – 'thank you!' – before running off into the house with her loot.

Justin laughed. 'Well, that went well.'

Ann smiled too, with relief.

With Sophie now introduced to Ann, she was at home more when Ann visited and they went out for lunches together, to the park and the cinema. Ann and Justin had agreed that they would be careful not to touch or kiss or hold hands around her.

And Ann tried to help as much as she could. She remembered what it was like to be the sole carer for her mother and how sometimes all she needed was someone to say, 'I'll sit with her for an hour, go for a walk.' She knew what it was like being the last stop, the person it all rested on, and she didn't want Justin to feel alone.

But that meant she was getting in faster and deeper than either of them had intended. Justin was coming to rely on her and she was, much to her surprise, growing fond of Sophie.

Emily and Juliet argued with Ann constantly. 'What are you doing, Ann? We thought you were going to get your career back on track but instead you're babysitting this married man's kid and spending all of your free time upstate . . . you're throwing everything away. Try to think of yourself here, Ann. What if he dumps you?'

But what they didn't know was that Ann *was* thinking of herself. For the first time in a long time she was following her heart, going with her gut.

With Justin and Sophie, she could pretend that this was her life, her perfect family and perfect home and that her chaotic life in Brooklyn was happening to someone else.

Chapter Nine

'How come you don't have a kid?' Sophie asked. She and Ann were having a picnic in the playroom of Justin's house, the dolls laid out in a circle, toy cups and teapots filled with water.

'Well, not everybody has kids . . . '

'But don't you want one?'

'Sure, I'd love to have had a kid, but I guess I never really met the right person.'

'I could be your little girl if you like . . . ' Sophie said, pouring water down one of her doll's faces. 'My mommy is in the hospital and she can't come home.'

Ann felt tears fill her eyes and she hugged Sophie tightly, 'Oh Sophie, I would like that very very much. Thank you. You're the best little girl anybody could ever wish for.'

Sophie pulled free of the hug and smiled up at Ann. 'You'd be a really nice mommy.'

'What makes you say that?,' Ann asked.

'Because you make Daddy smile and you always buy me candy.'

Ann laughed; she felt so happy she thought she might burst. She hadn't thought she had any maternal instinct at all, but her gentle relationship with Sophie was teaching her otherwise, her feelings unfurling under Sophie's love. Perhaps this was what her sisters had been talking about all along, all of those times when they had told Ann what she was missing. For the first time, Ann started to feel that maybe she really was missing something. She had never really known this feeling before, a very pure love, one where she simply wanted to make this little person happy and would do anything to achieve that.

During the week back in Brooklyn, Ann found herself thinking of Sophie on her lunch breaks. On her way to the bodega for a chicken wrap, she found herself scanning the shelves for something cute – sweets, hair ties, puppets or princess crowns, washi tapes and origami, anything really – she would buy it for her without hesitation, even though money was still tight. As she got to know Sophie better, Ann took delight in knowing exactly what she would love and seeing the smile on her face when she presented her with that week's treat. She knew now, for example, that Sophie preferred neon colours to pastels. And that she preferred potato chips to sticky sugary sweets.

On the long drive from Brooklyn to Hudson on Friday evenings, she often imagined Sophie's delight, anticipating the moment that would give the child so much joy.

Ann's strategy of saying yes to every job was starting to pay off. Some editors were using her regularly now, but it was difficult balancing the unpredictable nature of freelancing with a new relationship. She was sitting up until 2 a.m. some nights trying to cram her work into five days just so she could jump in her car and be with Justin by Friday evening.

On weekends, Justin and Sophie would drive out to the hospital to visit Deborah. Sometimes Sophie would stay with Ann and sometimes she preferred to see her mom. Afterwards, they would all go for pizza in Sophie's favourite pizzeria, where Ann would drink a glass of wine and feel an unbelievable sense of well-being, like everything was finally just as it was meant to be. Justin always paid. He paid for everything, which, like Ann's newfound maternal feelings, surprised her as being something she liked. It made her feel protected, looked after, part of his life. Could it really be this easy? Could this be her husband? Her child? Could this be her family?

The weeks passed peacefully and uneventfully; their routine became established. Ann walked around in a haze of happiness. She felt so utterly grateful for what had become a relationship with

Justin and also the relationship she now had with Sophie. They made plans. Sometimes she let herself daydream about what life might be like two years or three years down the line, all of them living together, a giant Christmas tree in the main room, walking around the house with the kind of familiar entitlement that comes with being someone's wife, someone's mother. She found herself longing for it.

In town one day, before Christmas, shopping on her own, Ann went into the children's section of the most expensive department store. Sophie and Justin were spending Christmas with his family so he and Ann were exchanging gifts before then. Ann looked around the store. The prices! More expensive than adult clothes. A plush bunny that would fit in the palm of your hand – $50. Dresses that cost $180 and would be ruined instantly and permanently if they came into contact with spaghetti bolognese. But Ann let herself look around, pick things up and put them down again, behaving like a woman who did this on a regular basis, a woman who bought beautiful items for her beautiful children.

She was trying on an imaginary life. She wondered if this is where Justin's wife might have shopped before she got sick. Probably. He was rich. Concept electric car. Crazy waterside mansion. Designer clothes with no defining logos. Ann picked up a little dress that she thought would look beautiful on Sophie. She felt a rush at the idea of buying it for her, taking a little ownership in some way of her role in Sophie's life, letting the good stuff in for once instead of presuming it would all be snatched away from her. Why shouldn't she buy a little thing for Sophie, she thought? Maybe she would wear this dress with Justin's family on Christmas day. She liked that idea. This was the reward after all, wasn't it, for looking after children? You got let into that world of joy, dressing them up, playing with them, a way to reimagine your own childhood, reshape their lives to live the childhood you never had, a way to set right all the wrongs; this was the reward for the confinement and the quotidian. Ann saw it now, yes. She picked up the bunny too, threw caution to the wind. She walked up to the cash point where a perfectly presented sales assistant in her early twenties greeted Ann. She was dressed all in black with immaculate make-up and gel nails. She gave Ann a quick once-over. Ann wondered how much she was earning and what percentage of it went towards her beauty maintenance. It looked like it cost at least $100 a week. And then she hated herself for always having to think about money, not just her own lack of it, but also other people's apparent abundance.

The sales assistant smiled an innocent, friendly smile and said, 'I love this dress, it's so pretty.'

Ann smiled back at her. 'I love it too.' She paused. 'It's for my little girl. I just couldn't help myself.' Ann wondered if the lie had landed, if she had gotten her tone just right, but the girl didn't seem to notice anything strange.

'It's so gorgeous. And this bunny! She'll be a very happy little girl. How old is she?'

'Six,' Ann said, stretching out in the lie now, kneading the soft belly of it like a cat on a cushion. 'My husband says she has more clothes than either of us—' she laughed and she heard an edge of mania to it '—but I honestly can't resist this stuff.' Saying 'my husband' felt like a big risk, chancing fate, telling two lies in one go, but it also felt good to say the words. *My husband.*

It felt like Ann's life had been anointed with security. To have a husband and a child is to feel admitted to a secret club. A club that said, we know what we're doing with our lives, what are you doing with yours? Ann couldn't very well call Justin her boyfriend. She was too old to have a boyfriend; he was too old to be one. She thought the words sounded preposterous coming out of her thirty-eight-year-old mouth. She realised she actually wanted it all so much, and she knew she wanted it too fast. But who was it harming to try on the life she wanted for just a few minutes, talk about her husband and daughter as if they were real, as if they existed? Who would know?

As the girl wrapped Ann's purchases and tied them into the luxurious bag, she said, 'We're having a special evening next week that you might be interested in coming to. It's the Baby Antoinette label. They'll be showcasing their new collection and there will be discounts and some prizes on the night. If you would like to give me your number, I'll add you to the list.'

'Sure,' Ann said, aware now that she had backed herself into a lie and the quickest way to get out of it was not to fight it. 'That would be lovely!' Ann recited her mobile number. She looked over her shoulder, scanning the shop to see if anyone might recognise her. She saw a woman her own age looking directly at her and there was a man browsing near the door. Did Ann recognise the woman? Was she perhaps a neighbour of Justin's? It unnerved Ann a little to think this person might have heard her lie, but she shook it off. Nobody knew who she was. 'Have a lovely day,' the sales assistant said, handing over the bag. 'I hope your little girl likes them.' She said it brightly and loudly and Ann found herself wanting to shush her, not so loud.

As she left the store, Ann heard a snort of laughter from the till and turned to see the girl giggling with a colleague. Ann had a lot to learn about small towns.

What she didn't know yet about small towns was that everyone knew exactly who everyone else was, especially the outsiders.

Chapter Ten

Ann had been ignoring the very pressing issue of her mom's apartment being sold from under her, pushing it to the back of her mind, but with Christmas behind them, the new owners wanted to take possession in four weeks.

'Just find somewhere temporary, Ann,' Emily said, 'until the money from the sale comes through. Your share after fees will be substantial enough for you to get on the property ladder. We're all going to come out of this at least a quarter of a million dollars up. Just find something small and cheap, or an Airbnb until the money clears. It doesn't have to be perfect. It's just temporary. You'll be able to get a mortgage with the lump sum.' It was easy for Emily to say. Emily had an answer for everything. As if they weren't in the midst of a property crisis. As if the average apartment didn't cost $4,000–6,000 a month. As if Ann didn't have a pockmarked credit history due to her interrupted career. She was finally getting steady work now, but she hadn't been working long enough to have built up consistent savings or stability, the kind a mortgage lender liked to see. She needed something more permanent. She needed a job.

That weekend, Justin must have noticed how preoccupied she was, even though she was trying to hide it.

'You seem really stressed out, Ann,' he said, after giving her a hug. 'What's going on?'

Ann didn't want to dump on Justin; she was aware of wanting to keep things light with him. He had so much bad stuff in his life; he didn't need to add her worries to his too. But he urged her, 'Please, tell me Ann. Don't shut me out . . .'

In the few seconds of silence that unspooled, Ann made a huge decision. She realised she had kept her relationship with Justin at arm's length because she assumed it wasn't going anywhere. They had both gone into it with eyes open, some no-strings fun, nothing more. He was married. They were just two lost people offering each other some comfort. But to keep shutting him out only warped and stunted the relationship, cut off its oxygen. She knew that if she confided in him she was taking steps further into a relationship with him than either of them had planned, but she didn't want to play a part any more, the cheerful, supportive presence who flitted in and out. She was a real, multidimensional person. She had spent so much time tending to her mother, and now here she was doing the same with Justin, tending to his needs and feelings before her own. She realised she needed to talk to someone and Justin was ready to listen.

'It's my mom's apartment,' she said. 'They've found a buyer and I have to be out in less than a month … and I haven't been able to find anywhere. It's not a big deal, I haven't had much time to dedicate to it. I'll just rent an Airbnb or something for a while until I can get something sorted. And when the sale is finalised I'll eventually have a down payment for a place of my own … but it is stressful and emotional. It's the place where I grew up, the place where my mother died and now I'm expected to just be gone in a matter of weeks? It's stressing me out so much!' She felt her lip tremble and saw Justin's concerned face. He took her into his arms and said, 'Ann, why didn't you tell me? I can help … you can stay here with us until you find somewhere.'

Ann was shocked; her sisters, her own flesh and blood, had not even offered her a place to stay and here was this man whom she barely knew offering his home to her.

'What did you say?'

'I said come stay here with us. It makes sense. Most

of your work is done from home anyway, right? And if you need to be in the city, you can be there quickly enough . . .'

'I just . . . Justin, it's really kind, don't get me wrong, but I think it's all a little too fast, don't you?'

'I get it, I just don't want you to be stressed about it, OK? So, you have a place here if you need it but I don't want you to feel like things are moving too fast either. I must admit I'd love to have you around more, and I know Sophie would too.' He looked at her and smiled in a way that made everything OK. 'I love you, Ann. I'm in love with you. You came into our lives at the exact moment we needed you and I could not imagine being without you.' Ann couldn't believe it. Something had cracked open inside her and for the first time everything was as it should be.

She threw her arms around Justin's neck. 'I love you too, Justin. I love you both so much.' She found she was crying. Although her mind urged her to be cautious, she had never felt this way before. She was tired of trying to make ends meet, tired of being insecure, tired of waking up at night worrying about where she was going to live. Couldn't she just give in to this man who so clearly wanted to take care of her? Take what the universe was offering her?

Stop fighting everything all the time, Ann.

Maybe that was why she had been alone for so long in the first place.

Just follow your heart, she told herself, and see where it takes you.

Chapter Eleven

Ann was packing boxes in her mom's apartment the following week when she got a text from Judy.

> Ann! Sorry it has taken me so long to text but I am having a dinner party and I'd love you to come! Friday 8 p.m., at our place. Please say you're free! I'll send you a pin. X

Judy was always so warm, and it was kind of her to make the effort to reconnect with Ann. Ann realised she hadn't expected to hear from her. When had she become so cynical about people? It was time for Ann to start reconnecting with the world, with life. She was happy, and in love, and felt strong for the first time since her mom's diagnosis. She could drive up to Justin's early Saturday morning. She texted back and a few seconds later Judy sent her a pin on Google Maps. Ann was curious to see where Judy lived and clicked on the link.

The Olympia, the building that rose like the sail of a boat rippling high above the surrounding buildings, towering over the highest towers with an unparalleled view of the Manhattan skyline. It was, everyone said, even nicer than living in Manhattan. You got to look at it without having to experience everything that drove you mad about it – the heat in summer, the noise, the bustle, the crime – you got to watch it all from your double-height windows. She texted Emily and asked to borrow something to wear.

On Friday, Ann arrived wearing a simple black Prada dress and some Tamara Mellon heels grudgingly handed over by Emily, with a warning not to wreck them on the cobbles down in Dumbo. Ann tiptoed over the street to the entrance of the Olympia. The concierge unlocked the elevator for her and sent her to the floor below the penthouse.

The apartment was enormous and already full of people. So much for Judy's 'small gathering'.

Judy spotted Ann right away and brought a glass of champagne to her, and rapidly introduced her to a friendly group. When the party was running on its own steam, Judy found Ann and dragged her away from the crowd for a sidebar.

'So, how are things with you? Are you seeing anyone? I have a gorgeous venture capitalist here tonight who I think you'd hit it off with . . .'

Ann smiled.

'I have started seeing someone actually,' she said shyly. 'In fact, I met him that day we bumped into each other.'

Judy slapped Ann's arm. 'Ann! That's great. It must be serious so if you're still seeing each other?'

'Actually, he wants me to move in with him. It's a bit of a whirlwind but it feels right, you know? ... The only catch is he lives in Hudson.'

'Oh, Ann,' Judy said in a tone that would have been appropriate if Ann had just told her that Justin had just been released from prison having served a life term as serial killer but he was just misunderstood. 'You can't move to Hudson, for goodness' sake! Here, come with me and I'll introduce you to Sebastian ... '

But Ann put her hand on Judy's bony wrist. 'No, Judy, listen. I think it's the real deal. I know it's fast but it's like people say, when you know you know. He has a little girl and they live in this beautiful compound by the water and—'

'Compound?' Judy's eyes lit up. 'You never mentioned compound ... OK, this changes everything. Hudson is not so far away when you have a private jet.' She laughed and clinked Ann's glass.

Ann felt a little disappointed that Judy would change her attitude based on how much money Justin had and her face obviously showed it because Judy said in a serious tone, 'Listen to me, Ann: we have to look out for ourselves. If the world is going to stack things against us, we need to play the world at its own game. Find a way to get the lives we want. If you love him, that's just the cherry on top. We're not getting any younger. I know we were brought up to be independent but independence is so ageing. Come, let's sit.'

Chapter Twelve

Ann didn't really remember when Justin first started giving her money. She was working as much as she could but she was spending more on gas for the round trip to Hudson and nights out with Justin and little presents for Sophie. Nobody had told her just how expensive children were. Even a trip to McDonald's set her back $20. Ann could make $20 cover her grocery needs for a few days, but a trip out with Sophie could cost upwards of $50, and she hated to say no to her.

Money was so tight for her that it was becoming difficult to hide it from Justin. And she was still resisting his offer to move in with him, even if it was only temporary, because part of her knew it was just too soon. Things were moving too fast. She still had some time to consider it, but an offer of rent-free accommodation was very appealing. She was constantly worried and stressed about her finances, so much so that when

Justin innocently suggested a weekend trip away, Ann exploded.

'Can we please just drop it, Justin?' she snapped.

'But I don't understand, it will be fantastic. We'll get a private VIP area, Sophie will be safe and we'll have a nice spot to base ourselves for the day. What's not to love?'

'How much does it cost?'

'What? I don't know, not much, maybe five hundred bucks? Why?'

'Because, Justin, I'm waiting to be paid and I really didn't want to have this conversation with you but I'm a bit broke this month. Between paying for gas to drive up and down here all the time, and taking trips with you and Sophie, I'm working less, and the money I do earn is just not going as far.'

He looked shocked for a minute, and then he started to laugh.

'Oh my god, Ann, is this why you won't come with us? Money? Is this why you've been so on edge?'

'It's not funny, Justin. Some of us have to earn a living you know,' she said testily.

'I'm sorry, I'm not laughing at you. I'm laughing because this is so easy to solve and that makes me happy. I'm paying for this. And Ann? From now on, you don't worry about money, OK? It was extremely insensitive of me not to think about this before now. You shouldn't have had to tell me but you're so independent. Every time I try to pay for things you object. But from here on in, this will be taken care of.'

Ann started to cry. She felt so ashamed, humiliated and angry. Why did she have to be poor? She bet Deborah never had to tell Justin that she was stuck for cash. That's why he never thought to ask. He had probably never even dated anyone who hadn't got their own trust fund. Ann was a new creature altogether.

'Hey,' he said, and came to kneel in front of her, 'I don't want you to worry about anything. We are a team, OK? We're together now. Everything is going to be fine. Ann, please don't be upset.' He looked at her then something occurred to him. 'I'll be right back,' he said.

He left the room and, as he re-entered, looking at his phone, her own phone buzzed. Her Venmo wanted her to accept a transfer. She swiped it automatically, presuming it was a payment from one of the websites she was writing for.

Justin looked up. 'Did you get it?'

'What?'

'The money, silly,' he said with a smile.

She looked back at her phone, and opened the app. 'Ten thousand dollars accepted.'

Her hand flew to her mouth. 'Justin!'

'Now will you please come with us?' He sat beside her on the couch.

'I can't accept . . . '

He shushed her and told her it was just money. 'You're in our lives now, Ann. I told you, I love you. I have money, more than enough for us all. What's mine, is yours,' he said, taking her face in his hands and pressing his forehead against hers. 'So, no more worrying about money, OK?.'

Ann felt weird about it at first. But after she'd cleared the $3,000 that had been stubbornly sitting on her credit card for the last two years and put another $3,000 into the dusty savings account she had had since childhood, the next thing she did was text Judy.

> Judy, are you free for a coffee? I need your advice. Man problems! X

The text was cryptic enough to reel Judy in and Ann was happy to exchange gossip about her own life for the information only Judy could give her.

'Ann!' Judy squealed when she told her what was happening with Justin.

'Oh my god, this is great. He clearly sees you as his partner and wants to make things right. He's not in a position to marry you but he's treating you like you are already married. It's a great sign.'

'Really?' Ann asked. 'You don't think it's weird? You don't think it makes our relationship a little ... transactional?'

Judy smiled pityingly. 'Ann, dear, innocent Ann. Relationships are transactional. Now you can choose to deny that and make life hard for yourself, live without money and keep your romantic ideals intact, or you can get real, grow up and enjoy the benefits that come with it. We are forming alliances. Most of us form alliances we can tolerate but I find you can tolerate a lot in exchange for a little security, a little luxury, the idea of not worrying too much about how you're going to make rent this month, or how you wish you could buy something but you can't afford it. I'm not being cruel here, Ann. You're a great-looking girl, petite with amazing curves. This man is offering you all of that and it sounds like you like him into the bargain – you've hit the jackpot.'

Ann didn't know if Judy was being serious or not so she gave a laugh that was somewhere between nervous and indulgent. 'It just makes me feel weird . . . it changes the power balance. Like, if he's giving me money, we no longer feel equal . . . I feel like his employee, or worse.'

'But you're not equal, Ann, that's the point. He's rich, and you are struggling, but he's willing to overlook your imbalances for what you give to him . . . I'm assuming affection, love, sex . . . and he's trying to even things up a bit in the ways that he can – by giving you money. If you have enough money that you don't have to worry about things he doesn't worry about, you can get on with the relationship stuff instead of creating issues for yourselves. One hundred per cent guaranteed that's what he's thinking. Don't you see?'

'When did you get your feminism bypass?' Ann jibed.

But Judy didn't like it. Ann saw a frown momentarily disturb her perfectly smooth face. 'Listen, Ann, I'm as feminist as they come, which is why I do what I do in the situation in which I find myself.'

'I'm sorry, Judy,' Ann said, genuinely. 'I guess I just worry that I'll start to rely on him and then what happens if things don't work out?'

'Ann, I don't know who's been advising you, but money, jewellery and gifts all remain the property of the dumpee if a relationship breaks up. This is not a loan. It's a gift. Don't look a gift horse in the mouth, I say.'

Ann couldn't help but laugh ... she sounded like someone's grandmother, but there was part of Ann that knew Judy was just a pragmatist. And Ann could really do with the money. It changed everything. It certainly erased a layer of stress.

'Have you moved in with him?' Judy asked.

'Not yet,' Ann said. 'And I'm still undecided. I'm still looking around for somewhere I might be able to afford to rent alone but rents are through the roof. My sisters want me out of the apartment in a matter of weeks. It's not a great situation, to be honest. In my head I still think it's way too soon for me to move in with Justin but in my heart I know I've fallen for him. I've never felt this way about anyone before.'

'Well, stop doubting yourself then, Ann. Just go for it. What's the worst that could happen? If it doesn't work out you won't have lost anything! And you can still find a place of your own, maybe even in Hudson if you feel things are moving too fast ... use it as a stopgap to take the pressure off until you find your own place.'

'Thanks, Judy, you're right. Nothing is permanent. I'm just scared of messing it up. Things are moving so fast and it all feels too good, too easy. There was something else I wanted to talk to you about. Justin told me that I should treat myself with the money, pamper myself a bit after everything, so I thought who better to ask ... Can you please tell me who I need to see – aesthetician, hairdresser, Pilates, clothes – to take myself in hand?'

A smile spread across Judy's taut face. 'Well,' she said, 'now that money isn't an issue ... ' She threw her head up to heaven and whispered a prayer of thanks. 'Ann, you have such brilliant raw materials, your bone structure, your waist, your thick hair. This is literally my favourite thing in the world. OK, how's your diary this week?' she asked, pulling out her phone and her Smythson planner. 'Clear, flexible?'

'Totally empty,' Ann said with a sigh, reminded again that her career needed more attention than she had been giving it. 'I have to transcribe an interview for *The Edge* but that should only take a couple of hours.'

'Ah, it gets better,' Judy said, scrolling through her phone and gently tapping the screen with her gel tips. She swished her heavy hair extensions over her shoulder and pressed the phone to her ear. Everything about Judy was amazing. She looked like she had been designed by a computer programme. Her lips were moist and glossy and plump but not sticky or lumpy. Her whole body looked brand new, like she had been taken out of a box. 'Anastasia!?' she shouted urgently as the phone was answered on the other end. 'I have an incredible makeover challenge for you!'

She repeated the process several times over until the following two days were completely block-booked with beauty treatments seeing a series of experts who would make Ann look like she was Justin's equal.

As she stood in a tanning booth on Thursday evening, even she had to admit that she looked like one of them.

Like Judy. Like her sisters. Like the wives who swanned around Whole Foods and picked up things they might want but would never eat.

Judy then took her to Nordstrom in midtown. 'I know it's a bit basic,' she said, 'but you need the basics first, and then I'll take you to my secret boutiques. You have to walk before you can run.'

Judy picked out twenty-seven items that she called

'essential', and Ann paid for them without any sense of anxiety about whether her card would be declined.

'I'm so proud!' Judy squealed as they took their bags and left.

Ann was glowing, partly from the chemical peels and partly because she felt and looked good for the first time in years. Did it also have something to do with the fact that for the first time in years she momentarily did not have to worry about where her next pay cheque was coming from?

As she walked down 7th Avenue, a gorgeous guy with thick black hair trained up off his face gave her an approving nod. Ann smiled back and he winked as he strutted on. Had that really just happened? Ann had been invisible for the past three years. Now she felt giddy. When was the last time she had felt this alive, this hopeful, this fun? She couldn't wait to see Justin the next day. She left early so she could get there as soon as possible. She was wearing a little dress that exposed her newly tanned legs and décolletage perfectly. Underneath she had on her new, expensive underwear, which felt like it was going to spring apart at any minute. She just hoped Justin would like it. She texted him to say she was going to be early and could he get out of work.

When she arrived a few hours later, she bounded out of her car, ran up the granite steps to where he was standing at the door and she knew her new hair was bouncing as she went. She could see Justin's surprise turn to delight as she reached the top of the steps. She smiled and wrapped her arms around him.

'Hi,' she said.

'Hi,' he whispered back. 'You look ... amazing.'

'Thank you ...' She smiled. 'I have a surprise for you ...'

'You mean this is not the surprise?' he said, gesturing at her makeover.

'No. I spoke to a very wise friend, who told me I should stop worrying and just go with the flow. I've thought about it and I think I would very much like to take you up on your offer to stay here with you and Sophie ... and if it's OK, I brought some of my stuff.'

Sold to the highest bidder.

Chapter Thirteen

Ann started to split her time evenly between following up leads for work and helping out with Sophie. The money Justin had given her helped but she didn't want to rely on it or expect it. She didn't really like the idea of being 'kept' by Justin. Still, she had to admit that she enjoyed being able to focus more on the projects she had an interest in rather than taking on every assignment. And Justin said he liked looking after her. He encouraged her to treat herself. 'You deserve to be kept in the style all of the wives around here are accustomed to,' he said.

Her stomach had flip-flopped when he had said that. Did he think of her as a wife, as *his* wife?

Ann now had all the things that her sisters and Judy did as a matter of course – hair, nails, Botox, Pilates, yoga, HIIT, Laser, facials, filler, CrossFit, SoulCycle . . . the list went on.

'You deserve it,' Justin told her.

What did that mean, Ann wondered, considering most of those things felt like a punishment rather than a treat. Wax ripped, hypodermics pricked, laser stung, bleach burned, and the rest ... Maybe she did deserve it.

The following month, as Ann was checking her banking app to see how much money was left in the account after Judy's spree, she got an alert from her cycle tracker. 'Has your period started?'

Ann realised she couldn't remember her last period. High on how good she was looking, on the fancy new clothes and underwear she was splashing out on, she and Justin had been having sex non-stop. She counted back in her mind. When did she last have a period?

She opened her phone calendar. She wasn't always disciplined about marking her period in but there it was, thirty-seven days ago. Her period usually came every twenty-eight or thirty days, like clockwork. And she felt fine. She didn't feel pregnant. But nor was there any sense of imminent menstruation, no heavy feeling in her pelvis, no tenderness of breast, no sickly suggestion of imminent bleed. She had experienced a sharp pain low in her groin about a week before, but had put it down to the onset of her period. On reflection, by which she meant googling, she figured out that it must have been an implantation pain. She bought a pregnancy test and watched the result swim into view on the stick. She waited to see whether it would go away again in a little while, fading back just as dreamily as it had arrived. But no. It was real. She was pregnant.

First Justin and now this, she thought? Good things like this didn't happen to her. But however positive Justin was about their relationship, this surely would not be welcome news. It wasn't exactly a convenient time for either of them to have a baby. She needed time to process so she decided to stay in Brooklyn that weekend.

She called Justin. 'I'm really sorry but I have a few loose ends to tie up at the apartment and a couple of big deadlines too so I really just need to plough through it and it's easier this way.'

Justin sulked a little. 'But Ann, I don't understand why you're even taking commissions any more. You don't need to work. I told you I'm happy to look after you.'

Ann laughed a little disbelievingly. 'That's really generous, Justin, but I can't just live off you. I need to work for my own sense of self.'

He huffed a little. 'Well, it doesn't seem to make your sense of self very happy,' he said.

A few hours later he texted. Have I done something wrong? Did I say something stupid or insensitive? Please tell me so I can fix it.

Ann texted back. Not at all, I've just been really busy with work. I'm getting a lot of commissions and I don't want to miss out on the opportunity to build some regular work. And Emily needs me to sort a few things at the apartment. I'll be back next week, promise. x

Sophie misses you, he tried.

Then added: and so do I. Please call me.

She replied that she would be in touch after the weekend. She knew she would have to deal with it sooner or later but she wasn't there yet.

The next day, Sunday, Ann was dismayed to find Justin at her mom's apartment building.

'I'm in the lobby,' Justin said. 'Can I come up?'

Ann felt instantly panicked and ashamed. He had never been to her apartment. It was clean and sparse but it was in no way tasteful or luxurious. At least she could brush over the condition because it was in the process of being transferred to new owners. Despite her mortification at him knowing the modest place she had grown up, at him seeing her for who she really was with nothing to hide behind, she was also relieved that he had come.

They went for a walk, some coffee, and then later had lunch. He didn't notice that Ann was not drinking as he ordered a Bloody Mary for himself. It was incredible how little people actually noticed, she thought. She couldn't think of anything to say, anything apart from the one thing she wasn't yet ready to reveal. She felt like a hostage in a parallel universe, barely hearing him and wondering how she could tell him this enormous secret that sat locked in her stomach. She had to tell him but found it impossible to bring it up in conversation. In the end, she waited until they were almost asleep that night, the lights were off, the blackness of the nighttime a silencer that might muffle what she knew she had to tell him. 'I'm pregnant,' she finally whispered.

'What?'

The fabric had been ripped. She had her entry point so she pushed until things tore irrevocably. 'I'm pregnant,' she repeated, louder this time. She was more scared then than she had ever been. She started to cry but he comforted her quickly, wrapping his arms around her in the darkness.

'I'm so sorry,' she said. 'I'm so, so sorry. I know this is the worst thing that could possibly happen . . .'

He pulled away from her to switch on the bedside light. 'Ann, this is so far from the worst thing that could possibly happen. Believe me, I know what the worst thing is. This is good news, don't you see? We'll all be together now, a proper family. Maybe a little sooner than we might have planned but I think we both knew that this was never going to be a casual relationship. It was always going to happen, I think, don't you?'

He smiled at her kindly and she could see that he meant it.

'We'll all have such a lovely time, I know we will.' He squeezed her close to him and his words absolved her of the fear that had been growing alongside the foetus like a mirror placenta, melting it all away.

Ann never knew it was possible to feel this protected. Nobody had ever cared for her like this.

In Justin, it felt like she had gained a parent again, as well as a lover and a best friend, as if something had finally been resolved in her. Ann no longer had good enough reasons to fight against what Justin was offering her. Her sisters' suspicions that it was moving too fast or that he was a married man sounded hollow in the face of his actions.

Ann could no longer find compelling reasons not to give in to this feeling. She could think clearly for the first time in years.

Was this what living felt like?

Chapter Fourteen

One Year Earlier

After Ann's mother's diagnosis, and after Ann had moved in with her, back into her childhood bedroom, a darkness settled over their lives. They didn't know how to embrace the day, how to find the joy in the moments they had left with each other. Ann didn't seem able to jolly them along either, even though she knew that was her job now too: to try and keep her mother's spirits buoyant, even though she couldn't even keep her own spirits up right now. Both she and her mother knew too much about how the disease would end.

Ann did what she always had: with any new piece of information she didn't understand fully, she spent hours researching until she did. She read every medical research paper that she could find that was trying to delay or cure the miserable disease. But she also read all of the different ways in which people died, the life expectancies, the tiny differentiations between each patient's suffering. By the end, she knew everything there was to know and she had yet to find a concretely hopeful thing to cling on to. It was all just theory, possibilities, hypotheses that needed further research funding.

There were days when Ann rallied and threw herself at the positivity movement with all the enthusiasm of a dieter on day one. She tried gratitude journals and crafting, but her mom, understandably, felt patronised and infantilised by these things. She wanted to mourn the life that had been cut short, to grieve for what was happening to her. She chastised Ann for trying to get her to go along with what she called self-delusional hobbies in the face of her terminal illness. While she was well enough to travel, attend concerts and movies, they did that as much as they could. They did a few other things together, like art classes in a local art gallery, and a very expensive trip to Paris where they stayed in the Ritz and ate a meal in Les Deux Magots. It had cost Ann several thousand dollars, most of which she put on her credit card but she had felt it was important to do these things now, while she still had her mother. It was like speed-dating, trying to cram everything they might have done together in the future into the limited unknown amount of time they had left in the present. Ann tried to bank good memories and shared experiences as she realised she had left it too late to make new memories with her mother; she should have been doing these things all along.

Later, as her mother's mobility decreased, Ann read books to her, which created a gentle intimacy between them. But it also frustrated her mother, who never got over the fact that she was no longer autonomous. As her care demands increased, Ann's time was taken up with her physical rather than her emotional, spiritual and psychological needs, and she found herself too tired most evenings to read more than a few pages and instead their routine changed to turning on the television and letting a series of soap operas unspool. Ann couldn't sleep on particularly bad days, despite her exhaustion. Her anxiety kept her awake and so she sat quietly by her mother's bed, holding her hand while she slept, knowing that one day in the not-too-distant future there would never again be a hand to hold. She took a photo with her phone and slipped it back into her pyjama pocket. At least she would always be able to look at her mother's hands even if she could not touch them.

Just before she got her iSight machine, as her speech was beginning to fail, Ann's mother shared her plans with Ann.

'I have no intention of waiting this disease out, Ann. We can both see where it's going. And we both know there is going to be less and less of life for me to enjoy.'

Ann knew instantly what her mother was getting at, but she didn't want to acknowledge it. 'I know it's hard, Mom, but there are still things we can enjoy: the shows we like watching together; the early mornings; and I love our trips around McCarren Park. I know it's not the same as going for a walk, being stuck in your chair, but you get to be out in nature.'

Her mother waited patiently for Ann, let her exhaust her meagre list of defences.

'Ann, I've lived a good life. I had three beautiful daughters and I got to see you all grow up. I have grandchildren, a comfortable place to live. I have no ambitions left, nothing I feel a burning desire to achieve. This disease has already robbed me of so much. There will come a time, and soon, when I will be confined to these four walls. I can keep going for now, but when that time comes, Ann, I'm going to need your help. That's why I wanted to talk to you about this now, before I get the machine, before everything I ever say will be written down and committed to a computer's hard drive.'

Ann wouldn't meet her eye. 'Mom, please. I can't. Even if it wasn't illegal . . . I can't. How could I?'

'You won't have to do anything,' her mother said. 'I'll just need you to . . . supervise. I've already organised everything,' she said. She directed me into her old bedroom – she was set up in the living room these days – and said, 'In the left-hand locker. The one up high, the large jewellery box, in the panel . . . '

Ann pulled out the jewellery box and brought it to her mother. Inside there was a navy bag, what her mother called a 'suicide bag'. She had done it all legally, she said, just siphoning off painkillers and opiates from her early prescriptions and the stronger opiates that the palliative care nurse left each week but which her mom refused to take while she was gone. She said she would not wait until she had lost the power in both hands. She didn't want the police to be able to prove that she couldn't have killed herself alone. She didn't want to get Ann into any trouble. She had thought long and hard about it. But the chances were she would need Ann's help to prepare the tables, to get her a drink to make sure she went through with it.

'I've spoken to my doctors. I haven't mentioned my plans, of course, but I have asked them to give me some idea of the disease's progression, a timeline of when they think certain things will likely happen ...' she reached her trembling hand out and it took all of her energy to lift it up to touch Ann's face. 'I don't want to go too soon, I don't want to lose one second of time with you, Ann, the best daughter anyone could wish for ... but I can't leave it too late for the reasons I've just explained.' Ann was completely torn. Part of her felt that there would be a last-minute reprieve, a messenger skidding to the gallows just in time, a miracle cure that would arrive just before her mother put the glass to her lips and imbibed her lethal cocktail. But she knew it was just fantasy. Her mother's basic health insurance didn't give her compassionate access to new high-tech medication that could save her life. She was doomed and Ann was doomed to watch.

'Just think of it as palliative care,' her mother said, trying to calm Ann's tears. 'It's just happening a little earlier than we planned, before I lose all of my dignity and comfort and joy in life. You don't want to see me like that any more than I do. The only thing I want to do before I go is for all of us girls to have one last family dinner together.'

Those last months went by quicker than Ann could ever have imagined, as the endless summer evenings fooled her into thinking they had all the time in the world. That last family dinner came much sooner than Ann had expected. She had hoped they would have one last Thanksgiving together, but her mother's deterioration seemed to be exponential now; each step down happened at a faster and more severe rate than the previous one.

'I think I'd like to have our family dinner this Sunday, Ann,' her mom said one sweltering evening in August as the air conditioner hummed innocently in the background. 'Are you free? Can you organise the girls to be here? Just like we used to do on Sundays . . . ' Ann knew then, this was her code, her way of saying it was time. 'Tell them it's a pre-Thanksgiving Thanksgiving.'

Ann called her sisters – just them, not the husbands

or children. Her mother wanted just the four of them together the way they had been as teenagers, sitting around the dining table after service to eat her roast potatoes and beef before dispersing to their respective delinquent pursuits with their overlapping groups of friends. Only this time, her mother wouldn't be cooking. This time she would barely be able to speak. This would be the last time.

Ann cried for days before the lunch but she knew that her mom had no quality of life left. Ann had no quality of life left either at that point. She was also desperate for it to end, which is why she knew neither of them could go on this way. Ann's mother had great difficulty breathing now, and had requested no intervention, no ventilator, nothing like that. Her nurse had left muscle relaxants to help deal with the breathing issues, but Ann's mother refused to take them when the nurse wasn't there, adding them carefully to her bag.

After the dinner, they sat around reminiscing for hours. Maybe it was the fact that the kids weren't there whooping around the place or the husbands fidgeting as they waited to leave that meant Emily and Juliet were relaxed, accepting glasses of wine and laughing easily. They hadn't been that relaxed as a family for a long time. Ann was glad for her mother that the girls were in good humour and enjoying each other's company.

'Ann,' her mother said, 'be a dear and get me my

jewellery box from the bedroom, will you? I want to give you girls something.'

Ann knew this was part of the plan. It would be the air-tight alibi that showed how Ann's mother had gotten the jewellery box. The story was she wanted to give each of her daughters a piece of her treasured jewellery – a gold bangle, diamond earrings and – for Ann – her engagement and wedding ring, 'because Emily and Juliet have their own'.

It still stung Ann how much it mattered to her mother that she was not married. Ann would have preferred to have a husband, a family, a home too, but she had also come to terms with her solo status.

Ann laughed and said, 'Thank you, Mom, maybe you can stop worrying about me so much now that I have a ring on my finger.'

Juliet tittered while Emily took Ann's hand in hers, turning it this way and that to look at the rings. 'They look beautiful on you, Ann. How do you feel?'

It was a strange question to ask, Ann thought, particularly as it cut straight to the fact that what Ann was feeling with the rings on her ring finger was bittersweet, a mixture of sadness at the impending loss of her mother and the fact that she liked how she felt with the rings on her finger. How simple a symbol the wedding ring was, she thought. It was about status. Ann knew that was part of the reason her mother was giving it to her. Her sisters were married, rings stacked on fingers.

Ann's mother knew these rings added up to something in the eyes of the world, she knew how the world viewed women. With these rings, Ann realised, every shop assistant would take one look at her ring finger and know that she was loved. She wanted every car salesman, every plumber, every electrician, every nail technician, every goddamn job interviewer to know from one look at Ann's left hand that she was a woman worthy of love and support, that she had back-up.

'How do I feel?' Ann laughed. 'I feel silly but like a princess! I will never take these rings off. I love them. Thank you, Mom. I love you. I love you all.' And they hugged each other, pressing cheeks and squeezing shoulders to show, yes, they loved each other so much after all.

'Why don't you girls go out, hit the town, have a few drinks together?' their mom said.

'Now that Ann has a ring on her finger, she might actually meet somebody,' Emily deadpanned.

This was all part of her mother's plan.

'I'm game if you are,' Juliet said. 'We haven't gone for drinks in ages.'

'Just do me a favour, Ann, and prepare my meds for me before you go, will you?'

Ann went cold. She knew she had to do this. Her mother selected the pills and asked Ann to crush them for her. 'Actually, Emily, would you mind doing that for Mom while I get some lipstick on?'

'Oh Ann, you know I'm no good at that stuff; I'll make a mistake. You do it. You don't need lipstick.'

Ann steeled herself. She took the drugs from her mother, which she kept in her jewellery box and went to the kitchen. She had put away far too much, about four times more than even the biggest dose needed to kill the largest sized person. But she wanted to be sure. Ann took the several small tablets that looked just like Advil and looked down at her hands as she crushed them, the small diamond ring and wedding ring now glinting on her finger.

She came back into the room with the powdered drugs, the glass of water and put them on her mother's tray. She used her remaining good hand to lift the bowl and tried to tip the ground-up drugs into the glass.

'For god's sake, Ann, help her,' Emily said, walking into the room having reapplied her make-up in the bathroom.

Ann looked at Emily.

'Oh here, I'll do it myself.' Emily took the bowl from her mom and tipped it into the glass and got a straw to stir it in. 'Here you go, Mom,' she said.

Ann's mother smiled at Ann, one of pure love. She let the tears slip silently from her eyes.

'Now, you girls go, shoo! I'm going to watch something on television.'

Ann knew she had to leave now. This was all part of the plan too. She had to leave with her sisters for the alibi to work, which meant her mother had to die alone. As Ann and her sisters said goodbye, she told herself that if this was anyone's last day on earth, it was a good last day.

When she returned that night around midnight, Ann called out – 'Mom?', still hoping the worst hadn't happened, but there was no response, no movement. She slowly approached the bed and sat down on the floor and gently laid her hands on her mother's legs. She felt the solidity beneath the duvet and knew instantly that her mother was gone. Her tears soaked the duvet and she begged her to come back, to stay.

'Please, Mom, please don't leave me alone.' But it was too late. At that moment, memories of roast chicken on picnic blankets in McCarren Park with wasps hovering shot along light years to the stars with her mother's soul.

Ann held on to those sunlit memories while she picked up the phone and called the emergency services. 'My mom, I think she's dead. I think she's taken something,' she said.

Which wasn't so far from the truth after all.

Chapter Fifteen

The night before the apartment was due to be handed over to the new buyers, Ann, Emily and Juliet met one last time to say a final goodbye to the place where they had grown up and the place their mother had died. Ann was still firmly against the sale, not just because it had forced her into making a fast decision about moving in with Justin but also because it was her last connection to her mother. She worried her memories of their time together would fade if she no longer had access to them through the portal of the apartment. But life moved on and Ann had to learn how to move on too.

Emily popped the cork on a bottle of champagne and filled three beakers, passing them among the three of them as they sat on the floor of the now-empty living room.

'It feels so much bigger now that all of the furniture is gone,' Juliet said.

'It's so strange,' Ann said, 'that this will be the last time we all sit in this apartment together.'

'Cheers,' Emily said, raising her plastic cup. 'To new beginnings, moving on and new adventures.'

'To new beginnings,' Juliet said and bashed her cup off Emily's.

'Ann,' Emily said, waiting for Ann to raise her cup, 'it's bad luck if you don't drink when you toast.'

Oh god, Ann thought. This is happening.

'I can't,' she said.

'Why not,' Emily asked.

'Because . . .' Ann had not said it out loud to anyone apart from Justin. She looked at her sisters' expectant faces. 'Because . . . I'm pregnant.'

Emily looked absolutely stunned and for once in her life seemed lost for words. Juliet screamed at an unbelievable pitch then hugged Ann so tightly she thought she was going to hurt the baby.

When everybody had calmed down, Ann unscrewed her bottle of sparkling water and held it up to them.

OK, so let's do that toast again properly, she thought.

'To new beginnings!'

Chapter Sixteen

When Ann first arrived in Hudson, Justin had come up with a cover story for her. Ann was to be Sophie's new live-in nanny. It was the perfect cover. It explained why Ann was suddenly living with them, spending so much time with them, spending Justin's money and credit card around town, without having to reveal that they were in a relationship.

Ann had felt the desolate clang of a warning bell in her chest. The suggestion that she needed a cover story made her feel alienated, like she didn't know this man at all. She wanted to be away from there suddenly, somewhere safe, a place that she knew, somewhere she didn't feel she had to watch her manners and earn her keep.

'I hope you don't think I'm ashamed of you or us. It's just easier this way,' Justin said. 'You'll see, this is a small town, people wouldn't understand. People are just so quick to judge.'

Not as quick as they were to judge women, Ann thought. With widows, it was different. Women were left alone to grieve, to pine, to sweep the grounds of the grave and replace the dying flowers every week, withering on the vine, altered by grief.

Justin's case was different, Ann argued. It wasn't like Deborah was still a part of their lives. People would understand, wouldn't they? This wasn't an affair, this was love, inconvenient though it was.

'It'll just be for a little while, Ann. Please don't take it the wrong way.' Even though she felt a sense of fright spread through her body, Ann tried to seal off the chasm of despair as she said, casually, 'Justin, of course I'm not offended. I know what we have here. I know this is real and that it doesn't matter what anyone else thinks. If we have to say I'm the nanny to make things easier for us, that's what we'll do. We're good.' But it didn't feel good. It felt awful. She wanted to take her belongings and run home. But home wasn't there any more. Her sisters had no interest in putting her up, and what about the baby growing inside her? She had to be an adult now. Justin didn't mean to hurt her. He had been so kind to her. She was just homesick and grieving. And emotional since she had become pregnant.

Ann's fears receded as she settled into life in Hudson, and soon her concerns were overtaken by how busy they were, with plans to renovate the house for the new baby and figuring out the kind of family they would be. Ann researched baby items – cots, strollers, prams, travel systems, car seats and feeding chairs, baby gyms and bouncers, rockers and breast-feeding pillows, and which baby mobiles would make your child more intelligent. It was a full-time job but she was superstitious about buying anything too soon. There would be plenty of time for that later. They chose the brightest spot in the house for the nursery, a sunny but small room looking directly out onto the water, which made the light change by the hour. Ann thought her baby would be very happy here. Is this what it felt like when life suddenly went your way, she wondered. Easy? Happy? Peaceful? She started to hope. She felt like she was living the life she was always meant to, the one everyone had been telling her she should be living.

One or two days a week, she drove into the city for work. She had secured some regular contract work with *The Edge*, and was required to be in the city at least part of the week for editorial meetings and assignments. 'How long are you going to keep this up, Ann,' Justin said one day, smiling at her from bed as she prepared for her journey. It was 6 a.m. and she had been up for an hour.

'Keep what up?' Ann asked, distracted.

'Getting up at the crack of dawn and driving into the city to work for hours on pieces that earn you just enough money to cover your gas?'

'That's what it pays,' she said. 'You don't get into journalism to get rich.'

'I'm not criticising. I just mean, you don't have to do that any more. We're having a baby. We live together. When are you going to let me look after you, Ann? You won't be able to keep this up when the baby is born.'

Ann was shocked. 'Justin, I'm having a baby. It's not 1950. Women have babies *and* work now, you know. And we both agreed that us living together was just temporary, until the sale of the apartment goes through and I can find something more permanent.'

He looked offended but Ann didn't have time for this conversation.

'Will you at least think about it? Sophie and I need you here now. You belong here, with us. And I worry that all this travel, the stress of deadlines, it can't be good for the baby.'

Ann was slightly unsettled by the idea of becoming completely reliant on Justin. But she also accepted that she needed to look after herself; she was perpetually exhausted and there was a constant humming anxiety about work.

'I'll think about it, I promise,' she said, trying not to let her feelings show. 'I'll be back tonight; I shouldn't be later than midnight.'

Chapter Seventeen

As the weeks passed, and Ann lived a quiet double life as a nanny in Hudson and a jobbing journalist who commuted in and out of the city as required, Justin broached the topic of introducing Ann to a select group of friends. 'As your nanny?' she asked.

'No,' he said, 'as my girlfriend ... what do you say? You're going to have to meet them sometime.'

Ann was pathetically grateful for this gesture. Whatever she had said to Justin, she hated the idea of being hidden, a dirty secret. This was a step in the right direction.

'I'd love that,' she said. 'I'd really love that. Can I invite my sisters too? I know they'd really like to meet you ...'

'Great idea,' he said with a smile. 'Let's do it this weekend.'

*

Justin's friends were old, old friends. Men he had known since they had shared frat houses and married girls from the same sororities.

'Where did you study, Ann?' one tall, Waspy type asked her.

'NYU,' said Ann.

'Ah, a city girl . . . and where are your family from?'

This was excruciating. He was trying to place her in her socio-economic box.

'Brooklyn,' Ann replied. 'I'm sorry, would you excuse me. I need to check on my sisters,' she said, drifting off to find Emily and Juliet, who were standing together by the drinks bar.

'I feel like I'm on trial,' she told them.

'Don't worry,' Emily said. 'They're just trying to figure you out. We're about to do the same to Justin.' She smiled.

'Oh, go easy on him,' Ann pleaded.

'This house is amazing,' Juliet squealed. 'Ann, you didn't tell us how huge it was. Or how gorgeous.'

Ann smiled. It was a weird feeling to have her sisters' admiration. 'I'd better be polite, go talk to some more of Justin's friends.' She had overheard a few weird comments as she'd moved through the room.

'Does anyone know anything about her?'

'Where exactly does she come from?'

'Has anyone heard of her family?'

Of course, nobody knew Ann's family. They couldn't

place her because their paths had never crossed. She didn't go to their schools, didn't know their younger sisters or cousins because she didn't go to riding school, or ballet classes. Some of them knew this instinctively when they realised they came from the same city or universities but had no connections. They knew the reason why. They were from different milieus. Ann was different; that's what made them uncomfortable.

Nobody was actively hostile, but Ann was conscious of a wariness around her. She realised they were suspicious of her. She tried to see it from their point of view. Justin was fifty-three, she was still in her thirties, even if it was the tail-end of that decade. She had no apparent baggage, no lovechild stashed with a maiden aunt, no history of mental illness, no apparent financial ruin, albeit she had come closer to poverty and homelessness than anyone might guess. In fact, she was a catch. That's why it didn't add up for them. What was this young, viable woman doing with an ageing man with a whole airport carousel of baggage?

They couldn't get their heads around the fact that there might just be a mutual attraction, a meeting of minds, that old-fashioned thing called chemistry. They didn't believe that people forged relationships from such a thing. No. Just like Judy, they believed that relationships were political alliances or financial mergers. It was indicative of their status. They made arrangements, connections, cross-party coalitions.

Nobody fell in love. That's what you did when you were poor. Of course, she realised. They thought Ann was after Justin's money, and when she looked back over her accounts over the last few months, the change her finances had taken, she had to admit it looked bad for her. But she had never asked for money. Justin had insisted.

The atmosphere in the room was tense. The evening had been set up as an ice-breaker and yet there was a cold wind buffeting every interaction. Ann had the impression that people were avoiding her. Her attempts at small-talk were rebuffed. Ann had thought that they would be happy for Justin but it seemed more like they found the whole thing distasteful and wanted nothing to do with it. But they were careful not to be cold in front of Justin.

He called her over. 'Ann! Come here, I want you to meet Craig . . . Craig and I wrestled in college, would you believe?'

Ann smiled. 'I would believe . . . pleased to meet you,' she said, shaking Craig's hand.

'So, Justin tells me you live in the city; are you east or west,' he asked.

'Uhm, east,' she said and didn't bother to tell him just how far east of Central Park she was from because she was more concerned that all of Justin's friends thought she lived in Manhattan. Not Hudson. Or even Brooklyn. Justin smiled and mouthed 'sorry' at her.

'And you're a writer?' The doorbell went and Justin said, 'That'll be Randy. You guys get to know each other. I'll be right back.'

Craig watched Justin as he left the room and then turned back to Ann. She thought he was going to ask her again about being a writer and she was preparing her answer when instead he asked sharply, sotto voce, 'What's your game?' He didn't bother to disguise his sentiments as concern for his friend. Ann felt as if she had been slapped.

'Excuse me?' Ann asked, taken aback, although she had heard him well enough and knew immediately from his tone what he was inferring.

'What are you playing at, with Justin?' he clarified, his tone blatantly rude and accusatory.

'I don't know what you mean,' she said. Her voice had involuntarily jumped an octave and she heard a quaver in it that she felt all the way through her body. She went to move away from him, but he gripped her arm above her elbow as if he had a right to do that, and said, 'Oh, I think you know exactly what I mean,' he said. His voice was cartoonishly menacing, as if they were sworn enemies rather than strangers who had just met. 'You thought a grieving man would be a soft target, that you could milk him for everything he's worth and he would be too distraught with grief to notice what's happening. He said this last part as if addressing an invisible group of people. Men like this were always speaking to an imaginary audience, she thought. 'It's *immoral* what you're doing. But I don't know why I would expect someone like you to have morals. What are you, twenty years younger than him?'

Ann was almost too shocked to be angry, but she felt a silent rage bubbling inside her as she responded. 'I'm thirty-eight. Justin is fifteen years older than me. It doesn't feel like a very big age gap. We're both adults, after all.' Now it was her turn to sound icy. 'Besides, I wouldn't have thought you objected much to age gaps, judging by your wife,' Ann said, nodding towards the twenty-something Craig had arrived with. 'Or is she your girlfriend?' Ann asked. She could see that Craig had already made up his mind about her. Why would she waste her time trying to convince him otherwise.

Was that it? Was that what Justin's friends thought? That she was a gold digger, out to get what she could? If anyone was compromising, it was Ann, she thought, giving up her family, her city and her free time to move to a backwater, and try to ingratiate herself with hostile locals and a child who was not hers. Travelling vast distances, neglecting her work. And she was happy to do it because she loved Justin and he loved her ... but she hadn't expected there to be any suspicion around either of their motivations. She had thought naively that people would be happy for them.

'Well, what else is in it for you?' he asked, staring at her ...

What was in it for her? The money was nice but it didn't matter. In truth, what was in it for her was the first adult relationship of her life, and a chance at motherhood with Sophie and now her own baby. That's what was in it for her, the same thing everyone else seemed to think they were naturally entitled to but thought she didn't deserve.

'You're so young, why aren't you with a guy your own age?'

Ann laughed. 'I'm not that young. And that's exactly what I love about Justin. He's knowledgeable, mature. Sure, he has a few more miles on the clock than me but he is accomplished in his career and comfortable in his own position in life. He doesn't own a video games console like so many men my age do. Maybe that's why I'm not with someone my own age. My ex-boyfriends always felt like my children, adolescent boys in thirty-something men's bodies . . . Justin is not like that.'

Craig stared at her and then boomed a laugh as Justin walked back into the room with Randy. Justin stared at Craig as Craig said, 'You've got yourself a little firecracker here, Justin. I like her!' And he put his arm around Ann's shoulder and jostled her.

Ann smiled at Justin, who was clearly delighted with this judgement, and she saw Emily and Juliet beaming too. They had evidently forgotten all of their earlier objections to Justin and his wife upon seeing his house in Hudson.

Ann made her escape from Craig and went back to the bar. She ordered another seltzer and pretended it was vodka. She moved off to the side of the large marble fireplace and let her body lean against the wall. A moment or two alone was all she wanted. A thin, sharp-looking woman strode up to her. Ann smiled, straightened up.

'I'm Cookie,' the woman said. 'Randy's wife. We have been so curious to meet you,' she said in a mischievous tone. Ann didn't know if she was making fun of her or not. She was tired now and worn out trying to make a good impression on people who seemed to have already made up their minds.

'You are a pretty thing, aren't you?! Different to Justin's usual type. I hope you're not playing with our Justin. He's been through a lot, you know. You're not going to break his heart, are you?'

The questions were intolerably rude in their directness. 'Of course not, I rather hope he won't break mine,' Ann said. And what did she mean by his usual type? Justin had been married for years.

'Come now,' she said, 'Justin knows he's lucky to have you. Why else would he be making such an effort by hosting this night? He wants us to like you.'

Where had this idea of Justin as a helpless creature come from? They all spoke to her as if she was the fifty-foot woman who was picking him up only to put him down again when she got bored. As if reading Ann's thoughts she said, 'Don't take it the wrong way. We all love Justin and just don't want to see him get hurt.'

Sophie came running through the crowd to find Ann. 'Ann! I'm tired and I can't find Daddy.'

Ann lifted Sophie up in her arms. She could kiss her for rescuing her at just the perfect moment. 'I'll take you to bed, button. Say good night to Daddy's friend.'

'Good night,' Sophie said sweetly and wrapped her arms around Ann's neck, leaning her head on her shoulder.

After Sophie brushed her teeth, Ann tucked her into bed and switched on the nightlight.

'Can you stay with me, Ann?' Sophie asked.

'Of course I can,' Ann said, all too willing to take a time-out from being interrogated. 'Shall I read you a story?'

'Yes, please, the one about the cat in the train station.'

'Oh, I love that one too,' Ann said.

Sophie's soft little fingers found Ann's hand and tucked themselves into her palm. As Ann read the story, Sophie's eyes grew heavy. She leaned down and kissed her forehead. 'Good night, darling,' she said.

'Good night, Mom,' Sophie said, then opened her eyes and giggled.

Ann smiled. 'You know you can call me Mom if you like. I think of you like my own little girl. And I'm sure your mommy wouldn't mind. But I'm just as happy if you call me Ann. Sleep well, Sophie.'

'Good night, Mommy,' Sophie whispered again and closed her eyes.

By the end of the evening, Ann was shattered. She felt like she had just been through a five-hour inquisition in front of a panel of ten people. But Justin was elated as they closed the door on the last of his friends. He wrapped his arms around her and swung her around.

'They loved you! I'm so glad, Ann. They can be difficult at the best of times but they all adored you. I knew they would. How could they not? You did so well,' he said, standing back from her.

She had the feeling that she had passed a test, that the committee had spoken and given its approval. Their approval didn't matter to Ann but she was sure it meant something to Justin.

Regardless of what was happening with Deborah, regardless of the grilling Justin's friends had just given her, Ann was even more determined than ever to follow her own happiness. She had never been happier. She had finally found her place and she wasn't going to give up just because a few people disapproved of her.

Part of Ann had to admire his friends' loyalty. It was a testament to his character, she thought, that his friends cared so much about him. But the idea that she was trying to trap him into a marriage offended her. As if she was seductive enough to do that to any grown man. She had her charms but they were simple, not wily, and she didn't really want that to be the basis of any relationship, a confidence trick. That wasn't her style. That was one of the reasons she found herself still single. She was kind, and honest. All Ann really wanted was a relationship of equals.

The insinuation of gold-digging irked her. If anyone cared to examine both of their lives, they would find that it was Ann who should have been wary, Ann who should have been scared off, Ann who should have taken heed of the red flags. She was the one getting in too deep. She was the one risking everything. She was the one being lovebombed. But people love the tale of the wicked woman and the innocent man, the spider and the fly. Why let the facts get in the way of a good story? And what did it really matter anyway? Soon Justin and Ann could move on with their lives, without the opinions of his friends. Some other piece of gossip would come by soon enough to replace them both. Or at least she hoped so.

Chapter Eighteen

Later that week, Ann got a call from *The Edge*.

'We've got a position coming up for a full-time features writer. We've been really happy with your work and thought you'd be a great fit for the job. Can we put you forward for interview?'

Ann jumped at the chance. OK, she was pregnant, which was as slight hitch, but nobody knew yet and legally it shouldn't make any difference to her chances, therefore she could absolutely square her conscience about not mentioning it at interview stage. If she got the job, she would tell them. Besides, it's not like she would be pregnant for ever and, despite Justin's objections, it felt weird not to have her own money, her own income, her own career. She had taken so much time out with her mom, this felt like her first substantial chance to get back to work in a meaningful way, to create some financial security for herself. 'That would be fantastic,' she said. 'Please do submit my CV.'

She felt energised after the phone call but something told her not to mention it to Justin yet. She started working on her cuttings file and possible feature ideas to pitch at the interview.

The following week, after meeting with the panel of editors conducting the interview, she was offered the job. They wanted her to start full-time the following week.

'This is incredible,' she said. 'Thank you so much!'

After she got off the phone, Ann was walking on air. She couldn't buy a bottle of champagne to celebrate but she could make a special meal. Sophie was in the kitchen looking at her quizzically. Ann took her by the hands and danced her around the kitchen. Sophie giggled. 'Do it again!' And so she did.

'Oh, Sophie! How did I get so lucky as to have you and your dad in my life? And now I have my dream job too. How lucky are we?'

'Very!' squealed Sophie as Ann spun her around again.

Later that evening, as Justin emerged from the basement, he looked surprised. 'What amazing smells am I smelling? I'm starving!'

'Well, then, you're in luck,' Ann said, kissing him deeply and hugging him. 'Because I've made my special secret-recipe dumplings and my mom's apple pie for dessert.'

'Wow, what have I done to deserve this?'

'It's more about what I've done, if you must know,' Ann said, smiling.

Justin didn't really like surprises. He was immediately defensive, as if she was going to trick him.

'Nothing *bad*, silly! It's *good* news. I've been offered a job, full-time, with benefits and health insurance at . . . *The Edge!* Can you believe it?'

'Wow, I cannot believe it,' he said. 'When did this happen? I didn't know you were interviewing?'

The atmosphere had changed, the temperature dropped a degree or two. Ann felt wrong-footed. All of a sudden what she thought was cause for celebration felt like she'd done something wrong.

'Well, I wasn't looking. I got a call from the magazine because I had been doing some freelance work for them. I didn't mention it to you because I wasn't sure whether I'd have a chance or not and I didn't want to get my hopes up.'

Justin pushed his plate back from him, gesturing that he had lost his appetite. 'Wow, Ann, I wish you'd mentioned it to me.'

'I'm sorry, Justin, I thought it would be better to wait and see if I got it first. I didn't mean to upset you? Are you OK? I wasn't actively hiding it from you. I didn't tell anyone about it.'

Justin made a big show of staying calm and reasonable but she could tell he was really pissed off. 'Have you thought this through, though, Ann?'

'Of course, Justin! This is a solid full-time permanent job with benefits. Do you know how rare they are in journalism? This is a once-in-a-career opportunity. This will get me back on my feet in my career and it will also be nice to have some financial independence too. I know you've been really generous but I like to have my own income too, just because if I want to buy something frivolous I can do it without feeling guilty that I'm being wasteful with your money.'

This conversation was not going the way she had expected. All of the joy and excitement she had felt earlier had dissipated.

'But how's it going to work?'

'Well, they know I am based in Hudson and are comfortable with me working hybrid. I thought it would be a good idea to get a studio in the city so I could stay over one or two nights a week. The salary will more than cover that. And it will be nice to have a base in the city for us too; we can take weekend trips. And it will be good for me too, Justin. Think about it. It might help with how difficult I've found adapting to the pace of life around here. And I have no friends here. I'm lonely! I miss my old friends in the city.'

'But you have me,' Justin said, and Ann felt slightly

claustrophobic, unsure of him in a way she hadn't ever done before.

'I just don't think it's the right thing, Ann,' he said in a chillingly reasonable tone. 'I wish you had discussed it with me. If you need money, I can give you money. Think about it. The timing is all wrong. You're having a baby. Are we not building something here, a family, and you're planning on running back and forth to New York? Who's going to mind the baby? Who's going to mind Sophie? Have you thought about how it will work in practical terms?'

'I – I thought we might get a childminder for Sophie,' Ann said.

'She'd hate that,' Justin replied shortly.

Ann felt almost giddy. Had she made a commitment that she would be Sophie's childminder? He was being unfair.

'Are you really going to give everything up to write gossipy articles about celebrities?'

Ann hadn't realised a) that Justin read her pieces and b) that he thought of them so dismissively. She felt mortified. She felt like she was talking to a stranger. She wanted to leave, to run back to her mother's apartment, to her mother's arms, but neither was possible.

'I think you're being selfish, Ann. You're only thinking of yourself. I thought we were in this together? Do we have a future here or not?'

'Justin, we do, of course we do,' but inside she was

panicking, thinking – *do we?* 'I had no idea this is how you felt. I'm thinking of everyone here. This job will offer me some security, a solid salary, some consistency as well as routine. I need to rebuild my career, surely you see that?'

'*I* offer you security, Ann. I have more money than you could possibly need. Why would you want to go get a job?'

'Well, because I need to work, I like working, and it will help with my mortgage application if I have a full-time job. Plus, these kind of jobs rarely come up. But I'm sorry, I – I didn't think you'd be unhappy. I'm sorry. I didn't think . . .'

The following Monday, Ann called the editor at the magazine and told her with great reluctance that she couldn't take the job. Every cell in her body told her not to let the job go, it went against everything to pass it up, but she had to think of Justin, Sophie and her own baby now if they were going to be a proper family. She told the editor about the pregnancy. 'I just wouldn't feel right taking it knowing that I'll need time off in six months when the baby arrives. I'm sorry, I should have said something at interview stage.'

They agreed that Ann could continue her contractual work but she could tell the editor was annoyed. And she had every right to be. But Justin was right. Ann had been thinking as a single person. She had to learn to think about herself as part of a group now, a family. She had to start trusting Justin, to not always be so self-reliant. Hadn't that been the problem in the first place; hadn't that been what had left her alone and without support when her mother had been sick? If she had had a partner, a husband, she would have had help. No, Justin was right. But why then did it feel all wrong?

Chapter Nineteen

After the tension created by Ann's job offer, she and Justin decided to take a weekend trip away, clear the air and forget about things. Ann had grown close to Justin and to Sophie over the past months, and the three of them tended to do everything together now. They had moved on from romantic dinners and dates to staying in on the couch, cloistered in Justin's house with Sophie playing happily nearby or watching a cartoon. They were a tight little unit and now that they had a baby to look forward to as well, Ann knew they'd make a lovely family. Sophie would share DNA with Ann's baby. They would both share DNA with Justin. Ann saw them all as connected like one of those paper cut-outs of people holding hands.

The pregnancy had cemented Ann's bond with Justin and she couldn't imagine anything coming between them. She had been foolish to think that he wouldn't be upset by the idea of her withdrawing from the life they were building to take a job in the city. In fact, it just proved his commitment to her. He didn't transfer so much money to her account these days, but now that she was living with him rent-free he said she didn't need as much so he just gave her money when she needed something. It didn't feel great, but he reassured her that his money was her money too.

Ann and Sophie had been spending a lot of time together and Ann had never known the kind of open and accepting love that Sophie showed her. Ann liked to read her a bedtime story now, and she and Sophie read the Eloise stories over and over again every night.

That's where the idea for the weekend away came from. Sophie wanted to visit some of the sights of New York City as detailed in her Eloise stories. They would stay at the Plaza, just like Eloise. The plan was to drive up on Saturday morning and stay overnight.

'We'll just make a quick stop at the hospital on the way to see Deborah,' Justin said. 'Is that OK? You can wait in the car.' Justin and Sophie usually visited Deborah every Saturday morning, just a quick visit to say hello, even though Deborah was often unconscious.

As Ann waited in the car in the hospital car park, she listened to her favourite current affairs show. She browsed through the weekend edition of the *New York Times* and tried to eat a croissant without getting any flakes on her silk blouse. Another Justin purchase.

Justin said they'd be about fifteen or twenty minutes. He usually spoke to the attending doctor before saying a quick hello to Deborah. After thirty minutes, Ann checked her watch but didn't make much of it. She was fine waiting. She liked reading the papers in peace and working on pitches for the following week. She was aware that people might think it was weird for her to be there, waiting in the car, while the father of her unborn child visited his wife with his child. But that completely missed the nuance of their dynamic. It was special. Justin's loyalty to his first wife was endearing to Ann: it showed what kind of a man he was.

There wasn't much Ann could do about it anyway, and she was pragmatic. She knew it would be ridiculous to get jealous, or make a big deal about it. Time dragged on as she tried to concentrate on the papers. She couldn't figure out what was taking them so long. Seconds crawled over each other. Another hour passed, at which point Ann broke and texted Justin – Everything OK?

No response. The early spring sunshine pulsed down on the car. Ann suddenly felt suffocated by the heat and the small interior of Justin's sports car. She opened the door suddenly and stepped out. She gulped in fresh air and looked around the car park. She ate an apple and some cashew nuts to keep the rising nausea at bay.

Everything seemed calm in the hospital. What could be keeping them so long?

After two and half hours, it finally dawned on Ann what had happened. How could she be so dumb, she thought? The inevitable event that they had been dreading for so long had finally happened. Deborah had died, she realised with a sudden shock.

Although she had waited for this day, its arrival brought her no pleasure. She was surprised to feel panic and fear creep in. Everything had been going so well with Justin and Sophie and now the baby, she didn't want anything to change and upset their little bubble.

Ann found she could go on happily as things were for the rest of her life. She was comfortable in suspended animation. Why did things always have to change? But she knew in her heart that it was kinder for Deborah to die, after clinging to life for so long. It was selfish of Ann to want Deborah to stay in stasis like that just so her life could remain settled and calm for the first time in her whole adulthood.

Ann was spiralling, anticipating how Deborah's death would affect Justin and Sophie; it brought them into uncharted territory. Perhaps Justin would want to call things off between them and just be alone with his daughter. Deborah's daughter. After all, grief did strange things to people. She knew that from experience, had seen it with her own mother, how her sisters had reacted, how she had reacted. Now that his wife was dead maybe Justin wouldn't want to be tied down, maybe he might want to enjoy being a single man again. Ann realised she could be cut loose and in an even more precarious situation than she was before she had met Justin. But surely Justin wouldn't do that to her and the baby?

She tried to relax and wait calmly for him and Sophie to return to the car, but her heart was racing. She didn't send any more texts. She knew they'd be here when they were able. She tried to think of what she might say to them, some words of comfort. Would he have told Sophie or would he wait to tell her? Ann tried to make her face look sympathetic without it being annoying.

She was still overthinking when ninety minutes later, as the light was starting to fall, she saw Justin's figure emerge from the hospital. Sophie was behind him but overtook him quickly as she broke into a run towards the car. He shouted at her to wait, to slow down but she didn't heed him. He never shouted at Sophie. He sounded angry, but Sophie kept running. Justin looked furious and it scared Ann. But when Sophie reached the car, Ann could see she looked happy, excited. He must not have told her yet. Ann's heart broke for her as she pulled down the window to say hi, but Sophie's words flew in like bats.

'Mommy's coming home! Mommy's coming home! She's better! She's coming home!'

Justin's face was stony as he caught up with Sophie.

Ann's body went into immediate physical shock and she could barely speak, so strong was her confusion. Her hand went to her stomach.

'Justin? What's going on?'

'We'll talk about it in a minute,' he said tersely, making an emphatic nod towards Sophie, as he bundled her into the car. He had never dismissed Ann in this way, like she was an irritant. Maybe she had misunderstood Sophie, somehow got it wrong. Maybe what she meant was that Mommy's coming home for the funeral. Had Justin told Sophie something euphemistic about her mother's death? Of course, she would be brought back home for the wake afterwards.

Ann breathed out slowly in little bursts to try and bring her alarm under control. That must be it. It's all mixed up for little kids. They don't really understand death. Ann had gotten the wrong end of the stick.

But the prickles remained on the back of Ann's neck, the nauseating feeling of clammy coolness clung to her skin.

'Here, Sophie, let me help you with your seatbelt and get you set up with a movie on your iPad,' Justin said, strapping her in to the booster seat. 'Here are your headphones, pop these on ... good girl.'

When Ann was certain Sophie was watching a movie at full volume and they were driving out of the hospital, she looked at Justin. 'Are you going to talk to me? Are you going to tell me what's happened?'

Justin craned around to look at Sophie. 'Sophie, do you want some chocolate?' he asked. No response. This was how he checked if Sophie could hear them, by offering her something she couldn't resist.

He turned back around, shook his head and started to cry. 'I – I . . . I don't know how to tell you this. I don't know what's going on but it looks like Deborah is . . . getting better? They gave her that drug. That miracle drug, the one that was on the news a couple of weeks ago. She was one of the patients on the clinical trial.'

Ann tried to keep her eyes on the road but wanted to stare at Justin, to see if the words really were coming out of his mouth. All she could manage was, 'What?'

'It's reversed everything,' he said. 'The tumour is literally dissolving, all of her memories appear to be intact. She knows me. She remembers stuff about our life together. It's like she's been rebooted. She is exactly the same person she was six years ago, before she got sick.'

Ann didn't dare look at him. She stared straight ahead. 'This can't be happening,' she said.

Justin nodded. 'I feel like I'm living in a sci-fi movie. They said she can come home if this rate of recovery continues.' He couldn't bring himself to look at Ann either.

Home. Where was home for Deborah? And where

was home for Ann if Deborah was coming home? She held the wheel of the car with one hand and put her other hand on her stomach. It felt important to protect the baby in some way from what felt like waves of attack. The shock of every detail felt like a whip on her body.

'Home where? To our house?' she said. 'She might notice that there's a strange woman living there, Justin. Does she even know about me, about us, about the baby?'

'Ann, of course not; she literally just woke up. It didn't feel like the right time. I'm still in shock myself. I love you, Ann, I love our baby, I love the family we've all become but . . .'

Ann took in a sharp breath to brace herself for the words she knew Justin was about to say.

'. . . she's my wife, Ann. She's Sophie's mother. How can I tell her? How can I tell her she can't come home?'

'But you've moved on, Justin, you're with me now. We are an "us" now. It's not just about you and me. We have a baby to think of. Sophie will have a sister or brother.' Ann felt like she was making an argument for her life. 'Deborah has been gone from your life, from Sophie's life, for so long. I know it sounds callous but your lives have moved on and that's nobody's fault. Everyone, even the best specialists in the world told you that they couldn't save Deborah.'

'Believe me, Ann, I would never have started something with you if I had thought this was even a remote possibility. The doctor told me the chances were something like one in a billion. Who could have predicted this?'

Ann's fear was making her desperate, impatient.

'But what about us, Justin? What about us?' she almost shrieked. The car juddered from side to side as she lost control. Justin reached over and grabbed the wheel. 'Jesus, Ann, can you watch the road?'

Tears were brimming in her eyes and she could feel herself beginning to hyperventilate.

'Look, Ann, you know about as much as I do right now. I just don't know what's going to happen, but we have a few weeks to figure it out.'

A cry escaped Ann's mouth and she started sobbing hard. 'But how, Justin, how are we going to figure it out? We can't both be with you, you have to pick one . . . How can you do this to me, to our baby? I've given up everything for you, uprooted my whole life to move here and to be with you, turned down a job that would have given me security to rely on you and now you're pulling the rug out from under us.' She heard the wheedling tone in her voice and hated herself for it.

'This is my fault. I wasn't free to start something new. I was still married to her, no matter what. I cheated on her. I should never have cheated on her. I should have been a good husband and stayed loyal until she died. Then I wouldn't be in this mess . . . ' Ann wiped her nose with the sleeve of her blazer.

'I'm sorry, this mess? Is that what you're calling us now?'

'No, god, Ann . . . will you please watch the road? No, I'm sorry. You know what I mean. This whole thing is a mess – Deborah, me, all of it . . . How am I supposed to choose?'

'How can you choose her?! She was supposed to die.'

'I'm not choosing anyone,' he hissed at her. 'Jesus, Ann, can't you see how distressing this all is? It's not just about you and your baby. Deborah has no one. Her parents are dead. She is an only child of only children. Sophie and I are her only family! Where else is she supposed to go?'

Ann realised she was being selfish. She was not putting herself in Deborah's place. How would she feel if it was her?

'I'm sorry. You're right. This is a shock. I'm not thinking straight. Of course you have to be there for her. Forgive me, I don't even know what I'm saying.'

Justin reached over and squeezed her hand. 'Thank you, darling,' he said. 'And, really, the house is big enough for all of us anyway.'

It was too much. Ann screeched the car across three lanes of traffic amidst blaring horns and slammed to a stop on the hard shoulder; the rumble strip felt like it was shredding the tyres. She got out of the car, and vomited over the guardrail into the rough.

Chapter Twenty

Sometimes the membrane between the knowledge that her mother was dead and the idea that she might somehow find a way back to Ann was very thin. In quieter moments, meditating, or just before fully waking up early in the morning, Ann swore she could feel a sense of her mother.

She tried to imagine what her mother might say to her now about the nightmare she was in. Told you so? Get the hell out of there? Ann was so deeply in love with Justin and the life she imagined they were going to have when their baby arrived that she found it impossible to reverse out of this situation. She was dug in, up to her waist in it. And why should she be the one who had to graciously bow out? Didn't she have as much right to Justin, their home, this life, as Deborah did? She should have known. Everything was too perfect, too good to be true. She should have listened to her sisters.

They cancelled their trip to the city, turned around and drove home in silence. Later on, after putting Sophie to bed and explaining that they would do the trip another time, Ann and Justin sat in stunned silence in the study, the same room they had spent that first night together. It felt like an absolute lifetime ago.

'I should have guessed,' he said.

'Guessed what?'

'That something was up. There was a weird atmosphere from the moment we walked into the hospital. It felt like there was a secret party or something, you know, everyone bursting to tell me but not wanting to ruin the surprise. It was ebullient, not your normal palliative care atmosphere.' The tone was usually hushed and reverent, he told her, more like a church. That morning it had been jubilant. The doctors and nurses had all smiled and said hello as he and Sophie had passed on their way to see Deborah.

'I just figured it was somebody's birthday. You can't be doom and gloom all the time when death is your job,' he said. 'Sophie picked up on it too. She was beaming back at everyone she passed. One of the nurses said, "Isn't this an amazing day, Justin?" and I just thought she had lost her marbles. It never occurred to me that it might be related to Deborah.'

Ann sat quietly. She was still in a state of shock and exhausted from the adrenalin of the day. Her eyes were puffy from crying but she had stopped for now.

'When we got to Deborah's room, there was a crowd outside, a group of nurses, interns, porters; it seemed like half the hospital were there. I thought what you thought at first: she's dead and they've come to pay their respects. That's when I saw her. She was sitting up, talking to people, eating something, looking as if she had just been in a long sleep.'

Justin didn't tell Ann the next bit. When their eyes had locked, he'd felt a jolt of memory. It was Deborah. 'Hello, Justin,' Deborah had said, sitting up in bed and smiling at him. Her skin was pale and her hair lank, but her eyes were full of life, everything that had ever happened between them reflected in them. He'd thought he was going mad but then Sophie had torn the silence apart and screamed 'Mommy!!' as she'd rushed past him and burst into tears, diving onto her mother's bed. 'Mommy, Mommy, you're awake!'

'Deborah? Oh my god, Deborah, is it you? Deborah . . . ' He'd turned to the doctors. 'Is this real? What's happening?'

They had tears in their eyes too; some of them were hugging each other.

'I'm better, Justin,' Deborah had said. He had forgotten her beautiful voice. 'I'm back.'

PART II

Getting to know Deborah

Chapter Twenty-One

Ann

Deborah was coming home. It would be a matter of days according to the doctors. She was behaving normally. Her vital signs were positive. Her memory and brain functioning were perfect. She remembered everything. While the physiotherapists worked on her muscles, teaching her how to walk again, Justin and Ann grimly worked out yet another cover story.

Deborah had become something of a celebrity. Journalists wanted to talk to her. The tabloids called her Miracle Mommy. Scientists and doctors and researchers clamoured for access to her. Was she the key to unlocking the mysteries of all sorts of incurable diseases?

Ann thought of her mother, how this drug might have

saved her, how she might have returned to live a full life with a treatment like this, how Ann might still have had her mother if only her healthcare had covered this kind of drug access. God knows she could have done with her mother's help right now. The mood was jubilant. This was quite simply the best news. Except for Ann. For Ann, this was the worst possible news. Just as she had found herself in the most secure and happy relationship of her life, planning to become a mother, she felt it was about to be ripped away from her.

And the worst part was that nobody was to blame. There was no villain. It wasn't Deborah's fault that she had gotten sick, or that she had gotten well again. She was an innocent woman. And didn't she have a right, after everything she had been through, to go back to her old life, her husband and daughter with whom she had missed out on so much?

But Ann had done nothing either. Deborah was supposed to die. She never felt like she was a homewrecker until now, when everything changed.

The doctors had told Justin that the best thing for Deborah's recovery now was for her to go home, to a familiar, comfortable place, and to be allowed to get used to her life again. 'Try to keep life as calm, and low-key as possible,' her doctor had said. 'This is a completely unknown treatment. We can't tell how she will react to stress or shock or fright or even a common cold. Everything will need to be monitored.

The best we can do for her on a day-to-day basis is to keep life simple and easy, keep her on an even emotional keel and just look after her the way you would a child.'

It was this that demolished Ann's argument that they should be upfront and honest with Deborah from the start. Before she knew this, she said to Justin, 'If we just tell her everything upfront, total disclosure, come clean about it all from the start, then there is no deception. Everything is forgivable if it is revealed immediately. This is a no-fault situation anyway.'

'We can't shock her,' he said levelly, relating everything the doctor had said. 'Even if it means lying to her in the short term, we can't risk her health.'

'Justin, I really think timing is everything here. The only way the truth hurts is when it is kept from people. When we tell her is going to make all the difference. If you don't want her to feel betrayed, you can't keep her in the dark. Time is of the essence. She's coming home soon. I'm pregnant, that's got a finite time frame too. Events will overtake us.'

But Justin couldn't bring himself to agree. He couldn't see where things would go from there. What if there was a huge blow-out? What if Deborah kicked him out and didn't let him see Sophie? What if the shock made her relapse? Where would they live? No, it was too risky. He sided with the doctors in the end. 'We will obviously tell her but we may need to do it in a slow and controlled fashion,' he said. 'It's a delicate situation, Ann; we're just going to have to be patient.

Ann's frustration was huge. She knew she was being unreasonable but she couldn't help seeing Deborah as the obstacle between herself and happiness, this contentment that she had experienced for the first time with Justin and Sophie. Her life for the last three years had been grey, struggle, poverty, medical bills and antiseptic wipes, sterilised water and pre-packed cotton swabs. Very little joy or spontaneity crept through that bubble. Ann had been living for other people, sacrificing everything for her mom, and now she was expected to sacrifice everything again, for this woman. She was finally living and now it would be taken away. Justin tried to calm her down.

'Ann, I'm not going to abandon you or our baby. Please try not to worry about that. This is not a you or her situation. We just need time to figure it out.' But of course it was an Ann or Deborah situation.

Ann went for a walk along the edge of the water. While she was walking, her phone rang, a number she didn't recognise. She answered.

'Oh, hi Ann, it's Cookie here, Justin's friend? From the party? How are you, dear? We've all just heard the wonderful news about Deborah but I thought of you when I heard and just wanted to call and say how sorry I am things are not going to work out for you. We all really liked you and could see how wonderful you were for Justin and Sophie.'

Ann was completely lost for words. This woman, who she had met once, was now on the phone commiserating (or was she gloating?) about Ann's catastrophe of a life. She was speaking as if it was a fait accompli. 'Are you still in Hudson?'

'Of course,' Ann responded. 'I live here now. Did Justin not tell you?'

Cookie laughed a brittle laugh. 'Oh, but you can't be serious, Ann. Surely you won't be staying now with Deborah coming home?'

Ann felt tears rising. Everyone expected her to just step aside, sacrifice her own life and feelings just because someone else was there first? That was not Ann's plan.

'I'm walking by the lake, Cookie, so I don't think the coverage is great. Perhaps we can talk another time. Thanks for the call though, I appreciate your concern.' She hung up on Cookie's babble. She was even more miserable now. She walked along the river for a long time but could see no obvious solution for her predicament.

When she arrived home her face was red and her hair was tangled from whipping about her face in the breeze. She had worn herself out with the walk and the thinking and the what ifs and the fruitless attempts to come up with a solution. And she realised she was starving. Since becoming pregnant she couldn't tolerate hunger at all. She just wanted to eat.

'I made chicken chasseur,' Justin said gently.

Sophie was in bed and he dished up two bowls and some bread and sat at an angle from her, across the table.

'I was thinking while you went for your walk,' he said. 'I have an idea that might be the bridge we need to get us across this crazy situation. What if we just tell Deborah – very temporarily – what we've been telling everyone else. That you're the live-in nanny who helped us out while she was in hospital, kept the house running and looked after Sophie while I dealt with my work, something like that? Think about it. People around here already know you as the nanny. They can corroborate the story.'

Ann couldn't believe her ears. Was he really suggesting this?

'It's not exactly a lie,' he said. 'You have done these things for us. What if we said that, just for now? Just so we can still be together ... Ann?'

It was a shocking suggestion. Ann didn't like it one bit. But it was also the only way she could think of that would allow her to stay where she was, in her place with Justin and Sophie, and for Deborah to be OK with it.

'I don't want you to leave, Ann,' he said, reaching for her hand. 'I love you. I need you. Sophie needs you.

After a while, as Deborah gets stronger, I can break it to her that our marriage is not working any more, that too much has changed, too much time has passed and we can amicably separate. Then you and I can be together. We don't even need to tell her that you and I are a couple straight off. I can tell her that the marriage is over, that we will parent our daughter together and that she can remain in this house and we'll find somewhere beautiful for us, Ann, to raise our baby together, and Sophie can spend half the week with us. It's complicated but I think we can make it work eventually if we are just strong now.'

Ann thought he sounded unhinged, but she had no alternative. She had no intention of leaving the man she loved; it had taken her so long to find him and she was carrying his baby.

'I just think a drip-feed of only necessary facts is the best approach. I might not even need to break it to her. She might decide that the marriage is not working for her.'

Oh god, Ann thought, did he really want to be that person. The kind of person who was so shitty and cowardly that they'd rather get the other person to make their decision for them than bite the bullet themselves? Ann pulled the fluttering red flag down to half-mast. She decided he must still be in shock.

'Justin, I know it all probably fits logically or plausibly but let's just take a step back here. In reality, what you're suggesting is that we all live together, pretending I'm the nanny while Deborah thinks she is back in the bosom of her family. And you and I, what, have trysts in the broom cupboard while she takes her physiotherapy sessions? Sneak around behind her back? Have a grope in the downstairs bathroom while she sleeps? How on earth do you see any of us getting away with this? How is our relationship supposed to survive if you're playing happy families with Deborah?'

'Ann, that's not what I think, obviously. I was thinking more that you could move into the pool house and keep that as your apartment quarters and I could come visit you, when Deborah is asleep.'

It got worse. 'Oh, wait, tell me if I've got this right: you want me to play housemaid and you're kicking me out of the house? I'm sorry, Justin, this is not really filling me with excitement.'

'No, no, you're wilfully misunderstanding me, Ann. I just meant if you'd prefer to be out of the house you can stay there but obviously stay in the house if you want. You could move into the room next door to the baby's nursery for now.'

'Justin, I don't think you're thinking this through fully. None of it works for me. I don't like any of it. I still think the best way is to be upfront with her. If we lie to her now and then two months in have to tell her or she finds out somehow, that's a shitstorm nobody will walk away from. How can I be in the same house with her and lie to her face? And where is she going to sleep? What are you going to do if she tries it on, if she wants to celebrate her resurrection by having sex. She hasn't had sex in years. She might be in the mood!' Ann was aware that she sounded crazy now.

'I won't tolerate you sleeping with her, Justin. I don't want you to cheat on me with her!' Was it even cheating if it's your wife? Christ!

'And have you thought about how she might feel having me around the whole time, cramping her style now that she's finally about to get her life back? She's going to want to spend one-on-one time with you and Sophie, make up for lost time.'

'Look, that's not going to happen. She won't expect to just jump straight back in. I'll tell her it's a shock, that we need to take things slowly, get to know each other again, work on our friendship first. I'll get the doctor to say that she should be in a room of her own, no excitement for the first six weeks. That buys us some time. I'll put her off. You don't have to worry about that. Think of what she's been through physically and mentally over the last few years; what she's endured will take a toll, and it will take a toll on Sophie too. She's going to need you. She thinks of you as a kind of mother now too. We just have to be strong and band together.'

'Justin, I'm terrified here. I've made myself completely vulnerable. I've given up my job to look after

Sophie, the one place that was home is now sold, gone for ever, but with no sign of money because of probate. I don't really have a lot of options here and I'm starting to feel really fucking vulnerable . . . ' She flung her head between her knees. 'Oh God, this is so sick. It's so fucked up. I just can't see the solution any which way. If I leave, I get to be a broke single parent and I lose Sophie and you. I love you both so much. My baby grows up without her dad and her sister so the baby loses out too. If I stay, I get to be part of some weird polyamorous situation except I get the short straw of being the nanny while you guys get to do fun stuff and I get to clean up after you,' she screamed in frustration.

She felt Justin's hand on her back. 'Ann, please, you can't get so worked up. It's bad for the baby.'

Ann shook her head again and came back up for air. 'I'm sorry, Justin, but the only way through this is the truth. You moved on for your sake and the sake of Sophie. Sophie needed a female influence in her life. Put yourself in her place. Wouldn't you want to know?'

'But she could make things difficult for me, Ann,' Justin said quietly.

'How, Justin?'

'My access to Sophie, for a start. I'd have to find a new place to live . . . '

'You are Sophie's father. You have legal entitlements. She cannot remove your access because you started having a relationship while everyone, including the professional experts, told you she would die, urged you to get on with your life. To transfer her to the sole custody of her mother now would be traumatising for her. That's not something you should fear just yet.'

'I just feel so scared. Why do I feel so guilty?'

'I don't know, Justin, but what has happened is nobody's fault. Nobody is at fault. It's just an accident. Whose idea was it to give her those drugs anyway, for god's sake? I thought she was under a non-interventionist Do Not Resuscitate order?' Ann said it more to herself than to him but he answered.

'She was. But I may have signed a clause saying I was happy for her to be used for research and the clinical trial was considered as falling under that. I thought it meant anatomical research, post-mortem research for medical students, after she had died. I didn't think it was research to save her life. Not that I didn't want to save her life ... god, you know what I mean, Ann. I didn't want to prolong her pain when there was no hope and no quality of life. But this is different. She has full quality of life back. She is herself again. Why should she not pick up where she left off?'

'Because it's not her life any more, Justin,' Ann snapped. 'It's my life. Mine and yours.'

Justin was shocked into silence. 'I don't know whose life it is. All I know is this is the best solution for right now. Just tell me you'll think about it, just for a month, to give us some breathing space, so we can figure out a way forward. It's all been so sudden, we just need a bit of time. We've all had a shock. We're not thinking straight. It's for us I'm doing this,' he said, gripping Ann's hands, 'so we can be together as a proper family. It will be worth it in the end, I promise.'

Sophie was one of the reasons Ann hadn't left yet. The idea of abandoning her, of her uncomprehending face, was impossible. She couldn't hurt her and she couldn't hurt herself by removing this relationship from her life. She couldn't refuse any request for Sophie's wellbeing. She felt her shoulders slump. Justin noticed the retreat and sat down beside her.

'Look, this changes nothing. We're still making a life together. That's not going to change. It's just going to take a little longer than we planned. I can't just abandon her. We'll sort it all out. I promise. A few weeks, I promise. A month tops.'

Chapter Twenty-Two

Deborah

I awoke to a world I didn't know. I had left behind a husband and a child who I still considered a baby, and now I was returned to a man I barely recognised and a grown child, with long hair, such beautiful hair, and so many words and ideas and articulation to arrange those ideas into sentences. And questions! She had so many questions. The miraculousness of it all struck me dumb.

'Did you miss me, Mommy?'

When I had gotten sick, Sophie used to call me Mama. I had never heard her say the word mommy. When had she stopped calling me Mama?

'Could you hear us when you were asleep, Mommy?' she asked, her curious eyes blinking up at me. 'We talked to you all the time. I sang you a lullaby,' she said but the l's sounded more like w's. How many of these adorable mispronunciations had I missed? How many had been corrected and disappeared before I even had the chance to hear them? I was here now and would listen to every word Sophie had to say.

'Would you like me to paint your nails? We can play salon?'

'I would love that,' I replied.

Strangely, I felt dissonance. I could just about trace the face of the child I remembered underneath the mask of this child. It looked like a canvas had been stretched out over the pins of Sophie's bone structure. The template underneath was of the baby I once knew, now superimposed with the face of this strange new person. My thoughts reached out like antennae, snaking around the room, tentatively seeking out this new reality. Questions tied my mind up in knots.

Justin felt unfamiliar, almost as unfamiliar as Sophie. He was older to start, that was the biggest surprise. Wrinkles and lines, but he was also ripped where he used to have a full dadbod. While I had wasted away, Justin had been working out. It made his face look cruel somehow. He looked like one of those men who ran marathons, all sinewy tendons and veins rutting up his forearms and neck. Maybe he was one of those men now? This was somehow the most ridiculous thing of all. Justin had never exercised. Maybe he felt he had to get healthy and fit when I had gotten sick. One of us had to be strong for our daughter. Or maybe he got ripped for other reasons, because he was single, or thought of himself as single. Had he dated other women? The thought was fleeting like a bird that had accidentally flown into a room but righted itself before it got trapped and flitted free again just as quickly. He had visited me every week and he was here now.

I wondered what I looked like now. I hadn't been out of the hospital yet and I somehow couldn't bear to look at myself in a mirror. But I knew that I must look different.

Justin was also guarded, uncertain, where previously he had a simple and open approach to everything. Now he seemed wary, as if all of our shared experiences, all of our times together, were as false as memories dragged from my hard-drive to his brain, false narratives that he didn't quite trust. It felt like he had spent the past eighteen months detaching himself from the pain of this situation, a satellite disconnecting from the mothership. He had been protecting himself. I understood. Wouldn't that be the most sensible thing to do? Wouldn't that be what I would do in his place?

Sophie's voice intruded. 'What's your favourite food? Mine is pancakes but no berries or cream, just chocolate spread. Ann makes them for me.'

My memories were jumbled. Some things were

completely lucid and detailed, others felt like the files had been removed for a certain year or years of my life. Funnily enough, Ann was the only person who made any sense to me, maybe because she was completely new. She didn't have a former ill-fitting template to poorly re-attach to, she hadn't existed in my before-life, so there was nothing to compare her to, no dissonance. With Justin and Sophie, it felt like I was lining up two images but the images would not align, and trying to recreate a dynamic that no longer existed. With Ann it was easy. Justin told me about her, how she had helped with Sophie and made life easier for him. Sophie talked about her non-stop so even though I hadn't met her yet I knew that she was a nice person. A good person.

'You'll love her,' Justin said. 'She'll be a great help to you.'

Sophie was excited, energised by her mother being back. Justin seemed tightly wound, nervous and reserved, so unlike the husband I had known before. And I was dealing with my own shock, my own strange existential experience while trying to be a mother and a wife again, things I hadn't been for years. I worried that I would be a disappointment to Sophie. She had probably spent the last couple of years imagining what her life with a mother might be like, but I knew from my relationship with my own mother that the reality would likely be less fun and more disciplined than she thought. Thinking of my mother made me sad. We had never been close but now I wished I had a parent to care for me, to love me unconditionally and help me navigate this situation. I felt like a frightened child.

Sophie had so many plans for us – cinema, swimming, beauty treatments, pizza, bookshops, holidays, colouring, shopping, playdates, school drama shows . . . all of the things I had missed out on. How could I ever make up for the time we had lost? How could I possibly live up to Sophie's hopes and expectations? And how could I ever say no to anything this child asked of me, even if it sounded exhausting?

But Ann, the childminder, would help, Justin reassured me. Ann's express purpose was to help Sophie, and by extension me. Justin had asked whether I wanted Ann to stay on and I had immediately replied yes because I would need the support. I remembered how absent Justin had been as a parent, how he had considered anything to do with Sophie my territory, my responsibility, my problem. I had made up my mind that I would take whatever help I could get. I was being given a second chance. Ann and I might even be friends. She wasn't much younger than me after all. It would be nice to have someone around. After Sophie had been born, the loneliness was almost unbearable. I had been isolated from friends and fallen out of touch with people. And Justin was constantly working so I could never get away. I would bond to Ann like a helpless lamb. Whether she was a wolf or not remained to be seen.

Chapter Twenty-Three

Ann

The day before Deborah was due to come home, Ann performed the heavy task of moving her belongings from the master bedroom, the room she shared with Justin, into the room next door to the nursery. At least it was a warm and bright room, facing out onto the water. 'Deborah never slept in here,' Justin said, as if Ann might suddenly develop a conscience about sleeping in Deborah's room but not about sleeping with her husband, mothering her child or living her life.

Even if Deborah had never slept in this particular room, she was everywhere. Underneath Ann's fingers as they glided the banisters on her way down the stairs, on the towels she pulled out of the closet, in the fabric of the curtains as Ann pulled them tightly shut at night. The neighbours had been calling regularly ever since finding out that Deborah was expected to come home, intrigued, hoping for a glimpse. Ann was suddenly just as intrigued now. She had never really taken an interest in Deborah before. She was supposed to die, after all. It was easy to be respectful then. Ann could afford to be magnanimous when Deborah posed no threat. What did her clothes and jewellery and belongings matter? They were just harmless objects. But now that Deborah was coming home, Ann was gripped with a burning obsession to know everything.

Now she moved methodically through the house, like a cat, from basement to eaves. She burned to know what Deborah was like. Was she reserved, outgoing, fun, cool? She had no way of finding out. Deborah was part of that generation that had little online life. She wasn't on Twitter, Insta or even Facebook.

'Jesus,' Ann whispered as her Google searches turned up nothing more than charity fundraisers. How was it possible that a search term of two names could yield so little, but it did. How she longed for a careless Facebook account, privacy set to 'public', an archive of a life with work colleagues, friends, afternoon tea with champagne in luxury hotels. Ann wanted a series of photos of a bachelorette party, an inflatable penis and veil. But there was nothing about Deborah online. Just a reference to her graduation, some corporate articles on her family's business and some pictures of the aforementioned charity events.

The passing of winter had transformed the house and it felt less gloomy now as the April sunlight filtered through the windows, bouncing light from the river. Justin had told her to make herself at home. In the quiet mornings, when Justin was at work and Sophie was in school, Ann could stare freely at the pictures of Deborah that were placed around the house. She was always posed. Good breeding, Ann supposed. Toes pointed, ankles crossed, eyes wide, chin down, she reminded Ann of the Miss World Contest that she used to watch as a child, but she knew these were all just vestiges of a proper upbringing, civilising classes in deportment, the kind of thing a girl from Brooklyn never got.

Ann couldn't believe how different they seemed. She compared her life with Deborah's like an AI program searching for points of recognition on a fingerprint database. Ann scanned the images. Deborah was pretty, but Ann was pretty too. Deborah was superthin, the thinness that only very rich people seemed able to achieve. Ann was athletic but curvy. Deborah looked like a middle-aged conservative wife, someone who might work in a museum with her sharply cut black bob and Moschino skirt suits. Ann was a Brooklyner; her clothes were made up of thrifted, vintage and designer. She liked to be casual.

She looked at Deborah's face in the picture until it

blurred into nothingness. She thought that if she stared at those pictures for long enough, absorbed every detail, she would gain some understanding of who Deborah was, *what* she was, but the more she looked, the more her features disappeared, became less distinct until she was nothing.

Ann could only know Deborah through the items at her disposal, her belongings, some discarded things, a tiny Pompeii of a day in the life, frozen in time. Ann touched each item thinking about how Deborah had touched these once. She tried to divine some insight into Deborah like a medium holding objects a dead person was close to. Was her energy here, on this item? What part of her lingered on these things, what molecules, what atoms? What part of her had now transferred onto Ann. Were those atoms morphing? Was Ann becoming more Deborah?

It didn't help that Justin had accidentally called Ann by Deborah's name a couple of times. The first time it had happened, Ann had been so shocked she'd thought she had imagined it.

'Did you see the remote anywhere, Deb?' he'd said. Such a banal and ordinary request, so casual that she might even have misheard. Deb. It didn't sound anything like anything else, particularly not Ann.

The air had changed immediately. Justin had known immediately what he had said, but he'd said nothing. So Ann had said, 'What did you say?'

'Did you see the remote control, for the TV?'

'Deb. You said Deb. You called me Deb?'

'Ann, it was an accident. Can we not make this weird?'

'Um, well, what if it is weird? I've never called you by my ex-boyfriend's name.'

'Deb is not my ex.'

Ann was silenced.

'I don't mean it like that . . . Look, it was a slip of the tongue. It doesn't mean I think you're Deb or I don't know your name or that you're a different person. I'm just tired, OK? I'm under a lot of stress at work and I'm distracted. Ann, please, Ann, can we not make a big deal out of it? It means nothing. I'm really sorry. It won't happen again.'

'It's fine,' Ann had said. 'It's just a bit weird. It feels like you see me as a wife-shaped blob that you're fitting into the space left by Deborah.' Her name felt sacrilegious in Ann's mouth. She never referred to Deborah by her name, never brought her up.

'Well, that's not what I'm doing, Ann. I'm just frazzled today. Have you never called someone by the wrong name?'

'Sure,' she'd said. 'Let's forget it.'

Did she really make so little impression on his life, she wondered? Was he so lazy that he couldn't be bothered remembering her one-syllable name, or was one wife's name the most any man could find room for in his brain? Or maybe it was just that Deborah was on his mind, she was his one big love and Ann was someone he stumbled across in a bar.

But why did Ann feel so insecure? She had never called her boyfriend by anyone else's name. She had started to worry as Deborah's return got closer. Was she in a precarious position? Could she trust the reassurances that Justin gave her or were all bets off?

Even though he'd said, and she tried to believe him, that it had meant nothing, Ann could feel the edifice of her confidence, once so solid and unassailable, begin to crumble. Him calling Ann by his wife's name made her feel like a generic woman, an understudy who had been shipped in but hadn't quite got the mannerisms down just yet, hadn't been quite good enough to win the role outright in the first place, but certainly good enough to stand in.

All was fine when Deborah lay dying in a hospital bed. But now Deborah was a living, walking, talking thing about to enter Ann's life. A person who wanted to take her life back from Ann. A person who didn't know that her life wasn't even hers any more but that it was Ann's now . . . that was something Ann needed to protect against.

As Ann unpacked her things in her new quarters, she noticed two little doors in the eaves, access to crawl spaces in the attic. This would be a good place to safely store her jewellery box, which doubled up as her medicine box. Keep it out of harm's way, she thought. She pulled the door but it was locked. The same with the second one. The keyhole looked antique, as old as the house. Ann ran her fingers along the architrave but found no hidden key. Where would Justin keep it? Surely in this room? And why keep the doors locked unless there was something to hide?

Ann walked around the attic room.

She tried to visualise the map of the house in her head and situated her bed directly above Justin's bedroom. The bedroom that had, until recently, been hers too.

There was some furniture in the room; it had clearly been used as an office at one point, with its shelves and box files, a decommissioned printer and a fabulous partner's desk pushed up against a window. It was a perfect writing spot, Ann thought. She pulled at the desk drawers but they hit against the metal lock. She rattled them a little then gave up. Also locked. Also no key. She opened the box files. Boring official documents, driver's licence applications, medical files, all in Deborah's name but revealing nothing. Mrs Deborah Forster. Ann clutched at the fact that Deborah had taken Justin's name as evidence of her inferiority. Who takes a man's name these days? It was such a deferential move for a woman to make. Or was Ann the outlier? Why did she have such a problem with it anyway? And if she had such a problem why was she was consumed with envy? She wondered what it felt like to be Mrs Foster and whether she would ever get to call herself by that name.

Ann jumped as she heard the heavy slam of the front door downstairs. She looked down at her watch. It was lunchtime already. She scuttled out of the room but her thoughts were still with the locked doors. What was hiding behind those doors, and in those desk drawers? And from whom?

'Ann!' Justin was calling her from downstairs.

She made her way down towards him.

'Ann! Where are you? I have news . . . are you here?'

'I'm here,' she said, emerging at the top of the first-floor staircase. 'I was just unpacking some things in the attic room.'

'Oh good,' he said. 'That's good because the hospital just called. They said Deborah is being discharged. She's coming home tomorrow.'

Chapter Twenty-Four

In the moments before Deborah arrived home, Ann looked at herself in the mirror. She tried to see herself as a stranger might, for the first time. She tried to formalise herself. Her relationship with Justin would become something else from now on. She was playing a role, a role that would hopefully save her relationship and ensure her family's security. For now, she was the childminder, the nanny, the help.

Her other persona – the moon-faced woman who was in love with Justin and his little girl, in love with the new sense of belonging and security she felt with this man – had to be buried, hidden and tucked out of sight, along with those tell-tale feelings, her very self.

Ann imagined her real self hidden away in the attic room along with whatever was behind those locked crawl-space doors. Deborah's secrets? Justin's secrets? Ann imagined she would spend a lot more time alone in her room. And maybe it wouldn't be so hard after all. She already played a role for Justin's neighbours, the reliable childminder who was helping him out in his time of need; surely it wouldn't be so hard to continue the act at home. It would just be for a few weeks, maybe a month, until Deborah was well enough to be told the reality of the situation. Ann could tolerate that. How bad could it be?

As she touched up her lip gloss and fluffed her hair, she reminded herself not to touch Justin inappropriately, meaning not at all. She needed to watch her body language, to get out of the way as much as she could. Every fibre in her body resisted it, but she heard Justin's voice in her head: stick to the plan and everything will be OK.

Stick to the plan, she murmured to herself as she straightened her t-shirt, tucking it tighter into her jeans waistband. She wasn't showing yet but she could feel her midriff thickening, her breasts leapfrogging bra cup sizes. She had given some thought as to how a childminder might dress. Jeans, a t-shirt, some flat espadrille shoes. Comfortable, flexible, casual, ready for the activities of the day – school run, playground, finger painting, meal-making. Extra-glamour not required.

She pulled her hair into a high ponytail. Better. More practical. Her phone buzzed with a message. She didn't recognise the number. Probably Cookie to give Ann another piece of her mind. But it wasn't Cookie.

Leave now. Leave while there is still time.

Ann's hand began to shake. She instinctively looked over her shoulder, as if she might find the anonymous texter behind her, but there was nothing.

Who is this? she texted back, but there was no response. She tried calling the number but it didn't ring. She was shaken and felt even less prepared to meet Deborah than she already had.

She looked down on the driveway from her bedroom window. The local media had arrived. It was a small news story but the kind that small-town newspapers thrived on, a good-news story that everyone was invested in. The local papers had covered it from the beginning, and had arranged with Deborah to film her journey from hospital to her home, her reunion with her daughter and her husband. Of course there was media interest. It was a rare happy story, wholesome, and one that they would be hoping to go viral. Ann could imagine the clips. See the moment this woman was reunited with her daughter after a miraculous recovery from a terminal illness! Would anyone notice the grim-faced woman standing off to the side of the picture?

As Ann scanned the driveway she noticed a couple of national correspondents outside. The story would make a perfect kicker for that night's six o'clock news – *Local woman's miracle recovery sees her reunited with family.*

Justin and Sophie were waiting on the steps for Deborah to arrive. Sophie was wearing one of those eye-wateringly expensive French dresses that made your child look like a Victorian aristocrat. Together they were the perfect family standing at the top of the grand stone steps that led to the main entrance, the entrance nobody ever used so it felt significant, ceremonial, like the lady of the house had returned, and now everyone should celebrate by putting on their good manners and good clothes and opening up the curtains and the doors to let the warm spring air and the sun flood in. She heard the crunch of tyres on the gravel drive and waited for Deborah to reveal herself. She knew her life would never be the same again.

Chapter Twenty-Five

Deborah

The day I went back to the house felt like a dream. I couldn't understand why I had agreed to do it the way we did it, local media, national media, all filming me leaving the hospital and on the drive from the hospital to my home, the home I hadn't been in for almost two years. They told me it would be better this way. If Justin and Sophie waited for me at home, instead of picking me up from the hospital.

I hadn't realised how utterly raw and exposed I would feel. I wanted to collapse in the dirt, roll around in the earth, tear at the grass and flowers and trees. I wanted to cry and scream, I'm alive! I'm home, home! I didn't think I would feel like that. I usually felt very little. I had been brought up to be stoic, reserved; any sign of emotion was weakness. I had developed an insulation between my emotions and the outer world, which meant my feelings never crossed that barrier. I was the person people asked to read at funerals. I was always the one to hold it together. I could see children being born and couples being wed and be happy but never moved to tears. Those old habits learned in childhood die hard. But as we rounded the corner that led to the avenue up to the house, I was scared, like I couldn't breathe.

When we drove up the avenue and the house came into view on the cusp of the bend, falling away to reveal the water, my breath caught in my chest and all of the insulation was torn away. I was completely naked. It was just as I had remembered but more beautiful. The shrubs were more mature, of course they were, the flowerbeds more densely planted. Memories filtered through my brain like images on a screen, sunlight shuttering past my eyes, memories I didn't even know I had of this house strobed through my mind. I felt like my whole body was palpitating. I had brought Sophie here after she was born. Those memories had not been accessible to me until this moment, unlocked now as comprehensively as if I had finally entered the correct password and every single file was downloading simultaneously. Sophie grabbing my face and laughing, us sitting together in the quiet night light at 3 a.m., her huddled on my chest in the living room under a sheepskin blanket. Me trying not to move so I wouldn't wake her. Time was a deceiver. That felt like a memory from a hundred years ago. But it also felt like a memory from today. But Sophie wasn't a baby any more. She was a different person, I could see her standing at the top of the steps now with Justin, tall and slim, with long lustrous hair that flowed like liquid. The tears began coursing down my face. The cameraman sitting opposite me twisted the magnifying ring to zoom in and I said, 'Please, don't. Can you give me a moment please?'

He slowly lowered his camera, so it was pointing at the floor. I still had a say. I still got to say who I was. Even though I didn't really know who I was any more.

As the car circled the crescent at the front of the house, I took a moment to brace myself. I dabbed my eyes and nodded at the cameraman. 'It's OK, I just needed a minute. I know you have to do your job. I'm OK. Sorry.' I stepped out and looked up to Justin and Sophie waiting at the top of the steps, and just behind them I saw a blonde woman, youthful and voluptuous. I could see the curve of her stomach as it disappeared into her jeans. There was only one word for her – ripe, not whittled by illness like me. She smiled a tense smile and waited where she stood, at the entrance to the house. I had the strangest sensation that she was welcoming me to her home. This must be Ann, I realised. I saw her face change as she watched Justin and Sophie skip down the steps towards me and their embrace almost knocked me over.

As we finally made our way up to the steps to Ann, she smiled awkwardly. She seemed a little weirded out by the situation, and I suppose I was too; the cameras followed every response. I guess we had something in common.

The cameras shuttered endlessly and Ann gracefully moved out of the picture. I watched the curve of her breast and waist and stomach, the fall of her blonde ponytail and how her highlights caught the sunlight. The cameras closed in on me and Justin and Sophie, and I smiled until my face hurt. Justin had told me about Ann. How helpful she had been. How much she loved Sophie. But he had never mentioned how beautiful she was.

Chapter Twenty-Six

Ann

Ann felt like someone had played a confidence trick on her. Deborah arrived like a queen to reclaim the throne that Ann had temporarily occupied. Anyone can sit on a throne, she thought, but it doesn't make them queen. Ann and Justin always used the side entrance, the one that led to the old servants' kitchen at the basement in the back of the house but Deborah used the grand entrance.

When Deborah finally made it to the top of the steps, she smiled warmly and said, 'Hello, you must be Ann,' and extended a slender hand.

Ann took it and had the strangest sensation of being a servant welcoming Deborah into her own home. Both thought they knew who the other was, and yet neither of them knew anything about the other. Both thought they were the primary woman, but both were the other woman.

'I've heard a lot about you,' Deborah said. 'Justin has told me how indispensable you have been, how kind to Sophie. I can't thank you enough.' She gave Ann's hand a confidential squeeze that seemed to say they were going to become the best of friends.

Ann felt guilt knife through her. This woman trusted her. She wanted them to start on the right foot. She was showing Ann warmth and kindness. Ann thought she must be able to read the guilt that was pulsing through every cell in her body. The photographers were jostling, calling Deborah's name, trying to get a picture of her at the top of the steps. Justin and Sophie had walked up behind her and now they were all standing in the doorway.

A photographer shouted at Ann. 'Miss! Miss! Yeah, you! You're in the shot. Can you step aside? We want one just of the family, please. Deborah, Justin, Sophie please. Sophie! Sophie! Can you stand in the middle between your mom and dad? Perfect!'

Ann walked down the steps and out of frame. She stood in the shade of a tree and looked up at the three of them from where the photographers were standing. It made a pretty picture.

From this vantage point, it seemed only right that Deborah should recover, that she should not die, that she should laugh in the face of Hades and leave the underworld unscathed. Tragedy had no place in this perfect family's life.

And where was Ann in this picture? Where would she stand? Just off to the side, brimming with bitten-off words and simmering envy? If she walked away, would anyone even notice? She felt like a spectre at the feast, the evil spirit haunting their lives, Rothbart at *Swan Lake*, the one obstacle left that might stop the family from living a long and happy life.

Ann should do the decent thing and step out of the picture fully, remove this dark spot on this otherwise perfect image.

And how could she stay, she wondered? She would always be the second-class citizen, the one who got to pick up the crumbs left behind after everyone else's feast. And how could it not turn out that way? Deborah and Sophie deserved everything. They were here first. Ann was spiralling. Justin had sworn to her that they would be together. They just needed to stick to the plan. She knew rationally that he was doing the right thing, that Deborah was the mother of his daughter, and that he was just being a good husband and a good father, the things she expected him to be, the things that made her love him. But could he also be a good boyfriend while being a good husband?

Deborah called down to the photographers, 'Please, come in out of the cold. Join us in our home; this is the home I thought I would never see again. And I am so overjoyed to be home with the two people that matter most to me in the whole world: my husband and my daughter.' She beamed up at Justin and put her arm around his waist, leaned into him and kissed him full on the mouth. Ann felt physically sick as the photographers aw-ed and cheered. It was like she was an actual princess or a politician. How did she know how to behave around cameras, TV, news people?

'Ann,' Deborah said. Ann thought she might faint when she heard her name. 'You too, come!'

When Ann made it to the top of the steps, Deborah turned to her quietly and said, 'Would you be a darling and mind making some tea and biscuits for everyone, maybe some sandwiches too?' She turned to ask the journalists, 'Are you hungry?' They all nodded eagerly. They loved her already.

'Of course not,' Ann murmured, and actually bowed her head.

'I'll help you, Ann,' Justin said, keenly aware of how she must be feeling, his face showing it, but Deborah put her hand on his arm.

'Oh, please, stay with me Justin. I need you. I need my husband by my side.'

Fifteen minutes later, Ann shuffled into the room with a large tray of sandwiches and coffee. All she was short of was a housecoat. But she was no shrinking violet; she looked good. She had thrown on an oatmeal cashmere sweater over her t-shirt. Justin bought it for her when she had paused over it while browsing online. 'You'll look great in that,' he'd said. It slipped off one shoulder, and it looked casually luxurious with her simple jeans and flats. The sweater would have cost Ann a month's rent in her old life. But what was that to her now?

She placed the tray down on the table in the living room and had already decided that she would leave immediately. If she was going to be staff, she would work to rule. She wanted nothing to do with this pantomime and it wouldn't cause offence if she was supposed to be just the childminder. She could stick to her role. But Deborah put a hand on Ann's wrist as she laid the tray down and dragged her into her hot little spotlight, saying to the gathered journalists, 'You must write something about Ann,' she said. 'Ann has kept Justin and Sophie going, she's our childminder, our guardian angel. She has practically given up her whole life to look after them and now she is indispensable. I am forever grateful to her for that.' Her grip was firm but Ann pulled her arm away.

'I'm not actually a childminder,' she blurted. She didn't know why she felt the need to refute the lie. Maybe because it was going on the record. She was thinking of what her old colleagues might think or say if they saw this. 'I'm— I'm just helping out . . . a friend,' she muttered. 'Anyone would do the same.'

'Oh—' Deborah gave a little bemused laugh '—I'm just getting to know everybody from scratch again,' she said to the cameras.

When the journalists had finally departed, Deborah settled herself on the couch with the tea Ann had made. Even though the days were thawing, the huge house was never warm and so Ann had lit and fed the fire for Deborah's return. 'Stay, please, sit, sit,' Deborah said.

Ann sat warily beside her on the couch.

'Justin told me you are expecting a baby,' Deborah said, and the unexpected shock of the statement made something gust through Ann, cold and icy. He had told her? She was immediately off balance.

'Oh, he did?' Ann was surprised and frightened for a second but realised of course he wouldn't have told her who the father was.

'When are you due?' Deborah asked.

'Oh, it's very early still,' Ann said, scanning Deborah's face for an indication of what Justin might have said. 'I shouldn't even be telling people yet.' She felt a surge of rage and betrayal that Justin had made this unilateral decision to tell Deborah without consulting her. Deborah was already coming between them, she thought. It made her feel in opposition to him. She wondered what he had told Deborah about the father. Had he made up some story about Ann having a boyfriend? Maybe a feckless lover? Or maybe even something closer to the truth, that she had gotten involved with a married man and now found herself in a bit of fix. 'I haven't really told anyone. I only told Justin because I thought he might need to plan something for Sophie when I have the baby ... but, maybe not now that you are back.'

'Where will you have the baby?' Deborah asked.

Again, Ann was destabilised by the whole conversation. She felt like a criminal, trying to second guess what her partner in crime had told the police in a separate interview room. 'I— I haven't really thought about it yet. It's still a long way off. Justin very kindly suggested that I could remain here in the house during my maternity leave. As I already live in, I don't really have anywhere else to go,' she said. 'We've ... I should say Justin and Sophie have been helping me to try out some colours for the room, to decorate it for the baby.'

'Oh, yes, that's right. Justin mentioned that the dad wasn't in the picture. That must be tough for you. Of course, you must stay here then, when you have the baby. This is your home now too, after all. And we have more than enough space. It will be lovely to have a baby in the house again.' Deborah's eyes brimmed with tears. She must have been thinking about all that she had missed with Sophie.

Ann despised Justin for putting her in this position. If he had listened to her, they could have everything out on the table now, honest, above board, no blame just adult understanding and conversation. But, instead, she had to be grateful to Deborah for her scraps. 'Thank you,' she said, as meaningfully as she could. 'That's very kind of you. Justin has already arranged to take some leave around the time and to get a local woman he knows to come help, to cover some of my duties while I recover.' Ann took some pleasure in giving Deborah information that she might not have been told.

'And I expect to be back on my feet quickly. I'm only thirty-eight, after all, and my doctor says women my age can still bounce back more quickly than older mothers.' Something small and nasty in Ann turned over inside her. She knew for a fact that Deborah had been forty when she had given birth to Sophie.

Deborah smiled. 'Is that all you are? I thought we were the same age.'

Ann deserved that, she thought. Pointing out their age difference was the act of a desperate, drowning woman, who would bring anyone down to gain a foothold for herself, ruin a life to save her own.

'What room do you stay in?' Deborah asked.

'Oh, the one under the eaves at the very top of the house, looking over the water.' Ann watched Deborah carefully as she said this for any hint of concern about the crawl space or the desk.

'The yellow room,' Deborah said, giving nothing away as she sipped her tea.

'Yes,' Ann said. It felt like Deborah had lost interest in the conversation all of a sudden. 'I used to use it as a home office sometimes. I found it very calming looking out on the water.'

'Oh, that's your beautiful desk, then?' Ann asked, but Deborah said, 'Oh no, that was my dad's. I gave it to Justin after he died but he only used it to store documents, never really used it for working at.' Justin walked into the room at that moment. Deborah turned to Justin. 'Oh, we were just talking about you,' she said with a sly smile, as if they had been saying something of interest. 'I think I'm just going to take a nap. Ann, would you mind checking that the journalists didn't leave anything behind on the lawn? Thank you so much.' And with that Ann was dismissed.

When Ann saw the day's events played back on the local news that night, she thought she looked a little too convincing in her new role as a deferential servant. She felt like a cuckoo in a nest, not quite able to make a life of her own so she had stolen someone else's. Deborah, on the other hand, looked like royalty. Ann made her excuses and said she was going to have an early night. She closed her bedroom door and tried the desk drawers again. She wiggled her hair pins in the locks like she had seen detectives do on television but they remained stubbornly unyielding.

Ann lay back on the bed. How had she gotten here? She felt that she had gone from lottery winner to Cinderella in a matter of days. The emotions she was feeling put her right back in her childhood, as easily as if someone had picked her up and placed her down, back in the wealthy Brooklyn brownstones that her mother had cleaned for a living while Ann and Emily and Juliet had been in school, a way of supporting them and feeding them after their father had died. Ann had hated it at the time; it always made her feel so jealous and resentful. Why did other families get to live like that while Ann had to live like she did? On days when she was sick, her mother would bring her along with her, telling her to stay quiet, sit still and not touch anything. She was usually cross with Ann for being sick and off school, for inconveniencing her, slowing her down. Ann understood it now as an adult, but as a child it always hurt her. She felt it was her mother saying she didn't want to be with Ann, but really Ann's mother was simply busy, under pressure from too many jobs, too many chores and not enough support.

There was one house that Ann loved the most. She still passed it sometimes in Brooklyn and couldn't resist straining to catch a glimpse of the place through the elevated double-fronted windows. Was it still the same as the house she'd had access to as a child, she wondered, the house that had given her so much to dream about? She remembered the desperation she had felt on those days she went inside the house with her mother, that feeling of wanting just a tiny piece of someone else's riches, just a tiny corner of their world. If she took something, would they even notice? She felt the same now, that she was nibbling at the edges of Deborah's feast of a life and hoping that she wouldn't notice.

Chapter Twenty-Seven

When she woke up the next morning, Ann was alone on the edge of the bed. Justin had said he would come to her in her room last night once Deborah was asleep, but the other side of the bed was untouched. Ann wondered where he had slept. She was desperately lonely and unhappy. Did she have the nerve to continue with this charade? Wouldn't it be best to get it all out on the table or else just leave, cut her losses and disappear, go back to her old life? But her old life was gone. She was having a baby. And what would she be going back to anyway? Poverty and grafting?

She got out of bed and walked downstairs. It was almost 6 a.m. She walked towards Justin's room – her room until yesterday. She followed the noise of gentle voices coming from the room; the door was ajar and some soft light was spilling out in a little triangle on the hallway.

Ann pushed the door gently, saying 'Justin?' but, as the door gave way, it was Deborah who turned from the bed to face Ann. She was wearing a full-length champagne silk nightdress with a robe thrown over it, sitting up, sipping tea from a china cup on a tray that Justin had clearly brought her. He was perched on the end of the bed in his boxers and a t-shirt. When she saw Ann at the door, her eyes widened with shock, and she pulled her robe around herself as if she had been naked beneath it; as if some fatal privacy had been breached. Her reaction felt melodramatic but Ann realised it was perfectly appropriate. What was she, the childminder, doing creeping around her bedroom door at this hour of the morning? Ann was in Deborah's private space now and she was not welcome. It was a transgression.

'Ann!' she said.

Justin spun around, repeating her name like a fool, then, 'Is everything OK?'

Ann was boiling up with so many thoughts and humiliations she didn't know how to contain. Did she dare speak? Dare to discover what might come out?

'Oh, yes, I'm so sorry to disturb you both so early; it's just I heard voices and the tap in my bathroom has come loose and is leaking – nothing urgent but I just don't want it to go down behind the sink and rot anything. There's nothing worse than the smell of rot.'

Deborah smiled and looked relieved.

Justin said, 'Give me a minute to get decent and I'll take a look.'

As if Ann hadn't seen him completely indecent before.

'Thank you,' she said, and turned on her heel, walking back to her room as hot tears ran down her face. She could barely breathe by the time Justin knocked on the door a minute later. She didn't have to say anything, ask any questions. That decent comment felt like a slap in the face.

'It's not what you think,' he whispered, making sure the door was fully closed behind him. 'We're not sleeping together. We are just sharing a bed.'

'I thought you said you were going to have separate rooms . . . I knew this would happen. I told you! How could you not have foreseen this, Justin? Of course she wants to sleep in her bed, with her husband. She's been practically dead and she might still be dying, for all she knows. She's not going to take things slowly. She has a whole life to catch up on . . . oh god, this is a disaster.'

'Ann, that's not what's happening here. You're overreacting,' Justin said. 'Please don't worry. We've discussed it but she was upset last night, she needed support and she will likely need more support. She's going through some huge stuff, this is existential. I have told her that we should sleep in separate rooms, for her recovery. She's under doctor's orders not to get . . . too excited.' Even he grimaced at the euphemism. 'But also, I've told her we need to get to know each other again, that we can't just step back in where we left off. That will buy us some time.' He sat on Ann's bed now, the same spot he had occupied on Deborah's bed a few minutes ago, and reached out to her.

She pulled her hand away, childishly. She hated him at that moment. Why did it suddenly feel like she was the imposter here?

'I hate that I feel this way. It's all so dishonest, Justin. Why do we have to be so deceptive? It's wrong to lie to her like this. We should have told her straight up; that was the right thing to do. Now it's a secret. Now she will feel betrayed and she'd be right to. Why didn't you come last night like you said you would?'

'I'm sorry. Deborah wanted me to stay with her until she fell asleep and I just fell asleep myself.'

'Please, Justin, I need to know I'm not crazy. I need you to tell me this is not crazy. This is so, so scary for me. I'm pregnant. I'm completely alone and I'm relying on you.'

'I know, I'm sorry,' he said, pulling Ann close to hug her to his chest, and something inside her wondered if he was doing this to shut her up.

'I'm just in a bit of a bind here; it's so conflicting, but you and I have our plan and that is still the plan.'

Ann didn't care about his conflicted feelings. She

cared about being dismissed from rooms, treated like the help, Justin moving further and further away from her. But what other choice did she have? Leave, and become a single parent, with no job, and no money, nowhere to live? Leave the man she loved, and the little girl that she had come to love too, who had also come to love her back and rely and depend upon her? It was an impossible situation.

'I'm sorry, Ann, I'd better get back. We don't want her to suspect . . . '

'Go, go,' Ann said, resigned.

After Justin left the room, Sophie came in wearing her uniform.

'Do you want to play with me before I go to school, Ann?'

Sophie was holding a folded paper fortune teller she had made at school. Ann already knew all the fortunes inside by heart but she played anyway.

'Now let me read yours,' she said, taking the fortune teller.

She fixed it so she ended on 'you will have a lovely day' and gave Sophie a kiss on the head.

'I bet your mom would love to play this with you too. Why don't you give her a turn before school.'

But Sophie shook her head and said, 'Mommy doesn't like these games. Not like you do.'

Ann was sad for Sophie. She probably thought she was going to get her mother back, full of energy, full of fun, but as far as Ann could tell, Deborah was still distant with Sophie, which must be tough for a little kid to understand. 'Maybe she's just out of practice,' Ann said. 'Now scoot or you'll be late. I'll see you at pick-up.' Sophie squeezed Ann tightly around the neck and Ann felt like Sophie was the only person who really knew how to love in this house. And she was grateful for it.

When Sophie was gone, Ann fell back on the pillows. She woke up to the sound of Justin returning from the school run with some fresh croissants. He had been taking Sophie to school while he was off work for Deborah's return home. Ann came downstairs to the kitchen in her vest and short shorts. Her hair was loose and golden and her legs were tanned.

She heard their voices murmuring quietly in the kitchen and walked through the open door. Deborah was sitting at the vast island, her face turned up to Justin's, who was looking down at her. But she saw the look between them, confidential, conspiratorial, close. They were mere inches away from each other. They shared a history of intimacy that Ann couldn't hope to catch up on, not even if she went at twice their pace, which she had done these past months with Justin. She heard her sisters' voices in her head: he's too good to be true.

Deborah looked up first. She seemed embarrassed and then, fleetingly, annoyed by Ann's lack of modesty.

Ann hadn't thought that she might look a little too at ease in the house. Deborah joked, 'I can lend you a dressing gown if you like, Ann,' but there was no warmth behind it.

She looked at Justin. 'Darling, I'm feeling a little dizzy, the doctor said this might happen. I'm going to lie on the sofa by the fire. I think I just need to rest. Will you keep me company for a while?'

This was her way of dismissing Ann.

'Ann,' she said, to make the point, 'would you bring me some tea if you're making some, please?'

What could Ann say? She was staff, after all, and her wishes, her desire to make herself warm and comfortable by the fire, to sip tea or nibble biscuits, were all inconsequential. Deborah came first now.

Ann made the tea and brought it to Deborah, Justin again perched at the end of the couch, Deborah's feet on his lap.

Ann held back tears at their intimacy. As she closed the door, she pressed her ear to the wood. What were they doing? They weren't talking. Were they embracing? Kissing? Cuddling? This was unbearable.

Justin emerged a couple of minutes later and Ann leapt away from the door. He looked stressed and exhaled loudly.

'She's asleep. I'm going to make myself a cup of coffee. Would you like one?'

Ann was furious with him but tried not to show

it. She didn't want to push Justin away, back into his marriage. They walked together to the little back kitchen, a kind of scullery in the former servants' part of the house.

'Deborah asked me about the baby yesterday,' Ann said, because that was as good a place as any to start a row. She wanted to poke him, frighten him the way she had been startled by Deborah. 'Were you going to tell me that you had told her?'

'I didn't tell her anything, just that you were pregnant.'

'Justin, you left me totally exposed and off-guard. She asked me about the father.'

'And what did you tell her?'

'That he was a cowardly married man who was never going to leave his wife!'

'Ann,' he said in the tone of voice he mostly used with Sophie when she was being naughty. 'Ann, I know this is hard but, please, be patient. Everything will be fine in time. You'll see. We just have to stay solid and firm, keep our plan in mind and get through it.' He pulled her towards him and she relented, letting him hug her, comfort her. 'This is awful for you, Ann,' he said stroking her hair gently. 'Just awful. I wish there was something I could do to change it but we can't be at each other's throats. This is going to be a long road and we need to stick together.'

Ann needed this reassurance, that Justin still

wanted her. She walked over to the door and locked it, then made her way back to Justin, and claimed him for herself.

Chapter Twenty-Eight

After a few days, Justin needed to return to work at the real estate agency, so it was just Ann and Deborah in the house. Deborah wanted company and, at around 11 a.m., she called Ann to sit with her.

Ann still felt queasy being around Deborah, being a walking, talking lie in Deborah's life. Her stomach rolled like a small boat climbing the wall of a wave.

'I'm so bored, Ann, please, join me. Tell me about yourself. And about all the things I have missed about my baby.'

For a minute, Ann thought she was talking about Justin but then she realised she was talking about Sophie.

'Where are you from and how did you end up here, helping Justin out with Sophie?'

Such simple questions that Ann couldn't answer simply because she could not tell the straightforward truth. She stalled by taking a sip of her drink.

'I kind of fell into it actually. I met Justin at a play I was covering – I sometimes write articles for magazines and online magazines in New York but I had taken time out to look after my mom when she was dying and so I was struggling to re-establish myself and more importantly struggling to pay the rent. I was in need of some regular work and Justin needed some help so I told him I would do it. I thought this would be a temporary way to earn some extra cash while I was getting back on my feet with journalism. I didn't think it would last this long, to be honest . . . Sorry, you know what I mean,' she said.

Deborah smiled. 'Don't worry Ann. I'm more surprised than anyone to be here.'

'Does it feel weird,' Ann asked, quietly, 'to go back to your old life? Does everything feel the same?'

'To be honest, everything feels different. I'm not sure any more whose life I have gone back to. My daughter is almost unrecognisable. My husband is changed too. There's a lot of distance between us, we're like strangers getting to know each other again. And I think grief and being a single parent has done something to him too,' she said, twisting her coffee cup around on the table.

'It must be very strange,' Ann said, 'to come back to your life, and see what your life would have looked like after you died . . . without, you know, actually dying? Most people never get to see that.'

'I never thought about it like that, but you're right,' Deborah said, 'That's exactly what's it's like. All of my stuff had been put away in vacuum bags. I don't even know where half my belongings are. I think Justin has everything in storage – notebooks, files, jewellery ... and then some stuff is still just lying around, like random lip glosses and half-used hand creams, those sort of things, as if I'd been out for the afternoon. And the pictures around the house! To see myself memorialised like that.' She gave a bleak laugh. 'There are so many pictures. I never had any pictures of me up before I got sick. Well, one or two of Sophie and me together but that was it. Now I'm everywhere!' She laughed again. 'I was always the one taking the pictures, putting up the pictures. It feels ... what's the word ... eerie, maybe? Like I don't belong here any more, like a new life has grown over the space where I used to live, and if I want my life back, I'm going to have to tear back the undergrowth, hack it away and I'm not sure I have the energy for it. It's almost like being alive and dead at the same time. There's a disconnect between me and my old life and my new life, it's as if a little bit of me got stuck in both worlds.'

She seemed to snap out of it and said, 'Sorry, Ann, you don't want to hear all this. I'm sorry for dumping on you. I need to start getting out, or get a shrink to offload on!'

'I don't mind,' Ann said. She was so curious to find

out about Deborah and Justin's relationship. 'If it makes you feel better, I don't really belong here either.'

'Have you made friends since moving here?' Deborah asked.

'Oh no, not really yet. There's not been any opportunity. The mothers at the school gate know I'm a childminder so they treat me like the temp in the office. Why bother getting to know her, right? She'll just be leaving in a year or two. And my job consists of looking after a six year old so I don't really get to meet many people outside of that sphere.' She smiled.

'You should join something,' Deborah said. 'The tennis or the golf club. Or one of the ladies' clubs. I could introduce you if you like.'

Ann's blood ran cold. The idea of getting involved with a group of rich privileged women who had nothing better to do with their time than organise fundraisers and squabble over committees filled her with dread. But also the idea of accepting any sort of generosity or kindness from Deborah felt like deception, betrayal.

'Oh, that's OK,' Ann said, 'I'm not too lonely. That's one of the reasons I'm keen to re-establish my career. And I go to the city to see my sisters when I can so it's not so desperate yet! Besides, I imagine the mothers at the school are right: I won't be here for ever. I'll be moving back to the city as soon as you and Justin and Sophie don't need me any more.'

Deborah looked sad. 'I hope that's not too soon. To be

honest, I've enjoyed having someone around. The mornings are quiet and Justin is so busy with the office, I don't know if I'll ever get back to work myself. It wasn't really a career anyway, more of a gentlewoman's job, a bit of a hobby. And Justin never really liked me working. He was adamant that I give up after we had Sophie.'

'Oh really?' Ann was surprised. She was interested to learn more about Justin from Deborah's perspective. 'Why is that?'

'He said he wanted our daughter to have a proper mother, someone at home. He's actually quite old-fashioned. I think he likes the idea of having a woman at home. But he also said it was his duty to support his wife and child. I think he sees it as a failure if I work; he thinks people will judge him. Which is clearly ridiculous. Just look at this house. It's literally a mansion. And besides, I don't need supporting. The business means I never had to work and I could always support myself. The fact is I liked working, I liked meeting people, but I think Justin's male ego needs to think he is supporting his family. I do miss the camaraderie of being in the office and the friends I made there. It's probably the same thing you miss about your old life.'

Ann couldn't help seeing Justin's recent protestations about her work in a new light. Did he want her to stop working because of her health, her pregnancy or did he just prefer her at home, where he could keep tabs on her?

Deborah looked down at her nails, her hands so delicate and small. She was a tiny person. She looked like she was thinking, biting her lip weighing up whether to say something or not.

Ann was thinking about saying something too. Surely Deborah would understand if Ann told her the truth, the awful, messy but blameless truth? Deborah was so understanding, not judgemental at all. Surely she would understand. They both started talking at the same time then laughed, like girlfriends.

'Go ahead,' Ann said.

'No, I was just thinking, well, we should do something together, Ann, go for lunch or something fun, before it's time to pick Sophie up from school. I'd like to get to know you better seeing as we're living in the same house and all. And Justin is so worried about my health he won't let me do anything fun, but I know he wouldn't mind if I was with you. He trusts you implicitly. And I'm going to go mad if I don't have a bit of fun. I'd love a glass of champagne,' she giggled.

'Why not?' Ann said. 'That would be lovely.'

'Really? How about now? I can go freshen up . . . ' she stood gingerly from the chair. She was still getting physiotherapy for her muscles after so many months spent in bed.

Ann's heart broke a little. This was not good. She could not become Deborah's friend. She was already betraying her just by walking around the house, asking if she would like anything, doing her laundry and sleeping with her husband, just biding her time until she stole Deborah's life completely.

Chapter Twenty-Nine

Ann drove them to town for lunch, a favourite place of Deborah's, a French-style brasserie where everyone seemed to know her. They discussed what women will always discuss: relationships, love, sex.

Deborah wanted to know about Ann's lover, the father of her child.

'I'm a bit ashamed to tell you this,' Ann said, 'but the main issue is he's married.'

'You should threaten to go to his wife,' Deborah said immediately. 'Say you'll tell her if he doesn't leave her.'

Ann squirmed. 'I don't know if that ever really works.' She sighed. 'And I don't know if I'd feel happy pressurising someone to be with me. How would you ever know that they wanted to be with you then? If you blackmail someone into being in a relationship with you, isn't that a little bit ... coercive? Besides, it's probably not fair on his wife. Like, what did she ever do to me?'

Deborah shrugged and bit one of her French fries. 'Should have thought of that before you slept with her husband.' She laughed.

'What would you do,' Ann asked suddenly, 'if someone came to you and said they were sleeping with Justin or having his baby?'

'Chop his balls off,' Deborah said. Then laughed. 'Can you really imagine Justin having the wherewithal to lead a double life?' She scoffed, then smiled. 'I don't know where people find the time to have affairs. But really, to answer your question, if someone told me that ... huh, I don't know. I have to think of Sophie really but I think I'd find it hard to find a way back to Justin if he had another partner, another child. The pregnancy thing would probably bother me more than the cheating. You know we struggled to have another child after Sophie? It was probably all to do with me getting sick, looking back now. But if I had to see another woman have Justin's baby while I couldn't, that would be really upsetting. Anyway, thankfully not something I have to worry about right now. And you certainly couldn't get away with anything in this town. The nosiness keeps us all honest.'

'Right,' Ann said. She wondered if Deborah could see her squirming.

'Don't tell me you haven't noticed the neighbours,'

Deborah asked, lightening the tone. 'It's like valley of the squinting windows round here.'

Ann smiled. 'People sure are friendly.'

The waiter brought a glass of champagne for Deborah and a sparkling water for Ann. Deborah took a sip. 'Oh, this is so good. Don't tell Justin.' Ann thought it was strange that Deborah should be so afraid of Justin knowing she had had a glass of champagne. Deborah suddenly leaned over and grasped Ann's hand. 'You're a strong person, I can see that. What you're going through is really hard. These men, they never leave their wives, you know, even if they're absolutely miserable, and if they do leave their wives, they also leave their mistresses. They like a clean slate and they never stop cheating. It's like a pathology. Believe me, I've been there.'

'You have?' Ann couldn't hide her surprise. She couldn't imagine a woman like Deborah being screwed around.

'Oh, believe me, I had my fair share of problems in the past . . . but I'm trying to focus on the present. That's one of the many gifts this second chance has given me. I find I don't spend so much time focusing on the past, on the wrongs people have done to me. I'm just happy to be here.'

Ann wanted to ask more about Justin but felt Deborah had made an effort to change the subject, so she let it go and asked instead about her recovery.

'What do the doctors say about your progress so far?' Ann asked.

'The doctors are amazed. They scan me every week and seem genuinely flabbergasted at how the tumour is retreating. I'm something of a novelty. All sorts of doctors turn up for my scans, from trainees to research academics. I'm like the circus freak they all want to catch a glimpse of. They expect the tumour to have fully disappeared within the month if it carries on at this rate. Everyone keeps telling me to take things slow but I want to start living again! If my illness has taught me anything it's that I've got to enjoy every moment. I don't know how long I've got, so I don't want to put anything off. And if I get the chance I want to have another baby. I'll be forty-six next month. I know this is my last chance.'

Ann grasped around for something to say but just stuttered, 'But didn't the chemo damage your fertility?'

'I never had chemo. I was a hopeless case. So, I know my reproduction hasn't been affected, well, apart from me being forty-five.' She paused. 'I probably shouldn't say this, but Justin is a better lover than I remember. Much better, in fact. It's like we have been given a whole new lease of life.' She tilted her glass towards Ann. 'To new beginnings.'

Ann could only muster a 'cheers'. Justin had sworn that he was not going to sleep with Deborah, and yet here she was, telling Ann about his improved sexual abilities. She put the glass down on the table but the wobble in her hand knocked it over.

'Oh! Are you OK, Ann?' Deborah asked, mopping at the table with her napkin.

'I am, I just think my blood sugar is low.'

'Here, take one of these,' Deborah said, pushing the silver platter of shortbread cookies across the table to her. 'It will help. I used to get low blood pressure when I was pregnant too. Better than the opposite, I guess.'

Ann smiled and scraped one of the biscuits off the plate with a shaking hand. 'Do you really think it would be wise, though, to put your body under that kind of strain, a pregnancy, after everything you've been through? Nobody knows what might happen, how your body might react?'

'I want to live. I'm not going to hide from life. I might as well have died if I do that. And I want another baby.'

She chanced a confidence. 'What does Justin think of this plan . . . ?'

Deborah smiled a sly smile. 'Justin won't even let me have a glass of champagne, never mind a baby! I haven't mentioned it to him yet . . . he wants us to take things slowly, says we need to get to know each other again and I can understand that, but it's only a matter of time before we grow close again.'

Ann felt cold. 'He might have a point. You should give your body a little bit of time, even just a few months . . . '

'Why would I give myself time I may not have? Who knows what tomorrow holds? If I've learned one thing from this whole experience it's you just don't know what's around the corner. Surely what makes me happy is good for my recovery. And if it's not good for my recovery at least I will have enjoyed what extra time I've been gifted instead of being so careful with myself that I live a sort of nothing life. It's a waste of this privilege I've been given. I want to live, dance, make love—' she giggled '—eat, sing, everything. I want it all.' She laughed again as she topped up her champagne glass and gulped some from her glass, wiping the bit that dribbled down her chin with the back of her hand. She held up her glass to Ann again. 'To life,' she said. 'And to living!'

'To life,' Ann said, but she couldn't help thinking only one of them was supposed to be living.

As they left the restaurant and made their way back to the car, Ann noticed a note stuck under her windshield wiper. She pulled it out and unfolded it.

LEAVE NOW BEFORE YOU GET HURT.

She crumpled it up quickly.

'What's that,' Deborah asked.

'Oh, just someone looking to buy a car. Obviously liked the look of mine.' She balled up the note and threw it in a trash can. Who on earth was sending those messages? And was that last one a threat? Who wanted to hurt her? Well, Ann didn't scare that easily. She decided to say nothing and ignore them. It was probably Cookie trying to run her out of town.

Chapter Thirty

The days ticked by uneventfully and Deborah continued to recover amidst Justin and Ann's simmering tension. They had settled into a kind of routine. Justin dropped Sophie to school, Ann did some light housework while Deborah rested and then they had coffee and sometimes lunch together before Ann went to collect Sophie from school. Some days Ann skipped coffee and lunch if she had an assignment. Deborah seemed so happy and trusting while Ann felt like a poisonous boil becoming more and more inflamed, swelling and throbbing and making its presence felt everywhere in the house.

Some days she felt as if she hardly saw Justin between work and Sophie and Deborah, and often he didn't come home from the office until late. She felt paranoia creeping in. Was he avoiding her? He still came to her room a couple of nights a week and she clung to those visits as evidence of their love, a conduit to their connectedness and a hope that, beneath the stress and drama, they could still find a future with each other. Ann had become desperate for these intimate moments together and often tried to force them, taking risks, making noise, risking Deborah walking in and catching them, but she didn't care. In some ways she was trying to sabotage them, get caught so she could force the issue to the surface, gain some closure either way. Ann worried that Justin might start to resent her, and how she had become a complication in his life. If it wasn't for the pregnancy, would Justin have broken up with her already? She worried that she was a constant negative reminder that he had to make a decision, that he had to take action in his otherwise perfect life. Could it be enough to make Justin fall out of love with her? She couldn't bear to think about it.

One night as they sat talking quietly, she asked him, 'Do you ever think what might have happened had we never met that night at the theatre?'

'Of course not,' he said, too quickly.

'I do,' Ann said. 'It's funny to think that you pursued me, that I had no interest in continuing things between us after that first night. I was willing to leave it as a fun one-night stand. I had already dismissed you as a married man. I told you that at the time. Several times. But you said you weren't really. You persuaded me to see you again and again and again until I was boxed into a position – homeless, penniless, pregnant with your baby. And now look at where it's gotten us! This is my punishment.'

'Nobody is being punished, Ann. Nobody is to blame. It just is what it is.'

'But, Justin, we can't go on like this, living in this weird fake triangle, nighttime visitations, having to look after Deborah as well as Sophie while I'm so tired myself that I could cry. Deborah is going to guess something is wrong the longer this goes on; she's going to want to restart your sexual relationship at some point.'

Ann dropped it into conversation. She wanted to see whether Justin would tell her that Deborah had been intimate with him, what his side of the story might be.

'I told you that's not going to happen. She's tried but I've put her off.'

'Swear to me,' Ann said. 'Swear that's all it is.'

'I swear, Ann, but I can't keep swearing this to you every day. You need to trust me.'

'I'm sorry. I feel half-crazy; I'm so paranoid living in this house.'

Justin looked crestfallen. He stared down at his hands. 'I just feel completely paralysed. I love you, I do, and I was so ready for us to start our new life together – you, me, Sophie and the new baby – but now I feel like I have an obligation to Deborah and Sophie, and of course I love them too. I never stopped loving Deborah but I had started to let her go, and now, here she is, a miracle. A fucking miracle! And I should be grateful but all I feel is: why did it have to happen? I have a responsibility to all of you, just as I would never dream of dropping you, nor can I just drop her . . . she's Sophie's mother, Ann. Please, trust me. I know we can't go on like this. I'm working on it, but just let me do it in my own time, in my own way.'

Ann's mind was stuck on the way he had used the past tense. *I was so ready for us to start our new life.* Was. She could also see how he had split them into factions and she could see he saw himself, Deborah and Sophie as one unit, and Ann and the baby as another. She understood it. His unit predated her unit. As the tension became unbearable for her, she had started to think about leaving Justin and what that would look like for her. Who was Ann to come in and make all this trouble? Who was she to stand in the way of a goddamn miracle? And yet, she felt this was her right too, her life.

If Deborah was going to fight for it, Ann could fight for her own miracle too.

Chapter Thirty-One

Ann and Deborah continued to go for lunch several days a week. At the start, Ann had seen the occasions as fact-finding missions but, against her better judgement, she had come to enjoy Deborah's company. She was funny and kind and seemed about as lonely as Ann was. Some days they went shopping after lunch, browsing the boutiques.

'Ann, you have to see this gorgeous kids' shop,' Deborah said one day. 'Have you bought anything for the baby yet?'

'No, I'm actually a bit superstitious about that,' Ann told her.

'Oh, for goodness sake, Ann! Don't be so silly. Why not let yourself enjoy the bits that you can?' Deborah took her arm and led her towards the shop. 'I used to buy all Sophie's baby stuff here,' she said. 'It's adorable. You're going to love it!'

The kindness of the gesture gave Ann a twinge. Deborah had turned from standoffish and suspicious to open and warm towards Ann over the past few weeks and the kinder she was to Ann, the worse Ann felt. Her guilt pounded away like a pulse in her temples, constantly there, a beacon of self-reproach.

Ann was deeply uncomfortable with this plan, but buried within her was the thrill of motherhood. How wonderful this experience might be, she wondered, if she and Justin had a normal relationship, a simple, straightforward one that allowed them to plan and get excited for the arrival of the baby. Ann tried to push those thoughts down and just be present with Deborah, take things at face value and push the guilt of the situation to the background. When they walked in the door, Ann took a moment before she recognised the shop. She realised to her horror that it was where she had bought the dress and soft toy for Sophie. Where she had pretended to be married and have a child. At the time it had seemed innocent, inconsequential. Now Ann searched desperately to see if the woman who had served her that day was on duty today. Would she remember Ann? Her insides clenched as she spotted her. She tried to think of an excuse to leave. But maybe she wouldn't remember her. Surely these assistants served hundreds of people every day.

'Oh my god oh my god,' Deborah squealed. 'Look at

these,' she said, picking up a pair of fluffy pink booties. 'Do you know the gender yet, Ann?'

Ann shook her head, no. Truthfully, she spent most days denying the fact that she was pregnant, but Deborah was dragging her into the reality of it all. Getting a gender DNA test meant acknowledging the pregnancy on a level that Ann wasn't quite ready to do since Deborah's return. She had thought about how this whole situation would be so easily solved if she could bring herself to have a termination. How it could all be so simple. She could just leave, go back to her old life, find a place to live, a job to work at, any job, and hand this whole episode over to an imagined realm, a nightmare, a momentary blip, a wrinkle in time. It would be like a distant bad memory; it might even eventually feel like it had never even happened. How easy it would be then to just walk away from this enormous mess.

But Ann couldn't bring herself to make an appointment at the clinic. She couldn't stop herself thinking about how good things had been between Justin and her, between Sophie and her in those first few months. And she knew that this would be the one and only time she would likely be pregnant. There would not be other chances. There would not be other relationships. And for that reason, she couldn't give up. But she couldn't quite acknowledge it either, without the risk of being overwhelmed. They had really started to feel like a family, Ann knew Sophie's needs so well, they had gorgeous conversations, she loved spoiling her and treating her and taking her out for the day. She also loved when people referred to her as Sophie's mother, and she and Sophie smiled and shared their secret. She needed to stay strong. This was what people went through to get the things they wanted.

While Ann had been lost in her thoughts, the shop assistant came over. 'Oh hi again,' she said. 'How did your husband and little girl like the gifts you bought for them?' she asked, smiling.

Deborah turned a bemused and curious look on Ann. 'Your husband?'

Ann laughed nervously 'I think you have me confused with someone else.'

'No, it was definitely you; you bought the pink teddy and the cute dress,' she said. 'For your little girl? And you said your husband would—'

Ann spoke over her, cutting her off. 'Definitely not me. I don't have a little girl or a husband, see?' Ann turned to Deborah. 'I think I'll wait outside.'

'What was that all about?' Deborah said, following her outside.

'I have no idea. But she must have confused me with someone else. I just didn't have the energy to get into a hypothetical argument with a snowflake about a case of mistaken identity. Or why I don't have a husband. Or a child.' To her horror, Ann started to cry.

'Oh Ann, of course these things are sensitive for you

right now but she's just a young dumb shop assistant who doesn't know anything. Don't let her get to you. Who needs a husband anyway?' Her tone was almost painfully supportive. 'You've got the best bit: a baby. You can find the man any time, but there's not such a great opportunity for women like us to have children. That door closes, all too soon. Believe me, I know. I was lucky to even have Sophie.'

Ann dabbed at her eyes, relieved that Deborah thought she was being sensitive about not having a partner.

They walked aimlessly along the streets and fell into easy talk. 'Didn't you ever want to get married?' Deborah asked.

'Maybe once; my college boyfriend wanted me to marry him but I didn't want to commit so early, so young, but now I think it was a mistake. I never met anyone . . . until . . . ' she nearly said Justin but stopped short. 'Besides, I've seen too many of my friends and family in unhappy marriages to ever fool myself into thinking it's any kind of silver bullet for loneliness. I can see the advantages. No single person I know can afford to live more than a rudimentary life by themselves, and I'm no different. I mean, look at me! I'm thirty-eight, pregnant and living in someone else's house. Why do you think my friends don't leave those unhappy marriages? Because they know they'll be impoverished and living like they had to live in college.

They love their lifestyle more than they despise their husbands, I guess, but I'm not sure I could do it.'

Deborah looked pensive. 'That was never my problem. My family were so well-off I always had my own money, and a really generous trust fund. My mother was adamant that I would never have to marry for anything other than love, but I've never really thought about it from the other perspective. I wonder if Justin ever felt that way about me.'

'Justin?' Ann said. 'What do you mean?'

'Just that I wonder would he ever stay with me just for money,' Deborah said. 'I hadn't really thought about it until you mentioned your friends.'

'But of course Justin is not with you for money! He has his own money, his family business,' Ann said, sounding more passionate than she should.

Deborah paused. 'Justin doesn't have any money. He came from nothing. He works for *my* family's business. The money, the money is ours, obviously, we're married so it's ours, but it's my family's money. Sometimes I do wonder if that's a part of why he's with me.'

It felt like a betrayal and it felt like the first time Ann had looked at Justin, and really seen him.

Chapter Thirty-Two

Things became strained between Justin and Ann. He visited her less and less at night, explaining that he was exhausted and confused, and needed head-space. He felt guilty when he was with Ann and guilty when he was with Deborah. And then he felt guilty for feeling guilty. Or so he said.

'You shouldn't,' Ann told him. 'You should only feel guilty for not being honest with her. We've been deceiving her, Justin, and the lie is starting to seep out of the pores of this house. I feel guilty and I'm not even married to her. It's like being in an Edgar Allen Poe story! Surely she can sense it too?'

To make matters worse, Ann and Deborah were becoming confidantes and companions.

'The closer we become as friends, the worse I feel,' she told Justin. 'I'm actively trying to avoid her now, I keep going out for long walks, taking on more work, just so I don't have to talk to Deborah, just so I don't have to lie to her. She's so nice, Justin, she's kind to me, and every time I feel like I'm twisting a knife in her life. She insists that we have lunch and shopping trips. It would be so much easier if she wasn't so nice. And how am I her only friend? Where are her friends, Justin? Why are they not visiting her, taking her out for lunches? How come I'm the only one she seems to have?'

'Her friends kind of faded out when she had Sophie and stopped working. Her world just became smaller. But she was busy looking after Sophie. You know how it is, life gets busy, people move on.'

Was Justin moving on, Ann wondered.

'I agree it's difficult,' Justin said, 'but we cannot risk Deborah's health. We have to keep that as our focus. The doctor said she mustn't have any shocks or stress and this would be exactly that. I understand how difficult it is for you, Ann, I honestly do. It's all so weird and not a nice experience for this time in your life. I feel that too. I've been thinking . . . this is not a particularly good environment for you. Why don't you take a trip home for a while, catch up with some friends, some old workmates, spend some time with your sisters, get your head out of here for a bit and take your mind off things? I'll book you into a nice hotel in Williamsburg, hmm? How does that sound?'

It sounds like you're making yourself out to be

more generous than you are, Ann thought as she was reminded of what Deborah told her at lunch. Justin was good at spending Deborah's family money it seemed. But he was right. Living the constant lie in the house with the three of them was taking its toll on Ann. Her heart leapt at the idea of getting out of there for even a few days. And maybe he was right. Maybe away from the house she would think more clearly.

'Maybe,' she said, 'And it might give you an opportunity to talk to her while it's just you guys here, to gently begin the process of breaking the news or at least beginning the idea of putting some distance between you as a couple . . . I'm sure it must be hard to talk with me here. It might be easier if I give you two some space for a couple of days. Maybe you don't even have to tell her that you're seeing someone. Maybe you could just say that the time apart has created a distance that you can't come back from . . . maybe we wouldn't have to tell her at all.'

Justin smiled and gave Ann's shoulder a rub.

'Now you're talking sense,' he said.

Ann hadn't thought that leaving might give Justin and Deborah the space they needed to fall in love again.

Chapter Thirty-Three

Ann didn't know who to text. Somehow she didn't feel like she had a friend in the world any more. How had this happened? She had neglected everyone when her mother was sick but she had cemented that isolation by not reconnecting after her death. Now it felt completely impossible to reach out because she had left it too long. She needed to talk to someone objective and her sisters were not that. She pulled out her phone and searched for the only person who had shown an interest in her life in the last six months. Judy.

Back in Brooklyn for a few days, she texted. You free for a coffee?

Judy responded immediately. Love to. Pilates till 12.30. Meet after that at the spot we met last time?

Ann felt relief. She really needed a friend.

She arrived at the coffee shop a little early and sat browsing a book from McNally Jackson. She'd gone in there again, this time with enough money to pick up a collection of stories by a young writer that looked interesting. But she couldn't concentrate on it. She lifted the milk jug, which held onto the greasy fingerprints of previous customers, and poured some into her coffee.

What was she going to do?

The door opened and Judy arrived, a walking advertisement for juicing, supplements, core fitness, Alpha hyaluronic acid and, above all, wealth. 'Ann!' Most things Judy said had an exclamation point at the end of them. 'How are you?! It's great to see you! Is everything OK?!'

She slid into the booth.

Ann couldn't launch straight into it. 'Are you hungry? Let's eat.'

'Sure,' Judy said, picking the tuna salad and sipping some water from the glasses on the table. Hydration was one of Judy's core beliefs.

'So, what has you pretty much disappeared off the face of the planet? Is the sex that good? What has you back in Brooklyn? Oh shit, have you broken up?'

Ann laughed despite herself. If she could get a word in edgeways, she would. 'I actually don't know where to start so I'm just going to tell you everything; it's all a bit shocking so prepare yourself.'

Ann told the whole sordid tale without ever quite looking Judy in the eye. She was vulnerable and exposed, but it felt good to be in charge of the narrative, to tell the truth for once. Judy's mouth had opened by increments until her jaw was almost on the table. There was a long pause at the end of her story as Judy considered how to respond.

'Holy shit, Ann. Talk about the fairy tale turning dark!'

'So, yeah, that's what has me back in Brooklyn. I had to get out of there, just for a while. It's so intense. I just hope with me out of the house Justin will have the opportunity to lay the groundwork to begin breaking the news to her about us, about him moving on.'

'What do your sisters think?' Judy asked carefully. Judy usually knew exactly what to say, what to advise, but she seemed to be keeping her powder dry for once.

'They don't know,' Ann said. 'I can't tell them. I was hoping I mightn't have to, that it would all sort itself out and I could just pretend it never happened, but it doesn't look like that's how it's going to play out at all. But I just can't stand to listen to them telling me they told me so.'

Judy looked sympathetic. 'I'm sure they wouldn't say that, Ann. I'm sure they'll only be worried about you.'

Ann shook her head. 'They're never worried about me. It's partly their fault that I'm in this predicament. They pressured me to sell Mom's apartment, even though they didn't need the money, and they knew I had nowhere to go . . . '

'Couldn't you stay with one of them?' Judy offered.

'They made it extremely clear that they didn't want me in their houses, in their perfect lives, even though they have the space. Juliet's basement is converted into a two-bedroom apartment and Emily has the pool house.'

Judy looked perplexed. 'I think they might feel differently if they knew what was going on. You're not really going to go back are you, Ann, are you? Surely it would be better for you to stay away until Justin has managed to sort things out, stay out of the whole thing completely until he has managed to . . . clarify things?'

'I've nowhere to go Judy, and besides, if I stay away he might change his mind and stay with Deborah after all.'

Judy pursed her lips. 'Would that really be so bad, Ann? It's not like you couldn't cope on your own with your baby. And surely Justin is wealthy enough to help you so that you wouldn't have to worry about earning a living.'

Ann shook her head. Justin might appear wealthy but he certainly wasn't as well-off as he had made himself out to be. In fact, Ann had no idea how wealthy he was at all. 'No, I need to be there. I can't just give up. You of all people can understand that.'

Chapter Thirty-Four

Deborah

The house felt serenely quiet with Ann gone. Much as I loved her, needed her, having her in the house took away the intimate private feeling of a family unit. Now that it was just me, Justin and Sophie, for the very first time since I got back from the hospital, it felt like we were a united front. It felt like home.

'Isn't this wonderful?' I said, luxuriating in the early-morning silence before the alarm went off. 'Just the three of us? Feels just like old times again, right?'

Justin smiled. 'It does, but you do need someone here to help at all times, Deb. You're not well enough yet to be fully independent, and Sophie loves Ann. And I also feel slightly responsible for her. I told her she could stay here for as long as she needed to. She doesn't have anywhere else to go really.'

'Oh, don't get me wrong, I love her too, and I'm also happy for her to stay with us as long as she needs to, the poor girl, I just mean, it's nice to have some time to ourselves, to be alone without anyone overhearing us or curtailing how we have to be around each other.'

I snuggled into him. I wanted to re-establish some intimacy between us both; we had only slept together a couple of times since I'd come home from the hospital. He said he didn't want to hurt me or set my progress back, told me I needed to take things slowly, but I didn't want to take things slowly. I wanted to feel secure in myself, in my marriage, in my life.

All I'd felt was displacement. Each room seemed unfamiliar, like a stranger had been there and their scent lingered behind them. Nothing was where it used to be, nothing felt like it should feel. But I was where I should be, of that I was sure. In my home, with my husband and my daughter.

'I just want things to go back to the way they used to be,' I said. I knew Justin had his faults, but he was Sophie's dad and my husband, and I didn't really want to start again. I pushed up against him, nuzzling into his back. I wanted us strong, connected. Things had been weird between us, naturally enough. Justin had moved on in a way, and I couldn't blame him, but I also knew I could get him back. 'I know it's a bit weird,'

I said, 'but it will get better. We just need some quality alone time together, like this, to get to know each other again.'

Justin turned around and smiled at me, taking me in his arms and kissing me like he used to. 'I'm enjoying getting to know you again,' he said, pulling up my nightdress and removing my underwear.

Maybe it was finally working. Maybe we were getting closer. I still felt like Justin was hiding something. Maybe it was just the fact that we barely knew each other any more, or perhaps it was the old feelings, the old paranoias, the fact that I still bore the scars of our past together.

Chapter Thirty-Five

Ann

On Judy's advice, Ann met up with Juliet and Emily for a coffee. 'You don't have to tell them everything but maybe at least intimate that things might go differently to how you all imagined at first.'

Ann was rattled when her sisters walked in. She had received another text.

> Smart move to get out of town. Even smarter if you made it permanent.

Who was sending these texts? She wondered if she should go to the police, but she didn't really want to have to explain anything about her circumstances to her sisters, never mind the local police department.

She'd discuss it with Justin that night, see what he thought about it.

They met in the old-fashioned diner, close to their mom's old apartment, for nostalgia's sake Juliet said, but it felt hurtful to Ann. She missed the only place that had ever felt like home.

'So, how's everything going, Ann?' Juliet asked. She was naive, romantic, saw every new relationship with optimistic eyes.

'Oh, it's OK, you know, we're still getting to know each other. It's a big change, living together, and it feels like I'm still trying to hide all of the normal stuff from him, you know – my razors, my bathroom visits, my face cream . . . it feels too early for him to see the human side of me.'

Emily snorted dismissively and looked up from her phone. 'Don't be ridiculous, Ann. He's a grown man and you're pregnant with his kid. What does he think you're made of, sugar and spice? You're adults, if he's got a problem with you pooping he's probably not someone you want to be with, and certainly not someone you want to raise a baby with.'

'That's not what I said, Emily; why do you have to be like that? I said I have a problem with him hearing me poop . . . it's just because we don't know each other that well yet.'

'Well, then maybe you shouldn't have moved in so fast,' Emily said, looking at her phone again.

'Emily,' Ann said, her voice trembling, 'I had nowhere to live, remember? He's the only person who offered me a place to stay. Not even my family did that.'

Emily had no answer to that.

'Let's not argue. I understand that feeling, Ann. It's tough but you guys are solid; you're going to have a family soon and you'll get over it. Plus there are enough bathrooms in that huge house for you to find one off in some hidden corner to use.'

Ann smiled. 'Sure. Forget I said anything.'

If this was how they reacted to Ann's minor relationship complaints, what would they say if they knew Deborah was back living at home. No, they had just proved her suspicions. Her sisters would not be understanding about her predicament. She would have to keep it to herself for now and hope for the best.

Chapter Thirty-Six

Deborah

I was intrigued by Ann. What was this woman, with seemingly better things to do, doing living in this house in the middle of nowhere keeping house for my husband and daughter? I didn't know much about her, even though we spent so much time together. But I did trust her. She had that air that good people have – you just know. She was probably a much better person than me.

I let myself into Ann's bedroom. She never locked her door. Another sign that she was a good person. Nothing to hide. I walked over to the chest of drawers, opened them, looked at the neatly folded t-shirts and sweaters, pulled the next drawer and the next, which revealed variations on the same theme. Ann was neat and tidy, orderly. I slammed the drawers shut a little too hard. Boring. What did Ann do for fun? Surely there was more to her than a pile of folded jumpers? I walked over to my old desk, pulled on the drawers but they were locked. Justin must have locked everything up before Ann moved in. I couldn't even remember if there was anything in there.

I sat down on the bed, clean and comfortable. The sheets were simple and plain but they felt soft to the touch. I pulled open the bedside table and my eyebrows shot up. So, here was what Ann did for fun. I closed the drawer quickly. I felt bad then for breaching Ann's privacy. I felt truly sorry for her. She was dating a deadbeat married man who didn't seem to care that she was pregnant with his child and living in a house with a family she wasn't part of. What a desperate fix she must be in. I left the room quickly then and vowed never to breach her privacy again.

Chapter Thirty-Seven

Ann

When Ann got back to the house, the atmosphere felt different. Justin seemed strained, distant.

'What's going on?' she asked.

'It's Deborah,' he said. Of course. It was always Deborah. 'She's really ill today. She thinks the treatment is failing. I'm sure she's catastrophising but I've left a message for her consultant and we haven't heard back. I'm so sorry to do this but can you keep an eye on her for me this morning? I need to go into the office for a meeting.'

Ann softened immediately. Justin was putting on a brave face but it was clear that he was shaken; he was obviously worried that there was some truth to Deborah's concerns. Could this be the answer to their problems? The drugs were too good to be true, Deborah was sick again. The thought flashed into Ann's head before she had time to register it, and she felt appalled at her callousness.

'Oh Justin, I hope she's not. Of course, I don't mind. It's no problem.' And Ann really didn't mind. She liked Deborah. She was easy-going and nice to be around. Despite everything, they had formed a connection. And, obviously, Ann wanted the best for her, even if ultimately the two women were in competition. But if Deborah got sick again, that was nobody's fault. 'I'll look after her, I promise. Go! Go!'

He stepped in and kissed her, holding her tightly and breathing into her hair.

'I've missed you so much,' he said. Ann felt her heart leap, as she had forgotten just how Justin could make her feel. 'Thank you,' he said.

Ann watched his car progress down the long driveway, around the curve that was lined with ancient trees. Trees like she'd never seen in Brooklyn. They had so much land here. She felt relieved as she watched his car disappear out of sight. She hated to admit it but when Justin was gone, all of the tension she felt lifted.

Ann listened all morning as Deborah moved between her bed and her en suite, throwing up. After a couple of hours, she appeared in the kitchen.

'Oh hi, Ann. When did you get back?'

'A little while ago. How are you feeling, Deborah? Justin said you've been unwell . . . '

'Not great,' she said, grimacing, and tears started to form in her eyes.

'Has your doctor called back yet?'

Deborah looked stricken, and shook her head before bursting into tears. 'I think my tumour is back, Ann.' Her hands were shaking. 'This is how it started before. This is how we realised I was sick last time. First the vomiting, then the seizures started soon after that, before the MRI/CT scan gave us the worst news, the news we hadn't even thought to consider. It's back, I just know it. I can feel it.' She buried her face in her hands. 'What am I going to do, Ann? How can this be happening again? What about Sophie? How will she survive going through this loss twice?'

Ann had no idea what to say to her. She was right. Was there anything worse than this, for her, to have her second chance at life snatched away? For Sophie? To have her mother returned then revoked a second time? For Justin? Ann didn't want to think about how Justin might feel about the whole thing. She reached her hand across the table and squeezed Deborah's.

'I promise you I will always be here for Sophie.'

Deborah's whole body was trembling. Ann realised she was terrified.

'Why has the doctor not called? She knows something. She must know that the treatment is not working. There was always a risk with a drug like this that anything could happen, that the effects would be short-lived . . .'

'Deborah, look at me,' Ann said. 'You don't know that. Look at how far you've come. It could be anything. You could have a tummy bug, for goodness sake! Sophie brings all sorts of bugs home from school all the time. I've had a few vomiting bugs from her myself. They catch everything in school and it barely registers with them but we're laid out with it for days. It's probably just something like that.'

She looked at Ann. 'Do you really think it might be?'

But Ann didn't believe her own words. Sophie hadn't been sick. Justin wasn't sick and neither was she. It was unlikely Deborah had picked up a viral bug.

'Of course it might, and you must remember that your immune system has been forced into compromise because of the treatment. You're going to pick up every little thing.'

Deborah started to cry. 'I just can't believe it. I've got this second chance. I should be dead and now it's coming back, I know it's coming back.'

The idea that Deborah might be dying made Ann generous. She stood up and walked around the table, squeezed her shoulders, as close as she had ever come to a hug.

'Why don't we go to the doctor's office instead of waiting here for a call that may not come? Let's just see what she says before we jump to conclusions. I'll drive you. I bet they'll be able to put your mind at ease.'

Ann stood as Deborah sniffed and dabbed her eyes. She was aware of the fucked-upness of the situation at all times. How did she end up comforting the woman who had stolen her dreams of a perfect life? She pulled away with the excuse of getting her phone and making a doctor's appointment.

'What's your doctor's name?' She asked, then googled the name Deborah gave her and found the number for the office. She made an appointment for 11 a.m.

'Whatever it is, Deborah, it's better to have an answer, than to be left in any doubt. I'm sure it's nothing.'

Deborah nodded. 'I really hope so.'

Ann pulled up at the doctor's office and told Deborah she would wait in the car.

Deborah looked panicked.

'Oh please, Ann, can't you come in with me? I'm so scared. I'm just so scared. I can't hear this news on my own.' Tears were running down her face and her hands were trembling.'

Ann swallowed another *how-did-I-get-here?* sigh and said, 'Of course. No problem.'

In the waiting room, Ann flicked through an old magazine, looking at quizzes that had been half-filled out by other bored patients, fashions that were already outdated, pictures of life, coming and going. It was all meaningless anyway. In fifty years, the models in these pages would be dead. In ten years, some of the people sitting here in this waiting area would certainly be dead. The cycle ground on relentlessly and still they fought it.

Ann allowed her thoughts to drift briefly into the fantasy of Deborah dying a quick and unavoidable death. Would that simplify things between her and Justin and Sophie. Could they continue as they had planned? Or were things already irreparable? The small flame of hope that Ann had been clinging to guttered.

'Mrs Forster?' a woman's voice said.

'Yes!' Deborah stood up.

'Good luck,' Ann said but, again, Deborah looked panicked.

'Ann, please, come with me. I need you.' At that moment, Ann felt good about how mature she was, how selfless, able to take care of her boyfriend's wife with such equanimity, able to comfort her and be kind. She was just a woman too, just doing her best to live the life she desperately wanted to live.

Chapter Thirty-Eight

Deborah

When we walked into the doctor's room, I instinctively grabbed Ann's hand. I was so scared. I didn't want to hear bad news again. I was surprised to find Ann's hand was clammy too. Was she nervous? Ann was clearly worried about what the doctor might say as well.

I knew the worst was coming. I had been here before. I squeezed Ann's hand. She looked at me and said, 'Let's just wait and see what the doctor says. It might not be what you think.'

But all of my symptoms were the same. I knew it the way you know a fundamental truth.

There were three doctors in the room. Every visit I paid to the doctors was now an event, an occasion for excitement among the medical team. It had actually really pissed me off, the way they treated me like a rare specimen to be prodded and observed. You'd think they would have a little more decorum around me. I was a human being after all. I took them away from their dreary day-to-day patients who presented with boring, mundane conditions that were easily solved.

The doctor had led us down to radiology for a CT and MRI scan and a gaggle of white coats had followed behind us. After the scan, we all walked back to my oncologist's office while we awaited the radiographer's interpretation of the scans. The radiographer had been kind, at least.

'Maybe the changing size of the tumour is causing some nausea as your brain readjusts – that would make sense – but let's wait to hear what Dr Drase has to say.'

Dr Drase analysed the images in irritatingly prolonged silence before eventually smiling.

'Everything seems fine, Deborah. There is no change apart from positive change. Look here—' She held up the plastic sheet with my brain imposed on it in blobs of varying shades of blue-grey. This part was always a weird thing. I don't think humans can really handle seeing our skeletons and our organs like this. It reminds us of what we really are. Mortal.

'—this is your scan from last month,' Dr Drase continued, pointing with her little conductor's pointer. 'This is your scan from today overlaid.'

Even I could see how the tumour had decreased. It was incredible. 'Your tumour has almost disappeared. But we have to take every symptom seriously, particularly ones that dovetail with the symptoms that preceded your original diagnosis. We're in uncharted territory here. You were right to come in. We don't have any precedent for how this drug behaves so we want to rule everything out every time.'

I knew I should feel relieved but, while the panic had died down a little, I still felt certain that my symptoms signified something awful. I glanced at Ann, who looked sicker than I felt. She gave me a weak smile as Dr Drase went through the motions of taking my blood pressure, getting me to stand on the scales, looking into my ears and eyes, listening to my heart and lungs, tapping on my back and asking me to cough, getting me to pee into a urine sample pot and connecting me to an ECG. A nurse came and went. I wanted to scream. I knew none of these things were going to give them any new information. Why were they putting me through this?

The doctor shrugged and used all of her seven years of medical training at Harvard University to conclude: 'I can only suggest that it is a stomach bug.'

The second hand on the clock ticked by loudly as she wrote and wrote and wrote in her notes and I waited for something more. I looked at Ann again, who still wore a tight little smile, the one she gave Sophie when she wanted her to be brave. I appreciated it.

The nurse came back and handed the doctor a kidney dish.

The doctor looked inside, then back at the nurse. With a nod that seemed to understand everything, she said, 'Thank you.' Then, 'OK, you can get dressed now, Deborah.'

I hated the way they treated me like I wasn't really there, as if I didn't really exist. They always acted surprised when I asked for some information about my body. I wondered whether the doctor was just going to keep writing in her pad and ignoring us, or maybe she didn't even notice that we were still there. After she had finished writing her notes, she pulled out her prescription pad and began writing in that.

I couldn't stand it any more.

'Doctor,' I said, a little sharper than I had actually intended, but it got her attention, 'should we leave?'

'Sorry, Deborah, I'm sorry. I just wanted to make a note of everything so we have it in your files. And I'm writing a referral note to your neurologist now, because of your unique history. I don't want to take any chances; we can't be too careful. I really don't want to overlook anything. And this—' she handed the prescription to me '—is for folic acid.' She broke into a huge smile. 'Because I think we've gotten to the bottom of your nausea . . . ' She held my gaze meaningfully.

'Are – are you saying what I think you're saying,' I asked.

The doctor nodded enthusiastically. How had I not considered *this* as an option? Why had I immediately thought I was getting sick again? It was so obvious now.

'I—I'm . . . pregnant?'

The doctor nodded again.

I felt the room rush towards me. But I didn't have time to think about it because, at the same moment, Ann's sweaty hand slipped from mine as she pitched forward and fell face-first to the floor.

Chapter Thirty-Nine

Ann

The words flew at Ann like arrows. Had she even put her arms up in front of her face to protect herself? Yes, she had. Ann had wanted to stop the doctor's words, let the words die in the womb of her mouth, but they'd come, and come and come. She didn't remember anything after that.

When she opened her eyes, she was on the floor. She didn't know how much time had passed but everybody was gathered around, looking down on her. She felt the baby move inside her and relief flooded her body. She had only started feeling the baby move about a month ago but now, at six months pregnant, she felt it moving all the time.

'Usually it's the expectant mother who gets a shock,' the doctor said, smiling.

'Oh, I think I just have low blood sugar or something. I've been having some dizzy spells since I got pregnant. I'm so sorry, everyone.'

'Wait, you're both pregnant?' the doctor asked. 'Let me just take your blood pressure. Stay on the floor, stay there. Don't stand up.'

Ann submitted to the checks and was finally allowed to stand up with assistance and sit back on her chair. Deborah was looking at Ann, laughing now as tears of relief and delight sparkled in her eyes, as if they were a couple who had been undergoing IVF together, as if they should both be so happy for Deborah's news, as if Ann's world was not falling apart moment by moment.

'Oh my god,' Ann said, trying to gather herself.

Deborah laughed. 'I feel so stupid, Ann. Why did it never even occur to us? I think I was just so scared that I was getting sick again that I had tunnel vision about it. I never thought it might be morning sickness! But I should have thought I might be pregnant . . . Of course I might be!'

Of course? How could it be such an obvious option if Justin and Deborah were not having sex? Ann felt like an idiot.

'This is the best news. Oh, Ann, isn't this just the best news? How lucky am I? First I get a new lease of life, and now a new baby? It just doesn't seem possible.'

It didn't seem possible to Ann either. How could it be possible that her boyfriend who swore he wasn't sleeping with his wife had somehow gotten his wife pregnant?

Deborah was laughing. 'Ann, you seem to be even more shocked than I am!'

Ann did her best impression of a smile. 'Oh, I think I'm just a little disoriented. I haven't eaten anything today and it's hot in here.'

'I'd like to have you checked over a bit more thoroughly if you don't mind,' the doctor said, 'just before I send you out into the world again.'

'I'll give you some privacy,' Deborah said. 'I'll wait in the car.'

The door had barely closed when Ann burst into tears.

'Is everything OK?' the doctor asked.

Ann was incoherent. She was so shocked by the news and so exhausted by the effort of acting like nothing was wrong that now she could not control the sobbing.

'Try to take a breath,' the doctor said. 'Just breathe.'

Ann managed to hold on to the ragged breaths which felt like dragging waves over shingle but finally she got her breathing under control.

'Everything you tell me in this room is completely confidential,' the doctor said.

Ann wanted to tell her everything, to tell her that she had just found out that the father of her child was also the father of Deborah's child. But she couldn't. She knew nothing was confidential in this town.

'You can trust me,' the doctor said.

Ann shook her head. 'I'm OK, thank you. I . . . just got some upsetting personal news today. It's nothing to worry about.'

'OK, well, I'll get the nurse to come in and check on you in just a minute.' But Ann didn't bother waiting. As soon as the doctor left the room, she slipped out too.

Ann made her way slowly but determinedly to the car park. The June heat was merciless. Deborah had the air on full-blast in the car and she was listening to pop music, turned up loud. She seemed high, almost uncontainable with excitement.

'I thought I was dying!' she squealed. 'But it's the opposite.'

'It really is the best news, Deborah. I'm so happy for you.' Ann said this mechanically, like a ventriloquist's puppet; someone else was moving her mouth, making her speak those words, smiling and squeezing Deborah back when she leaned across to hug her.

'What about you, what did the doctor say, are you OK?' Deborah asked, remembering herself.

'I'm fine,' Ann dismissed it. 'Just a dizzy spell.' She started the car and pulled out of the parking space. She needed an excuse to look away from Deborah, to concentrate on something, anything, other than the news that had just made the bottom fall out of Ann's world.

'This is such a huge relief,' Deborah said, squeezing Ann. 'Oh my goodness – we have to tell Justin. No wait. I want it to be a surprise. Please don't say anything. I've got just the idea about how to break the news to him. I can't wait to see his face.'

'Me too,' Ann said. There was no enthusiasm behind her voice and her face was set grimly towards the traffic that shimmered in the haze and yet she found the words she had said to be true.

She really couldn't wait to see his face.

Chapter Forty

When they got back to the house, Ann told Deborah she needed some air to clear her head after fainting and was going to take a walk. She walked and walked and walked, through the town, out past the shopfronts and diner, towards the opposite edge of town. And she cried. The baby moved in her stomach, squirming as if it knew how unsettled things were.

Ann thought of her old life in Brooklyn, how simple it was. Even though it was tough, it was never as emotionally turbulent as it was now. Was this happiness? Was this love? Did love really chew and mangle everything in its path? She thought of her dead mother, how simple her decision would be if she was still alive. She could just go home, move in with her, tell her her problems and she would make everything better. That's what it was like to have a parent. But instead she had to make her own decisions and be her own safety net.

She had to stay strong for the sake of her baby. She felt herself calming as she pounded on through the streets. Her phone rang. Justin. She took a couple of breaths and decided to play it as cool as she could.

'Tell me you love me,' she said as her greeting.

He laughed. Did he sound a little unnerved, a little paranoid? 'Uh . . . sure, of course I love you. What's brought this on?'

'I don't know. I'm just feeling a bit insecure. It must be the pregnancy hormones.' Ann felt wicked lying but she was not going to be the one to break the news of Deborah's pregnancy to him. She wanted to watch.

'How did you get on today?' Justin asked. 'Is Deborah OK?'

'She is. We went to the doctor and everything actually seems fine. They're happy with how she's recovering. They think she's probably picked something up. Her immune system is still low after so long in hospital.'

Justin sounded relieved. 'Oh, that's great. Thank you for looking after her today, for taking her to the doctor. I think she was really worried that she was getting sick again.'

'I don't mind. I just need you to tell me that everything will be fine. That soon all this will be a distant memory and it will be back to you and me and Sophie and our baby.' Silence on the end of the phone and a heavy sigh.

'Ann, I don't know if it will ever just be us . . . Deborah is Sophie's mother, she's always going to be in our lives ... but I can promise you that I am committed to you and our baby. You don't have to worry about that.'

Ann approached what felt like the edge of a deep cavern. She knew what she said next would lead her onto a road she might not want to go down.

'Promise me you're not sleeping with her?' She needed to hear him lie to her again.

He laughed. He feigned disbelief well.

'What has gotten into you, Ann? You're being para noid. Look, I know this is a messed-up situation but it will come good. We are getting there. Just hang tough, OK?'

She noticed he had avoided answering the question.

'Look, I have to go. I'm needed here but I'll see you for dinner tonight, OK? What about pizza?'

'Sure, sounds great,' Ann said.

She turned around and headed back towards home. Home. This was not her home and the longer things went on, the more alienated she felt.

By the time she arrived back, the light was starting to fade. Deborah was in the kitchen, sitting up at the island, staring at her laptop. She looked radiant with happiness. The developments of the morning rushed back in on Ann but she felt more capable of facing them now.

'Hi,' she said, throwing her keys down on the counter. 'How are you feeling?'

'Oh hi, Ann. I'm great. More importantly, how are

you feeling? Are you still dizzy? I was about to send a search party out . . .'

'Oh no, I'm fine. It was just the pregnancy hormones and I hadn't eaten. Totally back to normal now.'

'Great,' Deborah said, 'because I need your help with something. Look at this.' She swivelled the laptop towards Ann.

Ann read aloud: 'How to surprise your husband with your pregnancy news.'

'What do you think? I think I like the idea of getting a pizza delivery and the topping is "I'm pregnant" spelled out in pepperoni?' She giggled. 'Wouldn't that be fun?'

Ann smiled. 'I actually spoke to Justin earlier and he mentioned he would like pizza for dinner. He was calling to check up on you. Don't worry, I didn't say anything. I said you're feeling better and the doctor said everything is fine. He has no clue.'

'Oh, well done, thank you, Ann. What do you think? How would you tell someone if you were pregnant?'

It was too much. 'Well, I would probably just tell them. How did you tell him about Sophie?'

'Oh he knew about Sophie before I did,' Deborah said. 'He was the one monitoring my cycle. He really wanted us to have a baby, nearly more than I did . . . I think I'm going to go for the pizza topping,' she said.

Why would Justin be so invested in having a baby, more so than Deborah, Ann wondered. What Deborah had told her about her family's fortune crept in again. Was having an heir a way of securing his right to Deborah's wealth? It seemed cynical, even for Justin, but she had to admit it was possible.

'What do you think?' Deborah asked.

Ann smiled and told her, 'It's a cute idea, go for it. Where is Sophie? I'll go do some reading with her if you like?'

'Oh, thank you, Ann; would you? She's in the playroom I think.'

Ann had never been so grateful to leave a room but, as she walked away, she could hear Deborah chatting excitedly on the phone to the pizza delivery guy. Then saying, 'Thank you, thank you so much. It is such a blessing.'

Ann stayed out of the way until Justin got home, chatting to Sophie and feeling a little bittersweet about their relationship. Would it all end soon? Ann had grown to love Sophie and would miss her if she was gone from her life.

'How was your day, Soph?'

'Good. Mommy's going to have another baby.'

'What?! Sophie, how do you know that?'

'I heard her talking to you.'

'Wow, well, that's exciting news,' Ann said. 'How do you feel about it?'

'I'm happy. I always wanted a baby. I was really happy when you told me you were getting a baby because it means I'll get to play with it. Now I'm getting two babies.'

'Well, I'm so glad you're happy about it. But you know babies are a little bit boring when they're born. They just sleep and poop.'

Sophie ruched her nose. 'My mom's baby will be fun. I hope it's a boy.'

Ann could already feel the distance setting in. Sophie was now excited about her mom's baby. Ann's baby was surplus to requirements.

Somewhere in the house, a door banged. Justin was home.

Ann got Sophie into her pyjamas and left her with her storybooks. 'I'll send your daddy up to say hi in a little while, OK?'

Sophie stuck her thumb up without lifting her eyes from her book.

Ann took the stairs slowly; she could bear to prolong what was about to happen. As she walked into the kitchen, Deborah announced, 'Pizza shouldn't be too much longer.'

'Great,' Ann said, 'I'm starving!' but it sounded hollow.

'Oh, hey Ann,' Justin said. 'How was your day?'

'Eventful!' Ann said. Her tone was cold, unfriendly.

'Oh?' he asked but the doorbell interrupted him and Deborah widened her eyes meaningfully at Ann.

'I'll get that,' Justin said, happy to have an excuse to

step out of the soupy atmosphere of the room even for ten seconds.

He re-entered the room with a large pizza box. 'Who wants a slice,' he asked, opening the lid. Ann watched him intently as he did. it. 'What toppings did you g—' He stopped mid-sentence. He looked at Deborah, absolutely stunned. His mouth hung open. Deborah was smiling and squealing and hopping from foot to foot. Justin looked briefly at Ann, aware that she was watching him coolly, calmly, waiting for his reaction. He could see that she already knew. He knew then that the phone call earlier had been in that context.

Justin let the box's lid fall backwards and Ann could see the pizza now. 'WE'RE PREGNANT.' She had used the 'we' that people use; *we* are pregnant, as if the man was pregnant too. Ann had always hated that usage.

Still Justin didn't move, so Deborah walked towards him, took the pizza box from his hands and said, 'surprise!', before grabbing him into a bear hug. He looked directly at Ann, over Deborah's shoulder. She could see his mouth moving, like a fish gasping for air. He made no noise.

Deborah seemed to feel his shock in the limp hug, his reticence in the face of Ann's scrutiny. She pulled back and held him at arm's length.

'I expected you to be shocked, Justin, but I thought you might have some sort of reaction ... did you read the pizza? I'm pregnant. We're having another baby ...'

He still didn't respond.

'I ... I ... it's just such a shock,' he said after a few moments.

He didn't deny it, Ann realised. He could maybe have denied it if Deborah wasn't there but with both women in the same room, he couldn't deny it to Ann or Deborah would know that they were a couple, and he couldn't ask Deborah – *how did this happen?* – because she'd tell him how; all those nights they had slept together was how.

Instead, he stood there, talking about his shock and gasping for air, and for want of something to do, he pulled her in tightly to him again and hugged her.

'This is crazy, Deborah. What about your treatment?'

'They'll have to reduce my medication, to make it safe for the baby, which will have some side effects.'

'Such as ... ' Justin asked.

'Possible regression. But there's also a high chance that I'll have had the baby before the cancer comes back.'

That's not what the doctors had said but Ann stayed quiet. She was busy watching Justin's face.

He hugged Deborah again and, over her shoulder, he looked directly at Ann and mouthed the words 'I'm so sorry'.

Chapter Forty-One

Of course, there was a conversation to be had but, soon after that moment, Ann yawned theatrically and said, 'I'm beat, guys. Congratulations again, it's just amazing news.' She made her way to her room, leaving Justin and Deborah in the kitchen. She was still in total shock. Stunned. Hurt. Betrayed.

Just before midnight, the soft knock on Ann's door came.

'Can I come in?' he asked.

Ann's face was red and puffy from crying. She nodded and he tiptoed in and closed the door softly behind him.

'Ann, I don't know what to say to you ... I've been trying to work up the courage to face you for the last two hours.'

Ann stared at him. 'Perhaps start with *how*, Justin.

How, if you were not sleeping with Deborah, *how* is she now pregnant with your baby?'

He looked shamefaced. Caught out in a lie in the most undeniable way.

'I can't believe it. I really can't. It was just twice. That first time was the night she came home . . . '

'The first night!? The night you swore nothing was going to happen?'

'I swear. I didn't know which way was up. My wife who was supposed to be dead was home and used every trick in the book to get me to sleep with her. I wasn't thinking straight. It was a very emotional time . . . I guess I got swept away.'

'You said it happened twice . . . when was the second time?'

'It happened again when you were in Brooklyn.' Ann felt her heart harden. So, he'd packed her away so that he could sleep with his wife without his girlfriend interrupting him.

Justin must have seen the anger on her face, because his explanation got faster as he tripped over his words. 'Deborah and I spent a lot of time just talking and it felt just like it used to be when we were first married. You have to understand, Deborah and I have a whole history together, Ann, a child, a marriage, feelings, memories. We can't just switch these things off.'

'Come off it, Justin,' Ann said. 'What do you suggest I do with this new information? Your wife *and* your girlfriend are now pregnant. Have you any thoughts on this mess?' She was raising her voice now.

Justin shushed her. 'Ann, please, you'll wake Deborah.'

'Let her wake up. What do I care?! It's about time we all had a conversation anyway. I presume you're still planning on telling her that we're a couple, that we're planning on setting up a life together, that you're just waiting for the right moment to leave her. Or did you not have time to do that yesterday? I suppose you were too busy having sex.' Anne's voice reached a crescendo and she collapsed into tears.

'Ann, please,' he said. 'You'll wake Sophie.'

She was sobbing now, but her anger was ebbing. 'Do you still think it will all be tied up in a few weeks' time, Justin? A month, six weeks tops – weren't they your words? What am I supposed to do now? Are you just planning on living with us both for the rest of our lives, like some sort of involuntary Mormon sect?'

'I don't know, Ann. All I know is that I need you. I still want us to be together. I just need you to be patient. She's my wife ... what was I supposed to do?'

'Not sleep with her maybe?' Ann suggested sarcastically. 'But the more pertinent question is what are you going to do now?'

'I don't know, Ann. I'm so sorry.'

'Justin? Ann?' Deborah's tentative voice came from the door.

Ann looked up shocked and Justin spun around,

exclaiming, 'Deborah! I didn't hear you. How long have you been standing there?'

'What's going on?' she asked, looking between them. Ann was drying her face as discreetly as she could.

'Oh nothing,' Ann said, 'Sophie had a nightmare and both of us woke to go to her. She was crying and screaming for her mom. She was convinced you had died. She had just had a nightmare but she was inconsolable about it and for some reason it made me think of my own mom. It's so silly, but I just got upset thinking about her.'

Deborah looked from Ann to Justin and back to Ann again. Nobody said anything.

Justin spoke first. 'Well, if you're OK now, Ann, I'll head back to sleep.'

He stood up and took Deborah's hand.

'Coming, darling?' he asked and led her back to bed, closing the door firmly behind him.

Chapter Forty-Two

'So, how's it all going,' Juliet asked.

It had been a couple of weeks since Ann had gotten back from Brooklyn. She had still not mentioned Deborah's return to her sisters, preferring to keep quiet about everything. She needed their judgement like a hole in the head right now. She had thought that Justin would have started the process of sorting things out but instead, things were getting more and more complicated. Could she still hope that Justin would separate from Deborah or would Ann now have to face the prospect of returning to Brooklyn, tail between legs, and begging one of her sisters to put her up with her new baby? She couldn't bear the thought of it, but the thought of living with Justin and his pregnant wife was equally unbearable.

'Fine,' Ann said brightly. 'Much better, actually, than the last time we spoke. I think I was just a bit anxious but you and Emily—' Ann bugged her eyes '—made me realise I was being silly.'

'Any plans to come back to Brooklyn again any time soon? It was really nice to just hang out, like we used to. I know Emily was a bit scratchy but I actually do think that is just her way of telling you she misses you.'

Only Juliet could come up with that kind of explanation for Emily's rude behaviour but Ann let it slide.

'So, any news on Justin's wife? How is she doing? Not to sound morbid . . . ' Juliet trailed off.

'Oh no, no news. You know, we just have to live our lives and not wait for changes there.'

'But Ann, you'd be able to get married if Justin was a widower.'

Ann shrugged to herself. She realised that her hopes of marrying Justin had disappeared. She wasn't even sure if she could still be sure of a relationship, let alone marriage. 'It's not important.'

Juliet caught her tone. 'You're right,' she said. 'All that matters is your happiness. Nobody needs to be married. It's just a stupid piece of paper. Most people just end up unhappy or divorced anyway.'

'You're a terrible liar, you know that,' Ann said. 'But I appreciate it. And I prefer it to Emily's brutal honesty. Anyway, let's not talk about it. Tell me how is my favourite nephew?'

Ann knew how to get Juliet off the topic and she let Juliet ramble on for a good five minutes about schools and assessments and red flags and reading levels and numeracy before she interrupted her to say she had to go but she would call again soon and try to get down to Brooklyn again.

Ann hung up and felt the weight of her lies sit heavy on her chest. Justin was making a liar out of her with her sisters now too.

Chapter Forty-Three

Ann had no symptoms of pregnancy at all apart from the lack of periods. She felt well, strong, almost supercharged, the extra blood supply flowing around her body made her glow and feel capable. The opposite of Deborah's experience. Deborah was the most central-casting pregnant woman Ann had ever seen. She was vomiting urgently, running from rooms, covering her mouth and barely making it to a sink or a wastepaper basket or a toilet. Ann wondered about her own pregnancy, only a couple of months ahead of Deborah's but still barely showing. To most people she just looked like she had a round stomach. She wondered if it was the nature of having to keep her pregnancy a secret of sorts. The mind had an incredible power over the body, after all.

Deborah spent so much time vomiting that Ann wondered if it was normal. She had heard of hyperemesis but this seemed off the scale. Deborah's neurologist seemed to be having the same thoughts. They were wary of doing too many scans while she was pregnant but her symptoms were concerning him so he asked her to come in for an MRI. Justin was at work again so asked Ann to drive Deborah, as she was not supposed to drive for a full year.

As Deborah slid into the MRI machine, Ann watched her body disappear into the tube until she could only see the soles of her feet, like a corpse in a morgue, she thought. She was watching from outside the room, behind glass, behind the radiographer, looking at Deborah's brain appear on the screen piece by piece like a mystery to be solved. The outer edges still looked like coral but there was a dark splodge at the centre that she instinctively knew was not good. She looked at the radiographer's face. He caught Ann's eye and looked away too quickly. He didn't want her to ask the question but she did anyway, 'That's not good, is it?'

He shook his head. 'Let's just wait until the scan is finished. We'll have a better idea then.' But that was enough. He would have said if it all looked fine, if there was nothing to worry about. Ann had seen Deborah's earlier miraculous brain scans, the ones they had shown on the news as a before and after to show the extent of her recovery, the drastic difference between her brain with the tumour and her brain after the miracle medication. This black blot had not been there in the after pictures. But here it was. Irrefutable evidence. Deborah was regressing.

Was part of Ann relieved? Not then, not at that moment. She wasn't thinking of that. She was thinking about how sad Justin and Sophie would be, how hard it would be to lose her a second time, no matter what that might mean for Ann.

She waited for Deborah to emerge from the MRI. She saw her own ghostly reflection in the window beside Deborah. She nodded and swallowed. Deborah knew too, just by looking at her face, that the worst was happening.

Back in the consultant's room, Deborah's neurologist, Dr Reiss, spoke.

'Deborah, I'm sorry, it's not good news. The reduced dose of medication that we had been giving you to make it safe for pregnancy has not been enough to keep your tumour at bay. It appears to be returning.'

Everyone knew there was a decision to be made. Or more accurately, Deborah would have to make a decision. Whether to continue with her treatment, and her life, or to continue with her pregnancy.

'As I see it,' the doctor said, 'you have two choices. One: you have a medical abortion and aggressively increase your treatment to shrink the tumour and get your chances of life back. Or two, you continue with the pregnancy. As your doctor, I am advising you for your own health to take the first path.'

Deborah started to cry. This was an impossible choice.

'It's no choice at all,' Deborah said. 'I know I'm living on borrowed time. I know I'm not even supposed to be here. I'm just waiting for the universe to notice that I'm still here, that there's been an accounting error and I'll be corrected but, until then, I think I'm going to choose to live.'

There was a general sense of relief in the room. The emotional woman had seen reason, she wanted to live. She would put her life first. But no . . .

'The biggest miracle has already happened. Who's to say that another miracle won't happen? So, I choose my baby. My baby, who might have a beautiful life with me. Or maybe just with her sister and father. Or maybe not at all. But I want to live. I want to live as if every single day is the miracle that it is. As if every single day is capable of being miraculous. So, I choose my baby. I choose my baby.'

All the air went out of the room. The sense of deflation was huge. The doctors had found a miracle cure for cancer and maybe other diseases too. They didn't even know how it worked yet and here was this woman, choosing to trash it all because she wanted another baby.

There was a sombre tone in the room. The neurologist spoke as if Deborah had made a choice to euthanise herself.

'Of course. We can only advise you. The decision is

yours. We will continue with the lower dose of medication and the safe level of preventatives to do what we can about the nausea and the seizures that will come. And look at getting to thirty, thirty-two weeks to schedule a C-section. But I have to make it clear to you, Deborah, if you choose to continue with the pregnancy, we can't be certain that either you or the baby will survive. Looking at your MRI, I would expect you to be having debilitating migraines and seizures again very soon. We need to treat this aggressively and we can't do that if you're pregnant.'

Deborah wiped her eyes with the corner of her sleeve and shook her head. 'No,' she said. 'No, I won't terminate my baby. I'll go on. I know I'm strong enough.'

The doctor gave a heavy sigh and said, 'Well, if you're sure, there are some medications we can introduce to balance an increase in your treatment, to protect the baby. But it's important that you take these medications in the exact permutations they are prescribed, Deborah. This is life-or-death.'

'I understand,' she said.

There wasn't much anybody could do to convince her. Everyone tried to talk her round, get her to realise that maybe in a year or two, when she had recovered her health, she could try to have another baby, but she wouldn't hear it.

'Everything happens for a reason. Maybe the reason I came back from the dead was so I could have this baby.'

There was a sense of things coming undone, the whole thing starting to fall apart under the pressure. Ann thought of her mom, how she might have benefited from a treatment like this. It made Ann angry to think that Deborah was choosing to waste the gift that she had been given through this treatment, the second chance at life that her mother never had. Deborah didn't care that she was a miracle of science, that continuing her treatment might allow doctors to save the lives of many others. After a while Ann didn't know why she was trying so hard to save Deborah's life anyway. Wouldn't things be easier if Deborah wasn't around?

If she wants to die so much, Ann thought, let her die.

Chapter Forty-Four

Justin took the news badly. Worse than Ann might have expected. Deborah getting sick again was the natural answer to their problem. And Deborah was always supposed to die. But Justin seemed devastated. If he still loved Ann, the news should have been the news he wanted to hear. But it was clear to Ann from that moment that, at the very best, Justin loved them both, and at the worst, he only loved Deborah.

Ann started to wonder whether she had only ever been company for Justin, fulfilling practical needs. She was kind and loving to his daughter, a warm feminine presence, which was important for a little girl. Ann didn't need to be the real thing. Perhaps Justin was just being pragmatic in letting her into his life.

The news of Deborah's decline hit Ann in a different way than she expected too. She found she was upset. Deborah's wellbeing was so opposed to Ann's happiness and yet . . . Ann was utterly conflicted as to how she felt about this new turn of events. She suddenly wished that Deborah was not ill, that she could recover again.

Things between Justin and Ann were tense. Nobody was happy. Nobody knew where to go next. And nobody believed that this was a temporary difficulty that would ultimately lead to Ann and Justin living happily ever after. Ann couldn't even begin to figure out how she had allowed herself to become so hopelessly entangled, but all she knew was she was too far in to leave now. She had invested everything in the dream of having a partner, a family, a home, only to see it fall apart so dramatically. She had to try.

Justin seemed exhausted. She could see that. But she was tied up in knots over her own concerns. She was trying to be empathetic but at the same time so anxious about what was going to happen to her and her baby, and then she felt selfish for worrying about that instead of focusing on Deborah's health. But didn't Ann count for anything?

Chapter Forty-Five

Deborah initially appeared to be tolerating her reduced treatment quite well. She had some small seizures from time to time, which meant she looked like she had seen a ghost and would just stare at something out of sight until she returned to her body. But sometimes she had the big Hollywood seizure. The doctors had warned Justin and Ann that they were more dangerous and they would have to make sure that she didn't aspirate or choke. She would need to be put in the recovery position until the seizure passed.

Ann found these occasions frightening and prayed that they wouldn't happen when she was on her own with Deborah. She wasn't supposed to leave Deborah alone now but she did, just for short periods, to go to the shop or to her yoga class. She felt like she was back caring for her mother again, living for someone else. She told herself she was better able to look after

Deborah and Sophie if she had these small breaks for herself. Ann knew it was wrong but she couldn't help feeling a twinge of jealousy at how devoted Justin was to Deborah. He explained it away, told her it was easy to be kind and tender to Deborah knowing that she was dying and that Ann shouldn't feel threatened. They would be together soon. Justin still came to Ann's room the odd night, maybe once a week, but he always left straight afterwards. For the most part, Ann was an inconvenience.

'Isn't this weird, us being pregnant at the same time?' Deborah said to Ann one morning, when they were having their usual tea break. 'Like, what are the chances of that happening?'

Ann smiled and blew on her herbal tea. She was trying to keep her caffeine intake to two cups a day and had switched from coffee to a special pregnancy herbal tea, black cohosh root, that Justin had bought especially for her from the herbalist in the organic shop in town. Too much caffeine increased the risk of miscarriage.

'It's probably more common than we think,' Ann said. 'Women's periods synchronise, after all.' So, it makes sense if two women living in the same house and sleeping with the same man would also be pregnant at the same time.

'It's nice, though,' Deborah said, 'knowing someone else knows what I'm going through . . . '

Ann smiled again. These conversations made her squirm, like Deborah was forcing an intimacy.

'Ann, forgive me, and tell me it's none of my business if it isn't, but don't you think that maybe you should contact the father, ask him for some help, some support? I think most men nowadays realise they have a duty . . .'

'Oh, he is supporting me . . . it's just complicated . . .'

'But you can't lose anything by trying. I presume the relationship is gone now that he's not going to leave his wife?' Deborah seemed to really want to know.

'I haven't actually given up hope yet,' Ann said. 'He still says he's planning to leave, and for us to be together; he just has to be careful of his timing.'

Despite the uncertainty, they settled back into a routine quickly. Ann prepared breakfast for everyone and brought Sophie to school, then split the day between caring for Deborah and taking some time for herself. Justin looked after Deborah's medication as Ann felt too conflicted to be in charge of it.

On Tuesdays, she went to gentle yoga for expectant mothers. She hated it with a passion, how the instructor infantilised the women, and mythologised pregnancy and motherhood. At the end of the class, she told everyone to close their eyes and give their babies a hug. It made Ann want to punch a wall, but she knew it was important to maintain some physical health and also to take an hour away from the stone-cold madness of the situation she was now living in. For that hour at least, she could let her thoughts dissolve into her body and think of nothing at all. Sometimes she forgot she was even pregnant.

Most weeks after yoga, she walked to the store to pick up some groceries but this week she realised she had forgotten her purse so she went back to the house. She stepped inside and dropped her yoga mat in the corner by the wall, kicking off her trainers and padding gently further down the hall.

'Hello,' she called out. 'It's just me, Deborah. I forgot my wallet. Do you want me to bring you anything back from the store?'

Nothing.

'Deborah?'

No answer.

Maybe she was asleep. Ann called again as she stepped inside the living room. Something was wrong. The atmosphere was weird, a contrail of disturbance left behind by something alien.

As Ann turned to leave her eye caught Deborah, on the floor, convulsing. She hurried to her side. Deborah was making jerking movements with her hands and legs. Her body was tense and curled back, like a piece of paper recoiling from a flame. Ann panicked.

'Deborah,' she screamed. 'Deborah, can you hear me?' But she didn't answer. Ann was paralysed with fear. She didn't know what to do. Justin had always dealt with the big seizures. Ann called out, 'JUSTIN!!' even though she knew he was in work.

Ann tried gripping her face in her hands but she made a deathly noise so she stopped and instead tried to get her attention, slapping her face a little, calling her name sharply. Her eyes were open but unfocused. Ann needed help. She jumped up, ran to her handbag, which was thrown on the floor by the entrance. As she scrabbled through her bag looking for her phone, she slowed and then stopped, realisation dawning on her. How long was Deborah supposed to go on like this? How long were any of them supposed to go on like this? What if Ann hadn't forgotten her purse? She'd be at the supermarket now, browsing arugula and organic beef. She wasn't even supposed to be there. She was supposed to be at the shops. And Deborah was supposed to be dead. Her routine was always yoga, supermarket, home. It was entirely plausible that Deborah would have had this seizure while Ann was gone. Ann could even say that she had come back to dump her yoga mat, and grab her purse off the credenza inside the front door. She mightn't even have seen or heard Deborah. She might have assumed Deborah was asleep. She nearly hadn't seen her, only that she'd actively looked for her. But she *had* seen her. She knelt by her bag with her phone in her hand, her contacts screen open.

Life is all about what if's, sliding doors. The more

Ann thought about it, the more she realised that a massive seizure could be the perfect solution. Deborah was not getting better. Despite her doctors' hopes, her own hopes, she was not getting better.

What if Ann did nothing? Wasn't this just the universe's way of correcting the balance? She could hear Deborah gurgling from the living room. She picked up her keys and wallet from the sideboard, opened the front door and walked out.

Chapter Forty-Six

When she got to the store, Ann walked up and down the aisles in a daze, picking items off shelves and putting them into her cart. She was freezing cold. She felt as if she was trying to recoil from her very self. How had she gotten here? She started to shake as the adrenalin that had flooded her body left and she came to her senses. What had she just done? This wasn't who she was, was it? She was a Good Person, wasn't she?

She turned so quickly that her shoe squeaked on the tiled floor and she left the shopping cart in the middle of the aisle as she ran from the store. Someone called out behind her but she kept running until she got home. Her stomach felt heavy and her lungs small, but she took huge gulps of breath to try and keep up. She took the granite steps two by two and unlocked the door. It slammed back on its hinges, hitting the wall behind with a loud bang. She looked straight through to the kitchen where Deborah looked up from the table, surprised and shocked. She half-stood.

'Ann, are you OK? What's the matter,' she said, walking quickly towards her.

Deborah was alive? She was fucking alive? Ann started to laugh. 'Deborah, you're OK?'

Deborah looked bemused. 'Yee-es … should I not be?'

Ann snapped out of it. 'Of course, of course.'

'Ann, you're out of breath. What's happened,' she asked, walking towards her. 'Sit, have a glass of water.'

Ann walked into the kitchen and threw a glance into the living room. Nothing was amiss there, there was no furniture askew, no vomit on the carpet as there had been when she had left, no trace of what had happened. Had she imagined it? But no. It was real enough. She was relieved but she also realised with some degree of horror that she was disappointed. She had been sure that she would come home to find Deborah on the floor, dead, and all of her and Justin's problems solved.

The shock of finding Deborah making coffee and cookies was intense. She had been psyched up to ring the paramedics, ready to ring Justin and tell him he had to come home right away, that something awful had happened, prepared for the inevitable questions of what they would do now, where they would go from here, how they would put their lives back together.

Deborah pulled out a chair. 'Here,' she said, 'let me do something for you for a change. I've just made a fresh pot of that tea you like and a batch of cookies; why don't you join me?'

How had she managed that? She must have recovered as soon as Ann had closed the door. Ann felt something creep into her lizard brain. Did Deborah remember what had happened? Had she seen Ann? Had she heard her calling her name? And if so did she realise that Ann had left her for dead?

'Thanks,' Ann said, sipping the bitter tea. Deborah pushed the plate of cookies across the table. They looked fantastic. 'Did you make these?'

She laughed. 'No, I buy the cookie dough in a roll from the store and just slice it up into cookies. Sophie loves baking but I do not. This is a happy medium for both of us and there's no washing up afterwards.'

'Clever,' Ann said, taking a bite and then groaning with pleasure. 'These are amazing.'

'So, what have you been up to? Did you go to yoga this morning?' Deborah asked.

She stared at Ann. She seemed to be asking a trick question. Did she know? 'I did but I was too tired to go straight to the store, which is why I'm here. I'll go in a little while. How about you?'

'Oh, nothing really,' Deborah said. 'I rested, did a little reading and then had a sudden craving for cookies so I made these.'

Deborah had told Ann that after a seizure she lost a lot of energy and needed a huge sugar boost to restore her. But why didn't she mention the seizure? Was it because she knew Ann had been there or was she just trying to protect herself?

'Are you feeling any better since the doctors tweaked your drugs?' Ann asked.

'I'm OK, I made my peace with dying a long time ago. I've been here before and I'm not afraid any more. I've never done anything bad in my life, you know? I'm a good person.'

Ann gave a weak laugh. 'That's good, that's really philosophical, good for you. Well,' she said, standing up, 'those groceries won't buy themselves. I'd better get to the store or we'll have nothing to eat this evening. Can I get you anything?'

'No, thank you.' She smiled and watched Ann walk towards the door.

As Ann put her coat on and unlatched the door, Deborah called out, 'Ann?'

'Yes?'

'Don't forget your wallet.'

Chapter Forty-Seven

Deborah

From that point on, I knew that Ann was not the nanny, and that she was not my friend. Funny now to think I had been so naive to the fact that Justin was the deadbeat married boyfriend Ann and I spoke about at our lunches. But once the seizure happened, once I saw Ann paralysed and torn between helping and abandoning me, the connection had finally clicked.

I couldn't believe it had taken me so long to figure it out, actually. It explained everything: Ann's initial standoffishness, her weird behaviour about the leaky tap in her bedroom; it was suddenly as clear as if someone had sent me an anonymous message saying 'your husband is cheating with your nanny'. I could finally see Ann clearly for what she was: an obstacle that stood between me and my old life.

I hated Ann for her deceit. It hurt that she had sat with me so many mornings and confided in me, told me about her married lover and his plans to leave his wife. She had been gullible as to believe Justin was going to leave me. But she couldn't possibly know about Justin's past.

Justin had never left once. Despite all those promises he had made those women. And he never will. I'll make sure of that.

Over my dead body.

Chapter Forty-Eight

Ann

Justin was sorting Deborah's pills into her weekly dispenser. As he selected the varying strengths and colours from the generic bags that the pharmacist separated them into, and popped them into their holders, Ann wondered how long they would hold Deborah's illness at bay.

She knew her one job was to care for Deborah like a decent human being. Ann hated herself for having left her that day. She was still horrified by how she'd responded to her seizure. She would have been entirely responsible for her death. She vowed to look after her from here on in, come what may. She vowed to protect her and care for her. Her relationship with Justin would run its own course, but she couldn't make it happen.

Whatever she felt about Deborah's place in her life, she knew she had to do the right thing. There was a world of difference between wishing someone dead and actually killing them. Ann was lucky that Deborah had lived.

Ann tried to whitewash her thoughts but they kept coming back, like graffiti that showed under the paint. It was just like it had been with her mother. Deborah was not getting better. All it would be was an acceleration of the inevitable. Could anyone really be responsible if it was going to happen anyway? If it was going to happen, then why could it not happen in its own time? Ann had no answer for that question. Just please let it be quick, she thought.

'How is she doing?' she asked Justin.

'OK, she's just gone for a lie-down. She's not feeling great today, a lot of pain, she said. I might take this opportunity to nip out, if you don't mind? I need to clear my head.'

'Of course, take your time.'

Two hours later, Ann was getting worried. Justin still hadn't returned and Deborah was still asleep. She was reluctant to wake her and decided to check on her in thirty minutes if she wasn't awake. She got involved with an article on Instagram and swiped and swiped and read and read until she had lost all sense of time. It was an hour since she had last thought of Deborah.

She put her politeness aside and knocked on the bedroom door, Justin's bedroom door. It felt weird to have this bar now, not to be able to pass freely into that room where she had spent so many happy nights before Deborah came home. No answer. She knocked harder and called out her name.

'Deborah, are you awake? It's almost five o'clock, I thought you might want to be called. Are you all right? OK, I'm coming in . . . ' Deborah was asleep in bed but she looked ill. She looked dead. She had something coming from the side of her mouth.

Ann ran to her. She was breathing but clearly something was wrong. She was burning up and beads of sweat studded her brow. Ann called an ambulance and the operator talked her through what she should do. The paramedic told her it sounded like Deborah had had a seizure.

They found out that night that Deborah had lost the baby. The pregnancy had taken its toll on her, and as her body could barely support itself, it let go of the unnecessary functions it was supporting – hair growth, nail growth, baby growth. The doctors still didn't really know how or why Deborah's drug trial treatment had worked but somehow it had. They immediately reinstated the treatment and hoped that she would make the same recovery as before.

When Ann went home with Justin later that night,

it was the first time the two of them had been alone together in the house since Deborah had come home. Ann felt like she'd travelled a whole world since then. She remembered how they used to relax and cuddle on the couch together, how they couldn't keep their hands off each other. And now, she couldn't remember the last time she had felt light-hearted, the last time she had felt joy. Ann was bereft for Deborah. She had wanted a baby so desperately that she'd compromised her own health for the possibility of its future. And Ann couldn't help but imagine how she would feel losing her own baby now. It made her shiver. Now Deborah had no baby and she might not recover her health either. Ann cradled her own bump, thanking every possible deity that her child was still here.

The atmosphere was sombre now where once it had been playful.

'I think we have to face facts here, Ann. I can't fix this,' Justin said.

She didn't even feel angry any more. She knew they were both miserable. Was she even in love with him any more? Did she think they could be in love again, after this, after Deborah? That was why she was still here, but it felt less and less likely there would be a life after Deborah.

And she'd grown used to the comfort of this big old house, the heat, the aimlessness of reading in the mornings, the silence of the house ticking and settling as she made a cup of herbal tea, the manageable amount of work. They sounded like small things but they meant a lot to her having never had them. She knew if she walked away now, if she let go, she would fall and keep on falling until she hit the place where she had begun. She would never get back to this place. She saw a future. That was why she kept clinging on. She didn't want to go back to scraping alone for something that could never be more than substandard. But was how she was living now so much better? The sacrifices were so big, and she had made each one recklessly. She didn't want to go back to her old life as a woman without category. She was never going back to the solo travel and the inevitable questions every time she returned – well, did you meet anyone? The dinner invitations that paired her with the only single man the host knew. It was mortifying to live that way but increasingly it felt mortifying to live this way too, the way she was living with Justin. And Deborah.

She walked over to the rumpled bed and sat on it. She climbed in and lay down under the duvet. The pregnancy had exhausted her and all of her anger had been replaced with sadness.

'Now is the time to tell the truth, Justin. It has to be now, or never. Deborah is sick again. Now is the time to stop lying, to make a decision.' But he was still hedging his bets, putting off the decision-making so that he could have everything – Ann, Deborah, Sophie, Ann's baby, his life in Hudson, Deborah's family money, the family business, the mansion ... He didn't want to sacrifice anything, while Ann had sacrificed everything.

'You're right, Ann. This has gone on for too long ...' he said. 'I can't leave her. We're still married, we already have Sophie, this is our home ... It pains me to say it, Ann, but this is becoming more and more tangled. None of this is anybody's fault but it's not working and there's no solution in sight ...'

Ann knew instinctively that this was the beginning of the conversation she had been dreading, but she felt surprisingly little. She might even have felt the faintest hint of relief. She was worn out by the battle. It was death by a thousand cuts.

'And what about our baby?' Ann asked, but he skirted the question.

'It's just an impossible situation. You know I'll support you and the baby, but us living together as a family? I just can't see it happening in the way we could before.' He took a piece of paper from his pocket and laid it on the bed. 'There are still some options open to you, still some places who perform late-stage terminations. That's still an option to consider.' She looked at the anonymous white card for a women's health clinic. 'I'd pay for everything, of course,' he said. 'It might be best for everyone. You could go back to your life, your career, your hometown, your family, start a new life ... I'd help you financially, obviously, to get back on your feet, get a place, help with bills and stuff. I know you've been unhappy here, struggled to adapt to a smaller town, a slower pace of life, and I know people haven't been too friendly either. Don't you see? It could be a completely new start for all of us. What's happened here is nobody's fault. It's just lousy luck.'

Ann was so shocked by Justin's suggestion that she could barely speak. Asking her to get rid of the baby at this stage was like asking her to get rid of herself. The baby was real, part of her, moving in her every day, but she was too tired to fight with him now. Ann had had a taste of the joy of being a mother with Sophie. There was no way she was going to give that up just to make Justin's life easier. She was thirty-eight. She had no intention of having an abortion. She was old enough to know that this was probably her only chance to become a mother and she was certainly going to grab it with both hands. But she didn't say any of this to Justin; she just took the card and put it on the bedside locker.

She would have the baby with or without him.

'I'm sorry, Ann. I wish none of this had ever happened. God forgive me for saying this but I wish Deborah had never gotten better. I wish she had died like she was meant to. If she had died, there wouldn't be any issue; you and I would be together, welcoming our baby, a new chance at a family . . . '

That would all be very convenient, Ann thought, but

she doubted Deborah would like that idea much.

'You invited me into your home and told me to call it my home. This was my home but it has never felt like it since Deborah came back. I agree with you it's not going to work. This problem is just too big.'

He looked hurt but Ann thought she could also detect relief. He thought she was going to call the clinic tomorrow, he thought she was going to meekly disappear back to Greenpoint. She marvelled at how quickly the coin of love could flip to its dark side. How she abhorred him now, his weakness, his spinelessness. If he turned to her and said he had changed his mind, begged her to give it a go with him, she didn't think she would be able to. She had lost respect for him. Fatal.

'Ann, look at it from my perspective, from Deborah's. We never actually broke up. And you and I would never have been together had she not been dying. Those circumstances are all reversed now and it's affected everything between us.' It struck a false note with Ann. She knew how little he thought of his vows.

'I wish I'd never met you,' she said quietly. 'I wish you'd never come after me the way you did. Why couldn't you have left it at a one-night stand the way most decent people would have, the way I wanted you to? Why couldn't you have just left me alone?'

'Because we had a connection, Ann. We still do. And I thought my wife was never coming back. I hadn't felt anything for anybody since Deborah. Nobody could have predicted this would be how things turned out.'

She felt exhausted suddenly. She had no appetite nor energy for an argument.

'This is not your home any more, Ann. It's my family's home. I'm sorry things haven't worked out for us.'

Her voice was flat. 'I wonder whether you ever loved me. I certainly loved you but I was just a stand-in for Deborah.'

'It's not true, Ann. I did love you. I do love you, but I have to help Deborah through this. It's time to make a decision. Even though it's not the right one for you and me, it's the right one for me and Deborah and Sophie.'

'I knew you would do this. I knew you'd go back on your word.'

He scraped back his chair and crossed the room in just a couple of paces. He gripped her by the wrists before flinging her away from him.

'I'm keeping my word to my wife,' he said, dangerously quietly, and left the room.

Her wrists burned where he had gripped them. Justin wasn't afraid of hurting Ann. In fact, she started to feel that he wished it on her, wished it was her and not Deborah who was dying. If something awful happened to her, or to the baby, she saw now that it would be a relief to Justin. It would solve all of his issues. Ann suddenly felt very vulnerable.

She couldn't go on pretending, lying, keeping secrets,

keeping track of the lies. It was corrosive, burning away inside her. She had to concede that she had tried, and she had lost. It was time to let go.

It would be quick and easy this way; with Deborah in the hospital she wouldn't have to make any explanations, wouldn't have to cause a scene. Justin could come up with something. He was good at that. And that would be the end. She was done.

She packed a bag and then crept into Sophie's bedroom and sat on the edge of her bed. She was so beautiful, her perfect hands clutching at her teddy bear, her hair fanned out on the pillow like a mermaid. Ann didn't want to leave, but Sophie had her mom now; she didn't need Ann any more. She leaned over and kissed Sophie's head and said, 'Goodbye, my darling. I'll always love you.' In the morning she would be gone.

When she got back to her bedroom, she picked up her phone and called her sister.

'Juliet, it's me. I need your help … I need to come home.'

PART III

Getting to know Ann

Chapter Forty-Nine

It was time to come clean with Juliet and Emily.

Emily's response was predictable. 'Jesus fucking Christ, Ann, what are you still doing there? Are you in a thruple?'

'Oh no, Ann, are you?' Juliet looked like she might cry.

'Of course I'm not in a thruple! I am just in a very complicated situation that nobody could have foreseen and I can't take it any more, which is why I am here with you now, asking for your help, not your judgement.'

'We're not judging you, Ann. We're just shocked and really concerned for you. Of course we will help you. What happens now? Are things definitely over with you and Justin?'

Emily harrumphed. 'I really hope so.'

'It looks like it,' Ann responded.

Emily simmered. 'Do you think he's ever going to tell Deborah what he did to her? What he's done to you?'

'It would probably kill her,' Juliet said. 'It would kill me.'

'Can you both please!' Ann shook her head then sighed. 'He's not going to leave her, he said so last night. I didn't tell you this but Deborah was pregnant ... she lost the baby but she was pregnant with Justin's baby.'

All colour leeched from Juliet's face. Ann hated telling her. Juliet was so trusting. Every time Ann told her something awful, it was like telling a child there was no Santa Claus.

Emily looked frozen too. 'Are you serious, Ann? This is not funny.'

Ann confirmed that it was not a sick joke but the sick truth.

Ann tried to zone out from their 'I knew he was too good to be true' comments. She thought that if she didn't respond they would be over sooner, but it still took them a full hour of post-mortem before they could move on to what Ann was going to do now.

'You'll stay in Juliet's basement,' Emily said. 'It's the best place. Hers is converted; mine is too shabby for a baby.' Emily said this as if she didn't have a fully functioning and renovated pool house attached to her house. But Ann said nothing and Juliet was too concerned about Ann to object. 'Of course you will come stay with us, for as long as you need to, Ann. You should have said something sooner. We would never have sold Mom's apartment if we had known the true story.'

Too late now, Ann thought. She would have come home a lot sooner if she'd had somewhere to go.

'We'll get you set up. We'll go to IKEA, get some furniture for the baby, make everything nice. It will be so special to have your baby in the house with us, Ann.'

Ann felt the stress of the previous months build up behind her eyes as the tears started to flow. She hadn't allowed herself to engage with the stress while she was in it but now it threatened to overwhelm her. When she thought about the insanity of the situation she had found herself in, she felt like she had been brainwashed. Why had she stayed for so long?

'Oh Ann, everything will be OK,' Juliet said, squeezing her hand. 'Don't cry. It's all going to be OK. We'll support you, won't we, Emily?'

'Of course, as much as we can, Ann,' Emily qualified.

'You look absolutely shattered. Why don't you take a lie-down in my room? I promise I'll wake you after an hour.'

Ann was so tired of looking after Deborah, Sophie and Justin, she had pushed herself way down the list for months. The idea of somebody looking after her now made her so grateful to have her sisters, to have family.

Chapter Fifty

Emily

Emily gave Ann a good sixty seconds after she left the room before she spoke, just to be sure that she would not be overheard.

'I knew there was something up,' she said to Juliet. 'Have you ever heard of a situation this batshit? The wife living with the girlfriend and having no clue who she is? It's obscene! How could Ann ever had agreed to it?'

Juliet was refilling their mugs from the coffee pot. 'It's funny but I was thinking how could he? OK, so Ann is pregnant, but it would have been much easier for him to set Ann up in an apartment here and continue things secretly if he wanted to, rather than put her through the stress of living side by side with his wife. Do you think he gets off on it? The thrill of being caught or something? Maybe he's controlling? Likes to have Ann under his thumb? I've read about men like that.'

Emily considered it. 'Maybe ...'

'Do you think he's done it before, cheated on his wife?'

Emily had her phone open and was typing-typing-typing, and finally said, 'Let's see,' as she hit send and clicked her phone off.

'What do you mean? Who were you just messaging, Emily?'

'OK, you can't tell anyone this but I'm a member of a private Facebook group; it's called "Are We Dating The Same Guy?". I joined it when I thought Jackson was cheating on me—'

'What!?' Juliet said.

'Calm down, he wasn't – but I've stayed a quiet member of the group. I can't leave. It's so fascinating,' Emily admitted.

'I don't even know where to begin with that. How does it work?'

'Simple. You just post a picture of the guy you suspect and wait to see if anyone has any information on him. If any of the women in the group recognise or have had any experience with him, they post about it. Some women have been on dates or had one-night stands with the guys on there; others are in actual full-blown relationships with them. It's kind of a "solidarity among women" sort of thing.'

'So,' Juliet said, with a creeping feeling, 'let me guess, you've just posted a picture of Justin?'

Emily nodded gravely. 'And let's just see . . . no harm, no foul.' Her phone sat innocently on the table and they both jumped when it vibrated and lit up with a Facebook notification.

Emily smiled. 'Bingo.'

Chapter Fifty-One

Ann

Ann missed Sophie dreadfully but she knew she couldn't be in that situation for a second longer – it wasn't good for any of them, least of all Sophie – and as the weeks went by, Ann felt lighter and lighter.

Justin had been calling and texting non-stop for the first few weeks but she had decided a complete break was what she needed. They would talk in time. She hadn't told him that she wasn't going through with his idea for a late abortion, but right now she needed headspace as well as physical distance from him. It had now been a full week since she'd last heard from him and, with each passing day, she felt the benefit of the breathing space.

Later that week, Ann was squatting in Juliet's basement, trying to put together a crib they had bought on their trip to IKEA. Why did they make the instructions so impossible? While Ann was aware of how far from perfect living in her sister's basement was, she hadn't felt as light or as excited about the baby for her whole pregnancy. Walking away from Justin and his indecision had lifted a weight from her.

Where she was now wasn't ideal but it was somewhere secure, it was safe and she could finally let go of the stress she had been living on for the entire pregnancy. It wasn't good for her or her baby. The crib instructions showed a person alone with a sad-angry face and two people together with happy faces. Ann knew that this was just an instruction that this was a two-person job, but it still felt like an acute reminder that this world was not built for single mothers. She was trying to keep the cot frame up like a game of Twister when her phone buzzed and the distraction made her drop the whole thing, which collapsed like a bundle of Jenga. She clicked her AirPods, answering the call without taking her phone out of her back pocket. She should have screened but, as Justin had been respecting her request for a complete break, his was the last voice she had expected to hear when she answered.

'Ann! Please don't hang up. I need to talk to you. I'm in Brooklyn, please can we talk?'

Ann looked around her, the components of a baby crib she didn't know how to build strewn around her sister's basement. He had gotten her at a low point. She'd have to talk to him at some point anyway. She was having his baby. She sighed. 'I'll text you an address. I'll meet you there in fifteen minutes.'

She sent him the details of the coffee shop that Juliet liked to go to. It was lovely and Ann really needed something lovely right now.

Justin looked awful as he slid into the booth opposite her. He took in her pregnant stomach but didn't react.

'How are you ... and the baby?'

'We are both fine, thank you,' she said softly.

'I'm so pleased.'

She really didn't want to make small talk with Justin. She was here to find out what he had to say. She waited for the waitress to fill their coffee cups before saying, 'What's going on Justin, why are you here?'

'It's Deborah. She's home from the hospital but she's not really improving ... She's asking for you and Sophie really needs you. Deborah's not really well enough to look after her.' He said this so quietly Ann could barely hear him. 'She keeps asking when you're coming back.' He had the decency to look ashamed.

Ann couldn't quite believe what she was hearing. 'Justin, this is emotional blackmail. You made it clear you didn't want me there any more. You made it clear that you wanted to make things work with Deborah. If Deborah needs help, you should get a carer. If Sophie needs to be looked after, you need to hire a childminder.'

'She misses *you*, Ann. She needs *you*. They both need you. I'm not asking this for me. I'm asking for them. Please, please Ann . . . ' He was struggling to get his words out. 'Deborah considers you her friend. You're her only friend. And you're a second mother to Sophie. She's been wetting the bed since you left. I wouldn't ask this for me. It's for them I'm asking you to come back Ann.'

Justin slipped his hand into his trouser pocket and pulled out a folded piece of paper. He pushed it across the table.

'Sophie asked me to give you this.' It was a heart-shaped drawing that Sophie had made. It had pages which you lifted to reveal each person – Justin, Deborah, Sophie and Ann, and finally a secret message at the back: 'I love you'.

Ann was in turmoil. Sophie was an innocent in all this; she deserved better. How could Ann promise to be there for her and then disappear from her life? What message did that teach a young girl? And part of Ann knew she owed something to Deborah for the betrayal she had committed, for leaving her the day of her seizure. But Justin, what did she owe Justin? He had hurt her, he had taken the coward's way out, he had pushed her aside when she had needed him most.

'Justin I don't think it's doing me or the baby any good to be in that house.'

'I wouldn't ask, Ann, if it wasn't urgent. I don't think Deborah is going to make it, Ann. I don't think she's going to get better this time. The treatment is not working this time around. It's not making any difference,' Justin said. 'The doctors don't know why but she's getting worse, Ann, not better.'

It was the news she had expected to hear four months ago and yet now that it was finally here it brought her no joy. She felt only sadness, appalled at the idea that smart, funny Deborah should die after all.

'Please Ann,' Justin begged. 'They need you. Do it for them if not for me.'

Hadn't she already lived this part? Ann felt like she was stuck in a nightmare she couldn't wake up from. Did she dare go back, only to have Justin play with her emotions again, lie to her?

'Why is the medication not working now?'

'They have no idea,' Justin said, taking a sip of his coffee. He obviously felt the conversation was going well enough to relax, Ann thought, as she watched him. 'They don't even know how it worked in the first place. That's why they were so invested in Deborah. They think it's to do with the hormonal balance in her body, her chemistry, which changed when she became pregnant, obviously. They're hoping that when her hormone levels return to normal it will start to take effect again.'

Ann didn't like to be reminded of the pregnancy, of the fact that Justin had cheated on her, that he had lied about it. Was it even cheating if it was his wife he was sleeping with?

'So, what happens now?' she asked, deflated.

'They're going to keep monitoring her as an outpatient, keep trying the drug treatment, see if they can get her to respond to it again.'

'Oh Justin, I'm so sorry. It's too awful.'

She tried to imagine what things might look like if she came back now, into a scenario where Deborah was dying. Could she ever trust Justin again? She didn't think there was a future there and yet she felt she owed something to Deborah and Sophie.

'You've really hurt me, Justin, and I'm not sure how long it will take me to recover from that. I want you to know now that I'm coming back for Sophie, and for Deborah and I'm staying in the pool house. I will not stay under the same roof as you again.'

To her surprise, Justin started to sob in the booth.

'Thank you, Ann,' he struggled through his emotion. 'I'm just so glad we still have you.'

She would have to be made of stone not to feel something. She reached her hand across the table and squeezed his. It was the first time she had touched him in weeks. 'They'll always have me,' she said. Justin, however, would never have her again.

Chapter Fifty-Two

Emily

By now, Emily had several messages from several different women detailing their relationship history with Justin over the previous ten years, some as recent as the past month. 'Listen to this . . . One had an affair with Justin and only found out later that it was while his wife was pregnant. She lived in the same community as them, her husband found out about it on the grapevine – it turns out Justin kissed and told – and she lost her marriage as a result. She's moved up to Albany but she still sees mutual friends from time to time. Justin's wife had no idea, apparently. And she says he's still cheating on her. He had a new girl moved into the house who he was telling everyone was a childminder but the whole town knew she was in a relationship with him . . .'

'Oh my god, that's Ann,' Juliet said. 'They're talking about Ann! We have to warn her.'

'Juliet,' Emily said, 'Ann already knows he's a cheater; she knows he has a wife.'

'But she doesn't know that he's got form. She thinks he was only cheating on Deborah because she was dying. Ann doesn't know that he has always cheated and that he has made similar promises to other women. Might there even be other children out there? We have to warn her,' Juliet said.

'She won't thank us for it,' Emily said, 'but I agree with you.'

When Ann came home from her meeting with Justin, she told Juliet the whole story and that she was going to go back to help with Deborah.

'Ann, you're being rash. You haven't thought this through. Justin has shown he is not the man you think he is. You're not thinking straight.'

Ann didn't want to hear it. 'It's not for him. I owe it to Sophie and to Deborah. I'll be safe, I'll be staying in the pool house so I won't be under the same roof as them. As soon as he gets back from work, I'll go to the pool house and rest. I'm just there for Deborah and Sophie.'

Emily sighed and snapped, 'Ann, you're being ridiculous. These people don't need you. They need a home help. A nurse. Professionals, Ann, which they can more than comfortably afford. I know you care for Sophie but she is not your child. You've haven't even known them a year; it's possible you don't really know any of them *at all*. I'm telling you, Ann, this is a mistake. Save yourself and stay where you are, with your family who love you.'

'He's the father of my child.' Ann's eyes had filled with tears.

Emily rolled her eyes. 'Look, Ann, I didn't want to tell you this. I didn't think you needed to know because things with you and Justin had ended, but I think now's the time for you to hear it. After you moved back and told us everything that had happened, I did some digging into Justin.'

'What?' Ann said. 'Emily!'

Emily stayed calm while pulling her phone out of her handbag.

'It's not good, Ann.' She flipped through her phone, sliding it across the table once she'd found what she was looking for.

'What is this?' Ann asked. 'I don't know what I'm looking at.'

'These are the messages I got from a number of women. I posted Justin's picture on the "Are We Dating The Same Guy?" Facebook group . . . ' She watched as Ann read and scrolled and read. 'They go back years, Ann, back before Sophie was born. *Years*.'

Juliet chimed in, 'He's a cheater, Ann.'

'You knew about this too? You didn't think I should know about this?'

'I just found out five minutes ago!'

'We thought things were over with you and Justin,' Emily said. 'We didn't want to hurt you. We didn't want to upset you or the baby. And we thought you and Justin were done so there was no benefit to you knowing. But now you *do* need to know. You need to know the kind of man you're dealing with.'

Ann sat down shakily. 'Oh my god. I can't believe this. Deborah intimated but I never would have guessed . . . He swore to me that he had never felt this way about anyone before. Oh god, I'm such a fool.' Ann started to cry.

'One of the women said he was controlling, Ann. He isolated her from her friends and family, encouraged her give up her job, told her he'd support her and that she didn't have to worry about money. But pretty soon she realised she did have to worry about money because, without Justin, she had no source of income. Don't you see? It's a pattern. He cuts women off from their loved ones and makes them reliant on him so that when the time comes they can't leave him because they have no job, no income, no prospects and then he ends it, or threatens to, leaving them stranded, their lives in tatters. He must get off on the power. But you have options, Ann. You have us. You'll always have us.'

Emily felt herself getting sentimental, an unusual

feeling for her. Ann sniffed and Juliet put a hand on her shoulder.

'At least you found out now,' she said gently. 'It would be worse if you were still with him.'

Ann dried her eyes. 'You're right. At least he can't hurt me any more.'

Emily was triumphant. 'There, now you're talking some sense.'

'I'm still going back though,' Ann said. 'I'm going to tell Deborah everything that's been going on, and I'm going to ruin his fucking life.'

Chapter Fifty-Three

Ann

Ann hardly slept that night. She lay awake staring at the ceiling. Justin had sent a text earlier that evening.

So looking forward to seeing you tomorrow. X

She had stuck a thumbs-up emoji beside it. She was thinking. She didn't want Justin to know what she knew. Better to let him think that he was in control. She wanted to take him by surprise, let him think she was coming back for Deborah, for Sophie, let him think he was safe in having his cake and eating it too. Ann felt like she had finally developed perspective, come to her senses a little and regained some strength and confidence. Whatever happened, she knew she and the baby would be OK. Juliet had offered her a place to live. She would be fine. She felt a little less trapped; she had options.

By the time she pulled up to the house the next day, she was furious. She had spent the entire drive formulating what she would say, how she would make her entrance, how she would say 'shut up, Justin' if he tried to cut her off. She wanted to ruin him. He had ruined her and now she would return the favour.

She parked her car on the gravel driveway, her wheels kicking up the stones as she screeched to a halt. She stepped out and stomped up the granite steps. Let's get this over with, she thought. But as she let herself in, she instantly felt something was different with the house. The energy was off. She called out, 'Hello?' and heard Justin's voice from the living room.

'Is that you, Ann? We're in here!'

Deborah was on the couch, a blanket over her and the TV on quietly, apparently not watching it at all. Ann was reminded of the first day Deborah had come home, not that long ago, but it felt like a lifetime ago. She had dismissed Ann from the living room like the help. Things were different now. Deborah was a shadow. The transformation was stark. Ann was shocked and all of her anger fell away.

Deborah focused on Ann. 'Oh Ann, thank god you're back. We've missed you so much. How was your little holiday?'

Ann looked at Justin. Another lie he had told on her behalf. It seemed like everything that came out of his mouth was a lie. 'There was no holiday,' she said matter-of-factly. 'I just caught up with my sisters, tried and failed to build some flatpack furniture . . . ' Ann walked towards Deborah and sat down beside her on the couch. 'I'm so sorry about the baby. Are you feeling OK? You don't look like yourself.' She put her hand on Deborah's leg.

Deborah's eyes filled with tears. 'It's OK. I think I knew the baby wasn't ever going to make it but I really wanted to try, to give it my best shot. My body knew, you know . . . But I did hope the baby might make it. I just wasn't strong enough. At least now we can focus on my recovery.'

But Deborah didn't look like she was recovering. She looked like she was dying.

'Have you restarted your treatment?'

'Yes, the doctors are hoping with some rest I'll start responding and the symptoms will reverse again. Justin's been taking such good care of me.'

'Speaking of which,' Justin said, 'it's time for your medication.' He opened the pill sorter, the same kind Ann had used for her mom's medication, and he doled out several tablets, which Deborah swallowed with a glass of water.

'The doctors say it might take a little while for the drugs to take effect again because of the pregnancy hormones,' Justin explained, 'but also because the drugs need to build up in her system again. But we're hopeful we'll see some improvement soon—' he turned to Deborah '—aren't we, darling?'

Ann ignored him. 'Rest is the best thing for you now.'

Deborah took Ann's hand and squeezed it. 'I'm just so relieved you're back, Ann. Things have been chaos around here without you. But I've also missed my friend. Please say you're back for good now.'

Ann was completely off-balance. She had stormed into the house ready to expose all of the lies that had gone before. But faced with Deborah's sickness, she found she could not do it. She had planned on giving Justin a piece of her mind too, presenting him with the evidence from the Facebook group, but Deborah looked so ill. How could she hurt her or stress her more?

'I'll stay as long as you need me, Deborah. You just focus on getting better.'

It was clear that Justin wanted to get Ann alone to talk to her but she didn't want to talk to him. Deborah looked at him instead and said, 'Justin, would you make some tea for us, please? We have so much catching up to do.'

Justin was agitated for the rest of the evening. He was desperate to get Ann on her own but she avoided him scrupulously, leaving Deborah's side only to go to the bathroom. She knew he wouldn't bring anything up in front of her, even if she was sleeping, but he finally cornered her as she was leaving for the pool house that night.

'Ann, I'm so glad you've come back. Thank you for coming back to us.'

'I'm here for Deborah and Sophie, Justin. You don't have to thank me.'

Justin looked stung. 'I didn't mean it, Ann, what I said before you left. You've got to realise I was under so much pressure and I really didn't know where to turn. I felt so awful and so guilty about everything, I just wanted it to stop. I didn't think of how I was hurting you, hurting us and our baby. I just couldn't take it any more and I thought if I make just one clear decision, that yes I'd be hurting people but at least the awful limbo, the dilemma, would be gone. But I still love you, Ann. I still love you so much and I still want us to be together. And I really think we can. Any fool can see Deborah's treatment isn't working. I don't think it can last much longer like this. We can be together, Ann.'

Listening to him now, knowing what she did about his infidelities and his lies, made Ann's stomach turn. She could only hear the words of a selfish man, a man who had placed his bets on one woman and now wanted to switch bets late in the race. Ann may have been stupid once but she was learning. She had been here before, and she would not be bitten twice.

She decided to hold her tongue and see what emerged.

As long as she knew about his past, and Justin didn't know she knew, she held the upper hand.

'Let's just take care of Deborah, Justin. That's as far ahead as I can think for now.'

'But Ann, just say that you haven't changed, that you still have some feelings for me?' he begged her.

Ann was repulsed. 'Justin, I'm exhausted. I need to sleep.' And she left the house and didn't look back.

Deborah looked awful. Some days the pain was worse than others. On the good days, she made Ann tea and told her to rest up before the baby came. On the bad days she could barely do anything, regularly asking Ann for more painkillers than she was supposed to take.

'Please, Ann, anything. Do you have a prescription for something? Codeine, oxy, anything that might dull the pain a little? My doctors said my symptoms should improve any day now. I've done two full weeks of the medication and that's when it started to kick in before.'

'I wish I did, Deborah,' Ann lied. 'I have Advil if it's of any help.'

Deborah didn't need to know about the drugs Ann had left over from her mom's palliative care. Ann knew what pain did to people. If they were desperate enough for relief, they would take stupid risks. Ann had seen it with her own mother. The only thing that had curbed her mother's use of the pills was her knowledge that she needed to have enough to end her own life when the time came. But Deborah couldn't know about them. It would be too dangerous. A few beats of silence passed. Ann watched the light slither out from underneath a passing shadow.

'Have you ever thought about what you'd do,' Deborah asked, 'if you were in my shoes, Ann?'

'What do you mean?' Ann asked.

'If you were in my place, sick, in constant pain, probably dying . . . What would you do if you were me?'

'I suppose I have thought about it a lot. Not with you but with my mom. You know I cared for her until she died, and I came to think differently about suffering and autonomy and pain through watching her experience. She was determined to die on her own terms. There was nothing left for her to live for, and I understood that. From what I saw, practitioners are very caring, and very liberal about pain relief in the end. We all come to the same conclusions eventually if we see pain and terminal illness enough. I think the palliative nurse would have given her more than enough pain relief to help her on her way when it was time. But my mom wanted to decide the time, and for her that was earlier than the medical professionals thought. I was OK with that mainly because I knew there was no hope of recovery, no miracle cure for her, no way back. She wanted to go.'

Deborah looked as if she might cry and her voice cracked as she said, 'I'm sorry, I didn't know that. I mean, I knew your mom had died but I didn't realise it was like that.'

'I think a lot of terminal illness ends like that. We just can't really know about it because, well, technically it's against the law. But I think it goes against the law of nature to let someone suffer when there is no hope of recovery. Sometimes I think we treat animals better than human beings when it comes to end-of-life care.'

'Then you have me,' Deborah said. 'If Justin or the doctors had given up on me too soon, I would never have had the drug trial, never have had this second chance. You just never know what might happen.'

Ann found she was in disagreement here. Most of the time, people's suffering was prolonged. But she was uncomfortable having this conversation with Deborah. It felt wrong. It felt dangerous.

'I've spoken to Justin about it,' Deborah said. 'I've asked him not to let me suffer, not to intervene when the time comes. But he doesn't like to talk about it. I think he's in denial. Or he thinks he'd be somehow culpable.'

'He's right,' I said. 'The police always look at the husband first.'

'I know this illness,' Deborah said. 'I've lived it once already. They might tell me I have six months, a year, two years with experimental drugs but I don't. I have a couple of months maximum if things don't turn around quickly with this drug. Most of those months will be taken up with agonising pain that no drug can touch the edges of. If it comes down to it, I want to make sure that I'm ready, that I can die on my terms.'

Ann thought back to her mother, how she had seen it as her wishes, had distanced herself from the process and allowed her to take the lead. She found it impossible to physically help her, a philosophical impossibility to harm the woman she'd grown inside of and who had spent her whole life looking after her.

In the end, Ann did help her as much as she could, and it killed something in her. She was different after that. Maybe that's why she had been so vulnerable when she'd met Justin, or maybe that had been why she had been so calculating. She had made so many bad decisions so quickly she hadn't been able to see around the corners. With Justin, she had thought her life was going to go one way, endless wealth, no more financial worries and a baby to secure the deal. Now she was lost.

Ann couldn't believe this was happening again.

'Deborah, this is something for you and Justin to discuss. And I would actually advise you to not discuss it with Justin and to just make your own decision. Only you can decide really. I can't help you with this. I couldn't help my own mother. I'll go get you some Advil.'

Chapter Fifty-Four

As the days wore on, Deborah failed to improve. Justin was consistently kind towards Ann, paying her attention and keeping his feelings measured and concerned. Now that Ann knew what kind of a man Justin was, the tension was gone and they were no longer on a knife's edge in each other's company. They could talk easily to each other again. They talked about the baby. Ann told Justin about the DNA test she had done, revealing the baby's sex to be female. She told him now and swore she could detect a hint of disappointment on his face.

'You wanted a boy?' she asked.

'Oh, no, I don't mind as long as the baby is healthy. It would be nice to have a boy, considering we already have a girl. It would be nice to see the old family name continue,' he said with a chuckle that he wanted her to believe was jocular but she knew it was fake.

'Your family name will continue. The baby will have your name. You are her father . . . Your name will continue.'

'You know what I mean, Ann. Her children won't carry the name.'

'I think we're getting ahead of events,' Ann said. How had she not noticed before these things he said, the archaic opinions he held?

'Of course,' he said, 'you're right. Everything will be settled by the time the baby comes for sure. I'm sorry, I'm just a little distracted with everything that's happening. Come here,' he said, 'please, let's not be at odds. We're having a baby together, we need to stay united for that, if for nothing else.'

Ann bristled. She might be having Justin's baby but they were not having a baby together.

In the evenings, when Deborah was in bed sleeping, Justin insisted that Ann sit with him for tea.

'Do you really think she won't get better?' Ann asked.

'I don't,' he said. 'And it's exactly the same as it was first time she got sick, the same symptoms, the same degeneration. I remember it so clearly, Ann.'

'What do the doctors say? Do they give you any indication?'

'Of how long she'll survive?' he asked. 'It's hard to tell when there are children involved,' he said. 'The fight is always stronger then. She could last six months.'

She was here for Deborah and for Sophie, and she

would leave again when they no longer needed her. She wondered how she had travelled so far from the person she used to be. How had it come to this, a case of her wondering whether she could compromise herself so much just to be with a man, just to live in a nice house and drive a nice car? But it was Justin who had carried her so far away from who she used to be and he had brought her much further from shore than he had a right to. So, was it her fault if she now found herself sea-hardened with her mind focused on survival? No. That's what she would do – survive this.

Chapter Fifty-Five

Ann spent most days with Deborah now, except for the occasional day she needed to commute back into the city for work.

On good nights, Justin brought them herbal tea while Ann read to Deborah, classics from the bookshelves, sometimes children's stories if Sophie joined them.

Other nights, Deborah slept fitfully, waking with a start, frightened to be alone and Ann would sit with her until she fell back asleep. During this time, Sophie was clinging to Ann. She missed her own mother so much she drew closer to Ann, spending more time with her, giving her extra hugs and kisses.

Late one evening, as Ann went to say good night to Sophie, Sophie asked, 'Do I have two mommies?'

Ann smiled. 'Your mom is your real mommy but I'll always be here for you like a mommy too. So, maybe, yeah, I guess you do have two mommies.'

'I'm glad you're my second mommy,' Sophie said, squeezing Ann around the waist before turning over to go to sleep.

They'd spend the afternoon preparing a collage of pictures of Sophie and her mom. Sophie would remember all of this, Ann thought now, watching Sophie drift to sleep. Ann took pictures of Sophie and Deborah all the time recently; she knew it would be important for Sophie down the line.

The following day, Sophie was at school, and Justin was at work.

Ann sat beside Deborah and took her hand. It was so slender and soft but waxy to touch, the way her mom's skin had felt in the funeral parlour. Ann didn't say anything. She didn't know what to say. It felt stupid to ask her how she was feeling.

'It's nice that you're home,' Deborah said. 'The house felt empty with you gone.'

She sounded so genuine, Ann thought. She squeezed her hand and then Deborah said, 'Ann—' she looked exhausted '—we're friends, aren't we?'

Ann nodded, because despite all of the lies and betrayal, she did think of Deborah as a friend. She did care for her. Why else had she come back?

'Of course we are,' Ann said. But she couldn't be sure any more. Who was her friend and who was not.

Chapter Fifty-Six

Ann knew she should be taking better care of herself but all of the revelations of the past few days had left her numb, so she couldn't really say how long she had been experiencing the strange pains in her abdomen, like indigestion but also different. When she realised she couldn't pinpoint the onset, she went to the doctor, who sent her to the emergency room. The ED doctor chastised her for not coming in sooner. 'You're pregnant. It's not just you that you have to consider now,' he told her.

She was then seen by an obstetrician who informed her bluntly, 'You're in early labour.'

Ann was completely blindsided. 'Wait, what? What does that mean?'

'How far along are you?' the doctor asked, ignoring Ann's direct question.

'I'm almost twenty-nine weeks,' Ann said.

'Well, then, I would say it means it's not ideal that you're in early labour. We're going to inject steroids now for your baby's lungs and try to slow the labour as much as we can, just to give baby the best chance.'

Ann was shepherded off the examination bed and into a wheelchair so she could be moved to another room.

'Can I call . . . ?' Ann felt panic gust through her.

'Yes, I would advise you to contact your husband,' the doctor said.

Even in the midst of her shock, Ann was momentarily distracted by the doctor assuming she had a husband, but she was brought crashing back to the present when the doctor added, 'Your baby is coming and we will do everything we can to make sure she survives.'

Her baby might not survive . . . ?

Ann called Justin. He was the father after all, but it rang out. Of course. She called again but there was still no answer so she texted.

In hospital. Baby is coming. Please come ASAP!!

Then she texted Deborah. In hospital. Baby is coming!! She realised Deborah was her closest friend.

'Will the baby be OK?' Ann asked the orderly wheeling her, suddenly terrified.

'I'm sure everything is going to be absolutely fine, ma'am,' he said. 'Try not to worry.'

The doctor took her blood pressure, administered

the steroids, gave her pain relief and hooked her up to a monitor. Ann watched as a phlebotomist attached a canula, watched her screw and unscrew several little vials as they filled and refilled with her own dark-red blood.

Ann was fretful. The labour had slowed and the pain relief made her feel as if she was no longer in her own body, but she was aware that nothing was happening.

'Can anyone tell me what's going on?' she asked.

A nurse said she would have to ask the doctor.

Shortly afterwards, Ann saw the attending doctor pass the open door in a flash of green. 'Doctor!'

The doctor rerouted.

'Please can anyone tell me anything? Is my baby OK?'

The doctor flipped through her chart and asked the junior doctor at her side to call up Ann's blood work on an iPad.

'Huh. That's strange. Your blood gases looked a bit unusual so we did a toxicology screen and they came back showing very high levels of salicylate, which is essentially a blood thinner. Are you on any heart medication, Ann? Aspirin? Or have you been drinking energy drinks? Large amounts of coffee, tea? Do you know those drinks can trigger early labour?' There was the judgement again. Ann hadn't even answered the question and she was already being blamed.

'No, of course not. I mean, yes, yes, of course I knew

that. I've only been drinking herbal teas and decaffeinated drinks for the entire pregnancy. I have a single shot coffee as a treat.'

'Well, that's not what your bloodwork says,' the doctor said, infuriatingly refusing to hear her.

Ann went through her day in drinks for the doctor. Breakfast: the single-shot coffee. 11 a.m.: herbal tea with Deborah. Lunchtime: a walk to her local barista who gave her decaf for free some days. Then for the rest of the day, it was herbal tea.

'Is it possible your barista may have accidentally given you caffeinated? You'd need to be drinking twenty cups a day though for these levels.'

Ann was about to say no, of course not, but the question gave her pause. She didn't know what Deborah did when she was preparing their drinks. Could she have done this? Ann couldn't believe Deborah would do anything to harm her or the baby. They were friends. She was always so nice to Ann. Her mind went back to all the times she had argued with Justin, their words hissed out in stage whispers in an attempt to be quiet. Had Deborah heard them? Had she guessed? Or had Deborah known about them all along?

Then her memory unspooled to the day of Deborah's seizure. Though Deborah had been nothing but sweet since then, Ann couldn't shake the feeling that Deborah knew what Ann had done. She knew that Ann had left her for dead. She shook her head. Living like this was making her paranoid. Of course Deborah wasn't poisoning her.

The doctor saw the fear in Ann's face and said, 'Not something to worry about right now; that's something for later. Right now, we're happy with how your labour has slowed and how the baby's lungs will respond to the steroids, so it should be enough to keep her out of danger. She's small and will be in hospital for a while but I think in the next couple of days you will have a healthy little girl.'

Justin arrived a few minutes later. 'Ann, my god, Ann, what's happening? Are you OK? Is the baby OK?'

Ann was gratified to see that he seemed genuinely concerned for them both.

'The baby is coming. The doctor thinks it's because I have too much caffeine in my system. Justin, how is that even possible? I've been so careful! Do you think Deborah knows, about us?'

He looked taken aback, confused. 'What? No, no, of course she doesn't. What has that got to do with anything?'

'Maybe she was giving me caffeinated drinks or lacing them with aspirin in the hope that I would miscarry. Maybe she guessed who my married lover is and wanted to punish me?'

'Ann, I think you've had a lot of pain relief and it

might be warping things a little. Deborah doesn't know anything. She would have said—'

'Would she? Would she really? What if Deborah knows and has secretly been trying to poison me, our baby, with things designed to bring on labour?'

Justin started to laugh. 'Ann, no, that's preposterous. Deborah would never do something like that. Besides, she's too ill . . . '

'But Justin, even on her worst days, she makes sure I sit down and have tea with her. She's always said she wants to make sure I have a healthy pregnancy but . . . ' She trailed off. 'I just don't believe she is capable of something like this. There has to be something I'm missing.'

Justin was quiet. He was letting it sink in. He didn't want to agree with her, but she could see it made sense to him.

'Perhaps she has figured it out,' he said. 'That night we argued, in your room, do you remember, the day Deborah found out she was pregnant? Maybe she does know. Perhaps she felt threatened.'

Ann gasped and covered her mouth as she broke down in tears, imagining what might have happened to her baby, what might yet happen. Justin stayed quiet. She could see the shock of the truth sinking in, the reality that it might be possible.

'Let's not jump to conclusions,' he said.

'I'm not. I'm just coming up with rational possibilities

as to how I might have those levels in my bloodstream. Can you think of any other way?'

He had tears in his eyes as he moved closer to Ann in the bed. He took her hand. 'We'll get through this, Ann. You're safe now, our baby is going to be fine. I'm going to look after you. I'll look after you both. I'm here now. Let's just concentrate on getting our baby here safely.'

The next morning, Ann gave birth to a baby girl. She called her Agnes, after her mother, and got to hold her tiny warm baby on her chest for a few blissful seconds before she was whisked away to NICU, where she would spend several more weeks. Which was just as well. Because Ann could not bring her baby back to that house. She wasn't safe there.

Over the following weeks, Ann was bereft. She hardly knew what to do with herself without her baby. Though she herself had been discharged, Agnes would not be ready to go home for some time.

'Use this period to get some rest,' the midwives advised her, but she felt a supernatural attachment to Agnes that made it extremely difficult to leave the NICU.

'You'll run yourself into the ground,' the kind nurses said. 'You'll be no use to her if you're exhausted.' But Ann didn't want to leave Agnes. Ann made her excuses to Deborah, said she needed to be close to the hospital so had taken a short-term studio let nearby. At night she slept with the aching emptiness of not having her baby with her and returned to hospital as early as she could every day. She had nightmares about Agnes being switched or mixed up with another baby.

She couldn't work out what to do about Deborah, whether to confront her or bide her time. She still couldn't believe Deborah would do something like this. It seemingly made no difference, as Deborah's condition worsened by the day and she was growing steadily weaker. If she did pose a threat, it was diminishing rapidly.

Chapter Fifty-Seven

Deborah

Ann only called to the house occasionally now. She was caught up with her own baby, worried about her and pining for her. I couldn't help thinking about my own lost baby, how far along I would be now, what it would be like to prepare a room for him or her.

Ann seemed to be avoiding me when she did come to the house, spending most of her time with Sophie and was more affectionate with her than usual. I was so weak and she'd filled the gap of a mother. It killed me when she suggested that she and Sophie go outside and do things together, things I couldn't partake in.

I needed to keep my cool. I was becoming more volatile. Earlier, Sophie ran inside after she cut her knee, but when I opened my arms to comfort her, she ran to

Ann. I watched as Ann cupped the back of Sophie's head, smoothing her hair before kneeling down to kiss her scratched hands and blow on her cut knees. 'Oh, you poor thing. Let's go get these cleaned up in the bathroom. Would you like a plaster for those knees . . . '

I don't know what came over me, but I was so angry at Ann.

'She doesn't need a plaster,' I said. 'Better to let the air at it. It will heal more quickly.'

Neither of them listened to me.

'Yes, please,' said Sophie. 'Can I have a Cinderella plaster?'

'Of course you can,' said Ann and they left the room together, holding hands. I had the strangest feeling, like I was the imposter, with no right or authority over my own child. It was as if they hadn't even heard me or worse, they had ignored me as an irrelevance. But the most galling part was how Sophie had sought out Ann for comfort. Ann was her go-to mom. I felt a toxic jealousy spreading through me. Sophie was my daughter, and however much Ann pretended, or however many plasters she gave her, she would never be Sophie's mother; she would never be me.

So, later, when Ann chastised Sophie for not putting her dishes in the dishwasher, I was irked. Ann was not Sophie's mother. That was my job.

I spoke up then and addressed Sophie, ignoring Ann.

'Sophie darling, it's OK. You don't have to. Ann,

would you mind putting them away please? Thank you so much.'

It had felt good to put Ann back in her place, even if it didn't feel good to give in to my petty jealousies. But if Ann thought she could take my place as Sophie's mother, she would feel how wrong she was.

Chapter Fifty-Eight

Ann

Ann was still upset at how Deborah had spoken to her. Her mask had slipped and Deborah had revealed for a brief second the depth to which she disparaged Ann.

But now Deborah was behaving normally again, asking sweetly for more medication. It was clear she was in pain and Ann was sure it was affecting her mood. Ann went back to the pool house to get some Advil. Most of her belongings were still here. She opened the drawer of her jewellery box where she kept her mini first-aid kit. A smaller selection now since her mom had died.

She pulled out the different drawers and lifted out the secret compartments where she kept the stash of the serious medication that her mother had used to put an end to her pain and had given to Ann to hide. Ann wondered what might have happened had her mom received a treatment like Deborah had; had she been brought back from the dead, where would they all be now?

She touched her mom's wedding rings, twisting them around her fingers. The velvet lining of the jewellery box transported her back to childhood; the smell was like time travelling and made her think of nights her mother would get ready to go out with her friends or to play cards in one of their houses, and Ann would get to sit at her dresser and open the drawers of the jewellery box. Her phone pinged an alarm and she snapped out of her reverie. She needed to get to the hospital. She had already spent too much time thinking about Deborah.

She took two tablets and hastily tidied the rest back into the jewellery box drawer. She walked back to Deborah's room and placed the tablets beside the glass of water.

'Here you go,' she said, picking up the pills and the water and watching as Deborah gulped them back with a slug of water.

Chapter Fifty-Nine

Ann stayed in the hospital all day. She didn't want to go back to the house. She wanted to be with her baby, in the safe bubble of the NICU where everything was static and the outside world felt unreal or at least unable to reach Ann. She tried not to let her thoughts run as far as to what would become of her, how Agnes's life would be so different from Sophie's life of comfort and privilege, or how they would live segregated lives even though they were half-sisters.

Ann still couldn't get inside Deborah's head. Was this a woman who would try to harm a baby? She couldn't believe it. Could Deborah resort to something like this if she discovered Ann had been cheating with Justin, that she was not her friend but that she was betraying her all along? Maybe Deborah had changed the rules. Or was it Ann who had changed the rules when she left Deborah alone in the house that day of her seizure?

No matter how much she turned it over in her head, she could never conclude that Deborah would hurt her or her baby. If it was Justin Ann might have believed it, but not Deborah. Ann knew Deborah. She was not vindictive. She was kind.

Agnes was now four weeks old, not even full-term yet. She should still be inside Ann, but her lungs were getting stronger every day and her body was growing too, a stark opposite of what was happening to Deborah. Agnes was out of danger; her baby would survive and Ann would do anything to protect her. She was breathing with much less assistance and the doctors were happy that she might be able to come home in as little as a week.

At 4 p.m. Justin texted to ask would Ann like to come round for dinner.

Send a picture of baby Aggie, he said.

She took a photo of Agnes in her incubator and sent it back.

She followed with another message saying she would come for dinner by 7 p.m. and was happy to eat anything. She didn't like to leave before the NICU closed to parents.

At 5 p.m. her phone rang. Justin again. She wasn't supposed to have her phone in the NICU, so she stepped outside and answered. Justin sounded worried and upset.

'Deborah's really agitated. I think she's in a lot of pain. I've just been to the pharmacy but they said they already filled the prescription for you today so they couldn't give me anything more.'

'Oh Justin, I'm so sorry, I have her pills here but she can't take any more until tomorrow anyway. There should be two pills left for today in the pill organiser.'

'She's already taken those,' he said. 'Do you have anything I can give her, any strong painkillers like Difene or something? Anything?'

Every time she spoke to Justin now her instinct was to recoil completely. What had seemed like love just a few short months ago now seemed distasteful and like a mess she wanted to untangle herself from, she didn't want anything to do with him any more. But she wanted to help Deborah, to ease her pain. 'There are some strong painkillers in my jewellery box in the pool house. They're left over from my mom's treatment. But please, Justin, don't give her more than one. They're incredibly potent.'

'Of course,' Justin said, and the line went dead.

Chapter Sixty

Deborah

Justin came into the bedroom, just as I expected him to. I was in bed, in some pain but manageable as I had taken my full day's supply of painkillers.

'How are you, my love?' he asked, then said, 'I've found some painkillers for you that shouldn't react with your other medication. I called Ann. She had some of these,' he said, offering me a handful of pills.

'Thank you, darling. Would you mind getting me a fresh glass of water, please,' I asked.

An hour later, I went downstairs. Moving was slow but I was determined not to lie down until the end came for me. 'Whatever was in those pills has really worked,' I told Justin. 'Can we sit outside, just you and I? We haven't talked in ages and it's such a beautiful evening.'

'Sure,' Justin said. 'I'm glad you're feeling better.'

'I think I'll put some music on. I'll just get the speaker . . . ' I walked across to the pool house and opened the door. 'Would it be really bad to have a glass of wine too?' I called back over my shoulder.

Justin smiled. 'Of course not. You should have whatever you desire.'

'Here,' I said, coming out a few minutes later with two glasses of wine from the pool house fridge.

'Thanks,' he said. We said cheers and clinked glasses but drank deep in silence. Nobody dared say 'to your health' any more. Not in this house.

Chapter Sixty-One

Ann

Ann watched her phone's screen light up and dim down again as it rang out again, and again, and again.

'Everything's going to be OK,' she said as she rocked Agnes. 'It's all going to be OK now.'

She didn't bother checking the message. She already knew what it would say.

She felt the comfort of her alibi, the nurses, the cameras, the witnesses, locked in a watertight bubble around her.

It was after six now and she planned to stay longer even though she wasn't supposed to. The nurses never hurried the parents of the neo-nates out. They knew how painful it was for them to leave their babies. She wanted to prolong the moment between now and the new reality.

At 7 p.m. she said good night to Agnes and outside in the hallway looked at her phone, ostensibly noticing the missed calls for the first time. After listening to the voicemails she knew would be there, she hurried out of the hospital and made her way home.

It was done. Ann felt relief creeping through her body for the first time in months. It was finally over. She could finally breathe. Everything was going to be OK now. She was OK, Agnes was OK. They were not going to be separated or forced to live apart, she didn't have to go back to her old life, her old way of living.

Somebody had to take charge. She couldn't just let the situation go on and on as it had done. This way she got to keep her new life.

Chapter Sixty-Two

Six Months Later

The apartment was beautiful. Ann had never even imagined she might live in a place like this.

She couldn't believe she had been able to find her dream home in Brooklyn, the place she came from. She had bought the apartment with the money from the sale of her mother's apartment and a mortgage secured with her full-time job at *The Edge*. They had renewed their offer when Ann told them she was moving back to Brooklyn. And this time she didn't hesitate to say yes. She had finally found her place and it was where it had always been – right here, home.

Agnes murmured contentedly in her sleep in the crib next to the super king-sized bed. Ann couldn't believe she was already six months old. She went to the walk-in closet adjacent to the bedroom and pulled open one of the drawers built into the white marble island where she kept her jewellery and accessories. She picked up Agnes's name tag from the hospital. If anyone had told her a year ago the path her life would take, she would not have believed it. But hadn't it all been worth it in the end, Ann thought, looking at her daughter. Hadn't it all turned out even better than she could ever have hoped or planned?

She placed the name tag back beside her other keepsakes, the things that told the story of Ann's life. Her first tooth and her first lock of hair, which her mother had kept for her. School reports and sweet sixteen mementos, her prom ring and her mother's wedding ring and the diamond tennis bracelet she had given to Ann for her twenty-first birthday. The empty bottle that had held the drugs her mother had taken, the ones that Justin had called her about that day. She had finally found the proper way to dispose of the drugs but there was something comforting in keeping the bottle. She didn't like to analyse that feeling too closely. It was only when she looked at all of these items together that Ann could see the shape of everything that had happened, and the shape of what still might happen. She couldn't let herself forget. She needed these reminders of how easily a life can change in the most unexpected of ways. How, just because you find happiness, doesn't mean you get to keep it. No, Ann thought, carefully putting away the items and closing the drawer, sometimes you have to fight for it. You have to be willing to defend it to the death. Sometimes there can be no draw, no in-between. Not everyone gets a medal in life. Sometimes, the only options are win or lose, and if you lose, you don't just lose the game – you lose everything.

There was a gentle knock at the apartment door. Ann had been expecting it. She smoothed down her skirt and checked her appearance in the hallway mirror before opening the door.

Deborah was standing on the threshold, looking healthier and more relaxed than Ann had ever seen her. Her skin was glowing and she had put on weight, so different from the emaciated figure she had known in those final weeks back in Hudson.

They shared an awkward hug; the weight of everything they had been through together still hung between them.

'How are you feeling?'

'I couldn't feel better.' Deborah smiled, beauty radiating from her. Ann ushered her inside. 'I can't believe I'm getting a second – no, third – chance at life.' She laughed. 'I'm lucky, after everything.'

'How is Sophie doing?'

'She's OK. Some days are bad but there aren't too many of those. She's enjoying school and has a great circle of friends.'

'How are you feeling . . . about everything?' There

was a prolonged pause while Deborah considered the question. When she didn't answer, Ann prompted again. 'It must be complicated for you. No matter what happened, he was still your husband and you loved him.'

Deborah sighed.

'I did. But I know he never loved me. Even my father knew he was wrong, but I wouldn't listen. I was determined to marry someone "ordinary", not from the same background. I wanted to prove that everyone was equal; put my money where my mouth was, and really live by my principles. My father was furious, of course, but I thought it was because Justin came from nothing. I realise now it was because he could see Justin for what he was. Controlling. Obsessed with money. Obsessed with validation. I realised it all too late, after we'd had Sophie and after I found out about his cheating.'

She had never been so honest. Ann had expected her to be guarded, or mistrustful, but they'd been through so much together and there was nothing left to fight over.

'From how he described your marriage, it always sounded like you had an ideal relationship.'

Deborah shifted in her chair, pulling at the cushion behind her back.

'I think Justin had an idea of me, of us, as that – a dream – but it never worked out like that in reality.

My money was always a problem for him, even though I think it was a big part of his attraction to me. We argued a lot, there were resentments. Justin didn't like the prenup my dad made him sign; he didn't like that he wasn't a joint owner on the house, on my assets pre-marriage. I didn't mind sharing but my dad was protective and told me any man worth his salt would never mind signing such a prenup because all it meant was that he wasn't after my money. My dad wanted to be sure that I would not be preyed upon by fortune hunters. But when I got sick the first time, Justin convinced me to change my will to protect Sophie's future, he said, to make sure that he would have full power over my money, my trust fund, everything really, should he need to. That only kicks in if I die. My dad would never have allowed me to do such a thing had he been alive but he died soon after we were married.'

Ann didn't know what to say to any of this. 'Some people would call that motive,' she said.

'There were other things too. I'm sorry to say this but you weren't the first, Ann. He cheated on me repeatedly and told me it was my fault. I was too ashamed to do anything and then when I got sick I was too preoccupied. I'm sorry, I know it must hurt to hear that.'

Ann shook her head. It did hurt but it was only a twinge now and thanks to her sisters none of this came as a surprise. 'I did know actually. Like your dad, my sisters were always suspicious of Justin so they did some digging of their own and discovered what you have always known.'

Deborah took a brown envelope from her bag of documents. The trust fund for Agnes. A lump sum of $100,000 that was inaccessible until Agnes turned 18 and a monthly payment of $10,000 a month, for life.

'I don't know how to thank you, Deborah,' Ann said. 'You've given me and Agnes a life.'

'You saved *my* life,' Deborah said. 'I'll never forget that.'

'I just feel so guilty. I don't deserve this.'

'Ann,' Deborah said, 'you were in an impossible situation and your character shone through. You don't have to feel guilty. Consider it Agnes's birthright. If Justin was here he would have to make similar provisions for her.' She let the statement hang. Her look told Ann everything.

'You knew?' Ann asked.

Deborah nodded slowly. 'I've known for some time,' she said.

Ann froze. She didn't know what to say. 'There's no need to pretend any more. I was hoping you'd tell me yourself, but—' she held up her hand to cut Ann off ' —I understand why you didn't. And like I said, Justin was not a faithful husband. That part was not a surprise. But by the time the elation of getting better had worn off, I knew I had had enough. I knew I didn't love Justin any more. I had made a deal with myself that I would stay for Sophie's sake but when I realised what Justin had tried to do, I knew that we were better off without him. And Sophie was resilient. She had lost me, her mother, for years and she had coped. I couldn't use that excuse any more. When I realised he was cheating again, and that he was doing it right under my nose, I just made the decision that as soon as I got my health back I would finally leave him. My mistake was telling him. That's what made him turn against me recovering. If I recovered and left him, he lost everything. If I died in apparently natural circumstances, he had everything to gain. That's why he asked you for the drugs that day.'

'You know it was my mother's voice I heard in my head that day,' Ann said, 'the day that Justin called me in the hospital looking for painkillers for you. He let me believe that you would hurt Agnes but I never believed it. That's when I heard my mother's voice, as clearly as I can hear you now, telling me to call you and to warn you. After the day you had the seizure and I didn't know what to do, I promised myself that I would never leave you again, never not do what I could to help you. Do you remember what I said when I called you?'

Deborah nodded. 'You said, do you trust me?' She laughed. 'It was a crazy thing to ask considering the situation we were both in at that moment, but the strange thing is I did trust you. Certainly I trusted you more than I trusted my own husband.'

'I was so relieved to see it was your number ringing me later that day and not Justin's because it meant you were still alive. I never thought that Justin would be dead though.'

Chapter Sixty-Three

Deborah

I came up with the story all by myself. 'It's my fault,' I told them, weeping. 'He brought me extra tablets for my pain but I fell asleep again so he left them on the bedside table. When I woke up I was worried that Sophie would get them so I put them in the empty Advil bottle that was on the table just to keep them out of harm's way. I had no idea that Justin would take them.'

Nobody was going to question the miracle woman's story. Certainly not Ann.

Funny how we had both started off loving him, and tried so hard to keep loving him and in the end he'd forced us both to give up loving him.

As soon as Justin was gone, my health improved dramatically. The treatment started working within a week, and as I showed signs of improvement and regained my strength, the doctors rejoiced that I was back on track.

I rejoiced too. I think I had lost all hope that I would get a third chance at life. But they say everything happens for a reason.

Chapter Sixty-Four

Ann

Ann was not in any way sentimentally attached to Hudson. It had been a difficult time in her life but, that aside, it had not been a friendly place to find herself a stranger. Still, on her last day there, she stopped off at the diner to have one last cup of coffee and perhaps get some closure on the whole sorry episode. As she sat in the café, she made smiley faces at Agnes, who sat in her car seat beside Ann. She didn't notice a man standing at the edge of the table until he said, 'may I join you?'

Ann was wary. She had noticed that a baby attracted all sorts of people who were lonely or sad and wanted to talk. She hesitated.

'Do you remember me,' the man asked.

Ann could not. 'I'm sorry, do I know you . . . ' before a dawning realisation. The sandy hair was almost entirely grey now but the soft amber eyes were as kind as ever. 'Richard? Is it really you?'

He smiled and Ann was no longer in any doubt that it was Richard, from the summer she spent in Hudson as a student, Richard the man who had wanted to marry her, Richard the one that got away. 'You're still here? After all these years?'

'I sure am,' he said. 'I've been wanting to talk to you since I first noticed you but I wasn't sure you'd want to talk to me. I was in the children's clothing store that day you were there with Deborah Forster? And the time before that when you were there talking about your daughter and husband?'

Ann remembered now. 'You were shopping in the store. I did notice you, yes, but I didn't recognise you.'

'I wanted to warn you about Justin but I thought you might think it was sour grapes. So I sent those texts, the letters . . . I was the person trying to warn you, to get out while you could still leave. I should have been more explicit. I guess you finally found out what he's like without my help.'

Ann pulled Agnes closer to her.

'That was you? But why? It felt less like a friendly warning and more like intimidation. Just letting you know, your warnings could do with some finessing. Why didn't you speak to me?'

'Justin and I had a . . . history. He had an affair with my wife, my ex-wife, while Deborah was pregnant. It all blew up and our marriage fell apart as a result. He's got a reputation, certainly in Hudson, but it probably stretches further than that if you wanted to investigate.' Ann didn't bother telling him that it did.

'I'm sorry if I scared you. I heard on the town grapevine that you're leaving, that you're going back to Brooklyn. I just wanted to say good luck and I hope you have better luck in the future.'

'Thank you,' Ann said, and the silence settled between them.

'You look almost exactly the same,' he said after a few seconds. 'How is that possible?'

'It's funny, I was just thinking the same about you,' she said. 'I always liked you, you know,' she said. 'I had this foolish idea that New York was the centre of the universe and I needed to be there. For what it's worth, I was wrong.'

He smiled. 'Thanks,' he said. 'I might not have been so gung-ho about staying in the family business if I had my time over again. I moved to Manhattan after Natasha and I separated, to launch our NYC office. I come up here every couple of weeks to check on the Hudson and Albany offices.'

'So you're based in New York now?' Ann asked.

'Sure am,' he said, lifting his eyebrows. 'We should

get a coffee some time.' And with that his face broke into a smile that erased the last twenty years and took Ann right back to that summer, the summer she met the man she knew she was going to marry.

Chapter Sixty-Five

Deborah

With Ann gone back to Brooklyn, I was left with one last task. The task of sorting out the house before I put it on the market. My father had taught me never to let sentimentality get in the way of real estate but I knew I would never live in that house again. It wasn't sentiment, although there were many, many bad memories attached. It was a new beginning. I was tired of Hudson, I was tired of this old life. There was nothing to keep me here any more. Sophie and I were going to move to the city and start our lives again, and live the way we should be living.

It was when I was clearing out the eaves that I discovered the truth of what Justin had been doing. I pulled at the doors but they were locked so I went down to the servants' kitchen where Justin kept his tool box and the keys to every door in the house. He liked being the master of the keys, as he called it. Master of the house. Master of the universe.

I located the ring with the smallest keys and went back to the attic. As I unlocked the door to the crawl-space and switched on the light, I started to pull out the storage boxes that had been hidden there for years, decades probably. I wasn't gentle. These things were probably all for the dump, but I had to go through them, just in case. As I pulled away the last box I noticed stacks of padded envelopes left behind. They looked fresh, new even. I pulled one open and was faced with bags of pills. Pills I recognised. My treatment from the drug trial. And bags and bags of sugar pills. Placebos. I pulled at one of the bags and it came loose from the box with a rip, and a sprinkling of pills scattered onto the floor like the beads of a broken string of pearls.

This is why I wasn't getting better after I lost the baby, I thought.

I pulled apart every envelope and found more and more of the same, months' worth of drugs, all dated and made out in my name, all unopened, unused. Justin had been replacing my actual medication with sugar pills and because he had decanted everything into a weekly pill sorter, none of us guessed. Could he really be so abominable that he had wanted the mother of his child to die just so he could be rich?

It explained everything, I thought. It explained why I started to recover as soon as I was in charge of my own medication.

I walked over to the desk, found the key for the drawer and unlocked it. A phone, turned off. Most likely Justin's phone for Tinder. I didn't even bother turning it back on. Just threw it in the bag for garbage, where it belonged.

When I called Ann later that night and told her what I had found, we agreed to keep the information to ourselves. It could make things difficult, for both of us. It could reveal that all was not as perfect as it looked, raise awkward questions over whether I was as innocent as I appeared.

We kept our secrets well, even though keeping secrets is dangerous. Like keeping a pet tiger and trying to convince yourself it's tame. A wild animal is always a wild animal, just waiting for its chains to loosen, just waiting for an opportunity to reveal its true nature. And who can blame it, or even hold it responsible? You can't change the nature of a beast after all, just as you can't change the fact of a secret. A secret is always a truth waiting to be revealed. It's just the nature of the thing.

Some people said the truth will set you free but some things were best left as secrets.

I knew that. Ann did too for that matter. We were both better off with our truth kept secret. The truth could lock you up in a box just as quickly as set you free. Victim. Patient. Mother. Wife. Lover. Adulteress. Murderer . . . The truth was just an illusion and people treated you according to how you managed that illusion. If you could get people to believe your truth, well then, that was as good as the truth.

The only real truth was the one you created for yourself.

Of course, there was always a risk. The risk of being found out, sure. And other risks too. The risk that you might come to believe the illusion yourself. The risk that you might forget the difference between your truth and the truth. But with enough money, the truth became irrelevant. I knew that from experience.

Neither of us felt any sympathy for Justin any more. We had given him so many chances but he had been trying to kill me; he had tried to kill Agnes and he would surely have tried to kill Ann too. He had gotten what he deserved. What was clear was that he had never loved any of us.

As for the tigers roaming the cages of their consciences, what had happened to Justin, the reason why my treatment had failed the second time around, and the reason Agnes had been premature . . . well, these were just small secrets to keep after all.

Epilogue

Ann

Ann's life was stable now. She had a steady income, a job that she loved, a baby and a home of her own. Whenever she felt guilt creep in around the edges of her thoughts, she reminded herself that this was just how life fell sometimes: winners and losers, us or them. Would she prefer to have lost, just so she could feel less guilty? No, she could live with the guilt on those terms. What good is a moral victory anyway if you're freezing cold in your one-bed apartment? What good is the upper hand if you can't afford to feed or clothe your child?

Sometimes in life you have to make tough decisions. Ann didn't want anyone's life on her hands but she would defend her own life and her child's life to the death. Besides, if someone is willing to attempt to take a life, their wife's life, their baby's life, they know the risk they take is that they might lose their own life in the process.

When Ann discovered the tea that Justin had been giving her was an abortifacient that had brought on her early labour, she knew that Justin had never loved her and had no intention of being with her. He was using her.

And when he had called her about drugs for Deborah, she knew that he didn't want to end Deborah's pain, he wanted to end her life. That's why she had made the decision to call Deborah immediately and warn her of Justin's intentions. People will fight hard to keep power, to keep money, and they will sacrifice anyone or anything that gets in their way. Justin taught Ann that.

Ann saw Judy most days now. They went to the same Pilates class and usually found time for a coffee between that and the various commitments that made up their weeks. These days they fought over who would pay for lunch.

She grabbed an Uber and headed up to 7th Street, back to her favourite shops, where now she could afford to splurge on some gossamer-thin rings, a decorative plate to hold her keys in the entryway to her apartment. And sometimes she walked on up to McNally Jackson and bought a pile of books, anything that took her fancy, books in which she could bury herself for days until the bad thoughts stopped their clamouring and receded to a low-grade hum.

Ann had enough money now to last her a lifetime, should she ever need it to. Sometimes the cost of living is someone dying. It was a truth she found she could live with. As long as she didn't allow herself to stray too far into the past or the future, everything was fine.

Sophie and Ann had a bond that could not be broken. They had been through so much together. And she and Agnes loved each other too so they met up as often as possible. Ann and Richard had met for coffee and it was clear from the beginning that even though twenty years had passed, it felt as if no time had passed at all. She finally had the life she had always dreamed of. It just looked a little different. And did it really matter how she had arrived here?

From time to time, Justin still came to visit her in her dreams. But he could disturb Ann's sleep all he liked, drag her conscience back down into doubt, because the reality was, even on the longest, darkest nights of the soul, Ann could outwait Justin until he disintegrated with the dawn.

Acknowledgements

All of my gratitude goes to my agent, Marianne Gunn O'Connor, and my editors, Darcy Nicholson and Cal Kenny, for their patience and faith.

Thanks are due also to the production staff at Sphere and Little, Brown who whipped this book into shape and to everyone at Hachette Ireland for their constant support, particularly to Joanna Smyth and Elaine Egan.

Thank you to the editorial, sales, and marketing and publicity teams at Sphere, and to booksellers and librarians everywhere, who are so passionate about getting books into readers' hands.

Thank you to my friends, particularly to Aoife Kelleher, Ruth Murphy, Elaine Feeney, and Cormac Kinsella . . . and a special thank you to Tanya Sweeney.

Thank you to my family, the Coffeys and the Walshes, the Lappins and the Fahys, and to Jacinta Hannon without whom there would be no books.

Finally, thank you to David, Henry, Arthur, Edith and Frieda. You are my world. I love you more than books.